T0279241

ROBIN G. MERCIER

THE MARKSMAN

BY DANNY KRAVITZ & CHRIS CHARLES
WITH TED GOEGLEIN

This book is printed on acid-free paper.

Published by:
Level 4 Press, Inc.
14702 Haven Way
Jamul, CA 91935
www.level4press.com

Library of Congress Control Number: 2020939050

ISBN: 9781646305278

Printed in the United States of America

Large print edition.

1

Carlos walked quickly while dialing his phone and sweating like hell, not from the pulsing noontime sun or sidewalk thick with pedestrians or steaming food carts of central Nogales but because two men were pushing through the crowd after him, one tall and thin, the other a muscled block of flesh.

"Andale, Rosa," he whispered, listening to the phone ring on the other end.

She didn't answer.

A sharp buzz filled Carlos's ear and then static, the connection broken.

Fucking shit cell service, he was nearly running now, bumping the shopping bags of a heavily swaying woman who called him *pende-jo,* his fingers darting at the keypad.

"*Bueno?*"

"*Rosa. Escúchame,*" Carlos said. "Listen to me."

"*¿Porque estas sin aliento?*" Rosa said. "Why are you out of breath?"

Hurrying past a store window, he was alarmed by his reflection, a thirty-two-year-old man with good intentions, he didn't deserve to look so scared. The alley just ahead, he knew that it came out where the tractor trailers fueled up at Highway 15, some of the drivers parking in the lot for a night's sleep before carrying their cargo across the border into the U.S., Arizona. Glancing over his shoulder, Carlos was unable to locate the two men, which scared him even more. He ducked into the alley, jogging as he spoke to the phone. "Rosa, you have to leave."

Quiet a moment, she said, "Where are you?"

"Take Miguel and go. Now."

"What's wrong? Please, I only—"

"Rosa!" Carlos said, his sister's name caroming off the alley walls, the urgency in it stopping him. He looked behind at no one there, ahead at the rectangle of sunlight, and said what he'd hoped he'd never have to say. "They'll find you. They'll come for you, they won't wait."

A small intake of air on Rosa's side, not quite a gasp, she didn't reply.

"You have to hurry. Pack your things and call the number I gave you," Carlos said. "The person who answers knows what to do, it's all arranged."

"What about you?"

Moving again, he smelled diesel fuel and heard the groan and hiss of trucks. "Don't worry about me. Just follow the plan." He came to the end of the alley and pressed against the wall, peering out at the big rigs, some idling, others silent. If just one set of rear doors was unsecured or one cab was unlocked, there might be a chance. "I have to go. Leave now, get out of that apartment."

"Wait. Please—*wait!*" Rosa said, unable to keep the panic from her voice.

Carlos heard it, wished he hadn't, and hurried into the field of trucks. He yanked at the nearest set of doors. It was locked, as was the next, and he was climbing a short ladder to a cab when he sensed motion at the end of the row. One of the men who'd been following him, the tall one, stood watching. Carlos jumped down, turned in the other direction, and saw the block of flesh waiting down there. Nowhere to go, he scrambled beneath the truck's trailer. The men began to run. He rose on the other side and did it again, squatting and moving under a second truck, and would have to do it once more before sprinting toward the border patrol station with its guards and tourists, witnesses, and bent beneath a third trailer and froze there.

A pair of black boots waited on the other side, silver buckles coated with dust.

Unmoving, unable to, Rosa held the phone to her ear like a seashell, listening for the roar of the ocean that would not come. Since they were children her older brother had protected her and their younger sister, cut the paths, taken the blows. Supported Rosa and Miguel after cancer took her husband. Months later when Carlos told her what was inside the envelopes and to empty them into the new red backpack, that when it was full the three of them would run away to their younger sister in Chicago, Rosa didn't question him. But as time passed and he handed off more envelopes and the backpack filled, she watched his eyes begin to doubt his words.

Seconds fell away now.

6

Rosa understood that Carlos's plan did not include himself and maybe never had.

Maybe he'd suspected he'd never escape, or had known for sure. He told her to take her son and the backpack and flee, leave him behind, the reality of it cementing her to the floor. Still listening to the phone, she willed his voice to speak into her ear.

Instead hearing the doorknob turn slowly behind her.

They were beautiful, the translucent blues, greens, and reds of the *panditas*. Miguel held them up to sunlight before popping them into his mouth. Deliciously sweet, the gummy bears were his favorite. Lola's too. Hopefully she would figure out that the gift had come from him. He twisted the bag shut, stepped off the curb, and was nearly killed.

The 4x4 roared past so close Miguel could taste the driver's cigarette.

He watched the truck continue on, eyeing the figures riding in back, three older teenagers carrying guns, cartel soldiers-in-training. Two of them balanced rifles across their laps. The third, Felipe, with his stringy mustache, held a pistol in both hands. He rested his elbows on his knees and aimed the barrel skyward as if he were praying with it, glaring back at Miguel. Showing off, letting the neighborhood know he was armed. Miguel thought of his mother then, her opinion of the young men and their guns, her word for them on the tip of his tongue.

"*Animales*," he muttered, crossing the street to Lola's house.

It was small and plain, chipped stucco, and the porch creaked when he stepped onto it. Miguel hoped she might hear his footsteps, that she'd come out and be delighted by his gift, and that they'd eat the *panditas* sitting so close he could inhale Lola's smell, soapy and flowery. *Jesucristo,* he loved that smell. The house was shadowy behind the screen door, a radio murmuring back there. Miguel placed the candy carefully in front of the door. He considered knocking, but no, it felt too bold. Maybe next time. Yeah, next time for sure.

"*Estas muy chamaco pa' mi hermana, Miguel.*"

He turned from the front door. Felipe stood at the bottom of the porch, the butt of the pistol showing in the waist of his jeans. That glare, the tough guy look, still in place.

"Hear me? You're too young for my sister. How old are you anyway?"

"Almost twelve."

"So you're eleven," Felipe said. "She's thirteen, Miguel. You're a little boy."

With a shrug, Miguel descended the porch and headed for the street.

"Don't come around here anymore. I mean

it," Felipe said. "Shit, son, she doesn't even know your name."

Miguel stopped, stared at him. "You do. You know it, and you're her brother."

The young man thumbed his slight mustache, waiting.

"If you know my name I bet Lola does, too," Miguel said, seeing a flicker behind Felipe's tough guy look, a blip of respect. Maybe. No reason to push it. Miguel turned and walked away, picking up his pace as he descended the hill, heading toward his apartment. He thought of his parents, before his father died. Their heads bent together in conversation, fingertips brushing fingertips. A closeness that belonged only to them, Miguel wondered about such a thing with Lola. He'd need money if they were to be married, that much he understood.

Maybe his mother would give him some.

Paper bands around those American hundred-dollar bills in the backpack on the top shelf of her closet, she'd tried to hide it, but Miguel knew every inch of the small apartment. It belongs to your Uncle Carlos she'd told him, for an investment. For all of us, our futures, and instructed Miguel not to touch it again and he hadn't. Not a mama's boy but his mother's son, aware that he was her first priority. She didn't tell him things just to tell him. Work hard in school, learn English, she'd say, your life is only beginning. You must start off on the right foot. He could almost hear her response if he told her he wanted to marry Lola someday.

A hand on Miguel's cheek, she'd say a lot could happen between now and then.

The streets were blurry with heat when he passed the corner where the old men drank beer and pushed dominoes around a card table, farther on where the cabbies parked, argued, smoked, and napped. A gang of boys battled over a dented soccer ball, swirling in red dust. The scent of grilled chicken and bus exhaust clouded the air, blending into Nogales. Almost there, his building on the next block, Miguel thought of Felipe's gun. Something else he'd learned from his mother, to know danger when he saw it, and from his uncle, not to take anyone's shit but try to figure your way out of a fight, use his head, he was a smart kid. Miguel had dealt with Felipe and removed himself from the moment but didn't feel particularly smart. It didn't take a genius to know animals and pistols were a bad combination.

"Hola, Miguel."

Outside his building entrance Mrs. Diaz leaned on a packed shopping cart. She stood beneath the large hanging tooth, the sign for *Mejor Dental Ibarra,* which occupied the ground floor. The dentist's office was a one-chair operation, nothing like the slick tourism dental services down by the border. A bright elderly presence behind large eyeglasses, Mrs. Diaz lived across the hall from Miguel and his mother. He smiled at his neighbor, nodding at her shopping cart. "*Hola Señora. ¿Puedo ayudarte?*" he said. "Can I help you?"

"Oh yes, please. All those stairs." She led him inside, climbing slowly to the fourth floor while Miguel bumped the cart up behind them. She unlocked her apartment door, and he wheeled the cart inside, and she told him to wait, disappearing into the kitchen and returning with a paper bag. "*Polverones.* I know how you like them," she said, handing him the sugar cookies.

In the hall Miguel unfolded the bag and looked in at the crisp pink discs, tempted.

Even better, he'd save them for Lola. Stop by her house the day after tomorrow, early afternoon when Felipe wouldn't be around. This time he'd knock on the door, he promised himself, standing outside his own door now hearing his mother's voice.

"Wait, please—*wait!*" she said in a tone that put a chill on Miguel's shoulders.

He listened, wanting to hear her start talking again, calmly, getting the answer she'd demanded. Her shadow did not move beneath the door and it was quiet for too long, and Miguel turned the doorknob and slipped inside. His mother stood with her back to him, phone pressed to her ear. At the click of the door she spun around. Her large brown eyes, always intense, held something unfamiliar that chilled Miguel again. "Mama, what was that?" he asked. "Who is it you were talking to?"

"Your uncle." She licked her lips and pressed them together. "We have to leave."

"Leave? What do you mean?"

"I mean now. Now Miguel, take only what you need."

He gazed around the apartment at the small neat rooms, one pot boiling on the stove, two place settings on the table for dinner, and it made no sense. "But, I have cookies. For Lola,

I'm taking them to her, not tomorrow. The next day, so—"

His mother took the bag from him, set it aside. "Miguel. Either we leave now—" She swallowed the rest, choking it down, the thing in her voice and eyes coming alive to him then.

Panic.

He almost didn't hear her when she said, "Or we'll die."

On the outskirts of Nogales they passed a *maquiladora* and then several more, the vast, squat factories of the *Zona Technologico* where locals were paid modest wages to assemble products sold around the world. Among the factories stood dozens of outbuildings used for storage and maintenance. From the outside all of the outbuildings looked the same, windowless squares of concrete block. A person passed by the structures barely noticing them much less wondering what was happening inside.

The tall one had driven. The car eased to a halt and Carlos prepared for the worst.

Wrists joined by steel handcuffs, he was pulled from the vehicle by the block of flesh and shoved into an outbuilding. The tall one followed carrying a cattle prod. Overhead lights buzzed, the air flat and salty. A chain with a hook hung from the ceiling. Carlos struggled but it didn't matter, they hooked him to it by his cuffed wrists so that he stood on his toes like a ballerina. From outside came the crunch of tires, muffled music from a radio, and then silence. A black SUV had followed them, driven by the man in black boots. He entered the building and shut the door and slid the bolt.

Mauricio. What the tall one had called him.

Face like an Aztec mask, Carlos thought, all cheekbones and empty eyes.

Two things quickly, getting down to business, Mauricio removed his jacket to a plain T-shirt that showed a tattoo on his forearm, a skull and bloody knives, and then he pulled Carlos's phone from his jeans pocket and handed it to the block of flesh. Carlos's gaze followed the phone, watching the block of flesh moving his thumbs quickly over the screen. Mauricio began speaking in a slow voice then. Where is the money, where did you hide it, who has it, what's their name; he posed the questions sounding almost uninterested, as if asking were a formality. Carlos remained mute, his heart hammering in his ears. Mauricio glanced at the block of flesh and said, "Rigo, you got it? The screen's unlocked?"

"Soon."

"Someone knows where the money is. Clock's ticking." Mauricio turned the Aztec mask back on Carlos. "Maybe you'll tell me. Maybe not," he said, stepping forward, using both fists to crack Carlos's ribs like they were kindling. The pain took away Carlos's breath, his only thought a certainty, that no matter what he said, Mauricio wouldn't stop, but then he stopped. To look around, snap a finger at the tall one who handed him a billy club, which Mauricio used to batter at Carlos's lower organs. Afterward, Carlos didn't know when, he'd lost time by then, Mauricio burnt through his skin all the way to bone with the cattle prod. A knife came out, Carlos was aware of it but barely felt it, and then he twirled slowly, sliced raw and swollen from wrists to groin. Minutes away from being dead, knowing his body would be hung from the other place, not the bridge but the overpass, where other cartel functionaries could see what would happen to them if they too stole from the organization.

Rigo lifted Carlos's phone. "Got it."

"We don't find the money, what do we tell Ángel?" the tall one asked.

"We'll find it." Mauricio cleaned the knife with a cloth and set it aside. He took Carlos's phone from Rigo, scrolling through it. "Before we caught him, he made a call," Mauricio said, exhaling the name, "Rosa."

Not his last thoughts or maybe they were, Carlos apologized inside his mind to his sister and to his nephew, then told them to run fast and far and never stop running.

2

After a lifetime spent beneath the sky, it still surprised him that a thing making such graceful aerial circles meant that some other thing was dead.

Through binoculars Jim Hanson followed the wheeling pattern of a vulture, its long silvery wingspan punctuated by a blood-orange head. He stood on a rocky outcropping at the edge of the valley using the bird as a lodestar. Lowering his sightline from it to the desert floor, Jim saw his cattle trying to graze among sparse wheatgrass and sagebrush. Fencing stretched for miles. He'd planted the posts and strung the barbed wire himself, Arizona on this side, Mexico on the other. Adjusting the binoculars, he scanned left and right, and found it: head flung back, sprawled on its side, a freshly dead calf. Jim held the sight unmoving until the corpse jiggled, shifted from being gnawed upon. A coyote lifted its head, licked its muzzle, and returned to the calf's guts.

Damn it. Lost another one.

Barely enough grass for his cattle, and now it seemed lately the coyotes did just as much damage. He set the binoculars aside and lifted an old M21 rifle. Extended its bipod, set the weapon at the edge of the outcropping, and stretched out on his belly behind it. Sixty-three years old, he was wiry like those fences down there, agile despite the complaint of his knees on cold mornings. Blinking through the scope, he judged a windward breeze as enough to nudge the bullet off course. Jim shifted his shoulders in response. Without much effort he could hit a moving target from two thousand yards, hands steady, vision sharp. It was before sunrise when he stood staring into his eyes in the bathroom mirror. Steely was a term used to mean impenetrability. Jim saw it there in his gaze and knew it worked the other way too, holding things inside, misery he would not allow to roam free.

A whistling whine, a cold nose at his ear, he glanced over at Jackson.

The coffee-colored border collie a solid partner, waiting patiently while Jim prepared the shot. Jackson was checking in, ready for what happened next. "Soon," Jim said to the dog, lifting and aiming the binoculars. The coyote, sleepy from its feast, circled the calf with its snout in the air. Jim put an eye to the scope, adjusted it clockwise bringing the animal into focus, directly in the crosshairs. He curled his right index finger around the trigger. Gripping the stock, his left hand balanced the weight of the weapon while a faded gold wedding band caught the sun. Jim listened to his breathing, modulated it, told himself he had no choice, it had to be done, and then watched and waited, waited—

Bang!

On her feet, Jackson's ears moved at what she heard from the desert floor.

Jim stood and brushed himself clean and collected his gear. "C'mon, girl," he said, moving over the rocks, down through the brush. Jackson took the lead, several steps ahead while Jim felt the old regret. A rifle put into his hands as a boy, his daddy whistled and called him Dead-Eye, bragging to whoever would listen about his son's ability to shoot a gray hawk out of the sky, a sidewinder coiling across the cracked earth. Yet firing at living things had always felt to Jim like taking what wasn't his, a sort of thievery. The M21 slung over his shoulder, he'd been eighteen and fresh out of boot camp the first time he'd fired one like it. Shot another human being, the so-called enemy.

The young man as dead as if he'd never existed, his life turned to smoke. Jim sighed in his chest thinking of that distant moment.

Truth was, the moment never stopped trailing him, his own personal ghost.

That spirit and a few others drifted behind him during the ten minutes it took to reach the calf. No more than six months old, the thing was torn to pieces, innards open to the world. Jim gazed at the coyote. Sinewy and bristled, the bullet had pierced its neck. The animal seemed deflated. A stream of blood shaded the ground beneath it and Jackson barked once, high and short. "I don't know which, you tell me," Jim said. "Suppose I'll get rid of the calf first."

Jackson barked again, wanting Jim's attention.

"Agua."

Jim spun at the word, a dry rasp, and followed the dog's gaze.

Twenty or so yards away beneath a mesquite

tree lay a middle-aged man, sweat-stained and scorched, chest heaving. "*Por favor. Agua.*"

Jim raised his head and scanned the horizon, seeing what he expected: half a mile gone, a group of people moving slowly through the heat. Illegals were a regular sight in this part of Arizona, making the trek from Mexico, crossing the U.S. border only to encounter more sunbaked miles ahead, the long desert table of the Miracle Valley. What folks between here and Bisbee liked to say, for such a heavenly name the valley was its own patch of hell. Jim took a water bottle from his gear and went to the man. His lips were cut with scabs and one of his worn shoes showed a foot gone purple and split-wounded at the heel. Jim knelt and tipped the bottle to the man's mouth. The man gobbled at the water, ate it more than drank it. It was a known fact if someone couldn't make the rough crossing they were left behind. The shock of it faded years ago. Jim had seen it too often. More than a shame, it was a tragedy, a nightmare all around. The government was at fault, Jim believed, although he wasn't sure if it was because they didn't give a shit or because they couldn't get their shit together. In his experience it was some part of both.

"*Mas*," the man said.

Jim helped him drink again, then fetched a walkie-talkie from his gear and pressed a button. "Dispatch, come in. This is Jim Hanson, over."

A few seconds of crackle and a voice said, "This is border patrol dispatch. Hey Jim, it's Sarah, come back."

"Sarah, listen. Got some illegals down here in the valley, over."

"You have visual on them?"

"Yeah, let me see now." He squinted into the distance, using a finger to point at the receding figures. "Five by my count. Eastern edge of the ranch, heading due north toward Flat Rock Pass, just beyond the border wall, over."

"Copy that, Jim. I'll send agents."

"Need a medic, too. I found one left behind. He's in pretty bad shape, over."

"Will do," Sarah said. "It's been a little while, Jim. How are you doing out there?"

No easy answer to the question, he said what mattered. "Keeping busy."

"Good. Well," Sarah said. "Landmarks, where should agents look for the man?"

Shadows drifted overhead and Jim gazed up at the vulture joined by another, the pair skimming air currents. "Have them look for me. I'll wait with the man," Jim said. "Over."

3

He woke as the dark sky gave way to a nascent sun, soft oranges and pinks filtering through the blinds, knowing before looking at the other side of the bed that Christine would already be up. An early riser, eager for another day, she'd be in the kitchen now trying not to make noise but making just enough, eager for Jim to join her. The good burnt smell of coffee would travel up to him along with her whispered sweet talk to Jackson, maybe singing the dog a song, some little bit of Dolly or the Beatles or something.

Jim sat up slowly on the side of the bed and listened for his wife.

These were the hardest mornings.

Not that he forgot she was dead but when the memory of her was so alive that facing the day felt like that first day, the one after she passed. When he woke up listening for her and heard what he heard now, the silence of aloneness. Leaning on the edge of the mattress, the sensation of being cut from stone, that he'd never again move from this spot, and then Jackson nudged his ankle. Jim stared down at the dog. Jackson stared back saying a dozen things inside one look. Jim filled his lungs and exhaled. "Okay. You're right. Let's get started."

Like every other morning, it began with the flag.

More than an old Marine's patriotism, it was routine, what Jim relied on most. Patterns he could follow like road maps to get from the start of a day to its conclusion. The weathered clapboard house was framed by bougainvillea, rooted there by Christine. With Jackson in his wake, Jim stepped outside carrying the cloth triangle. As he unfolded it he noticed its fading stars and stripes and frayed edges, time to get a new one. Now he clipped it to the flagpole rope. He raised it, watching it catch the breeze like a fish's tail in water. Years of being trailed by that old ghost and all the other ghosts he'd set loose had separated the strands of duty from loyalty. It was enough that he hoisted the flag each day, believing it the right thing to do.

The sky began to vibrate then, a *thucka-thucka-thucka* above Jim's shoulder.

He looked up as a helicopter passed overhead. The Huey assigned to the border patrol had little to do with illegals, used instead in drug seizures. The cartels did human smuggling but it was narcotics the patrol cared about, an unending flow from Mexico to the U.S. Jim turned from the flagpole with a short whistle in his teeth. Jackson came off the porch, ambled to the pickup and into the passenger seat. The truck reminded him of the flag, frayed at the edges, a relic beat to hell except for the engine, the old monster 350 still grinding. Jim dropped the tailgate, made sure he had everything: hay bales, rolls of barbed wire, staplers and wire clips, a shovel. A dozen split-rail posts stacked beneath a tarp. The truck shuddered when he turned the key. As he drove from the house he was tempted to glance at the rearview mirror, wanting to see Christine on the porch there, waving goodbye. He kept his eyes on the dirt road instead.

Ten minutes later he hurried to shut the window so as not to chew dust.

Three Border Patrol ATVs sped around him, churning up a cloud. He watched them disappear and then eased onto a rocky trail, bouncing down into the valley to a grazing patch on his property not far from the border wall. Hungry cattle lumbered toward him, understanding what the truck meant. Jim kicked the hay bales onto the ground. Watching the cattle eat, he tried not to think of what he knew, that it wouldn't help much, they were almost too thin for slaughter. He looked away, gazing at a far-off line of fencing. Back in the truck, he drove south until he came to a ragged section. Jackson's head lifted at a whip-poor-will flitting from its ground nest, reddish-brown wings pinching the sky. Jim braked and climbed from the truck and stared over at the fence. Russian thistle choked the barbed wire in several places but it was two wooden posts Jim sought. Thirty feet between the pair, rotted and tilted inward, they dropped the fence to the ground like a sagging tennis net. Cattle, coyote, or anything else could clear it with ease.

Jim said, "Find a place. Got work to do."

He lowered the tailgate then and took out the posts, wire, and tools. Jackson leapt up, circled the tarp and curled up on it. The wind blew in whipping bursts, gritty and warm, threatening Jim's hat. He went to the rotted posts, clipped away the old wire before going to work with the shovel. Using it to hack away at hard-packed earth, Jim dropped the shovel and hugged the post, fighting it free. Sweat triangulated the back of his shirt. He repeated the process with the second post. With the shovel he deepened and widened the existing holes, tipping in water from a jug to soften the soil, drinking some himself. He worked the new posts into the ground using his body weight, heaving and twisting, legs and arms aflame. When the posts were in place, packed at the base with dirt and stone, he sat on the tailgate and shared bits of jerky with Jackson. The sun was higher now, orange and radiant. Jackson found her way into the shade of the truck cab. Jim stood feeling the welcome pain and spoke to himself, to Christine, needing his wife to hear his thoughts.

Telling her if he kept to his routines he might survive his days.

Because her eyes and mouth joined to his were gone forever, so were her hands on his shoulders, his on her hips, all gone. But if he continued to wake in their home, raise the flag, and tend the cattle, if the patterns held, then he might, too. Christine was woven into all he'd done when she was alive. She'd imbued his days with the sense of having tried his best, that he was part of something worthwhile, even if it was just planting posts and fixing fences. His wife was with him now when he did those things, necessary things that burned off the hours.

Jim returned to the fence, wanting the work. The day unwound as he cut scrub from the old wire in some places, stapled new barbed wire into others, repaired holes wrought either by a coyote's jaw or paw. Other types of coyotes too, those who guided illegals, Jim found a section clipped away just large enough for a body to slip through. It was alone out there in that wide stretch of world where he felt sharply what he was numb to on a moment-to-moment basis, the strangeness of his personal landscape. A place where one group of people badly wanted to be, where another group was determined to keep them out. It was almost enough for him to leave the hole as it was, but only almost. This land was his and Christine's. He could not help but feel a sense of violation and went to work on the wire fence. Jackson chased prairie dogs, nosed at toddling partridges. The sun was surrendering its heat when Jim dropped the tools into the back of the pickup. Jackson took her seat, riding shotgun. Ascending the valley, Jim glanced past the dog's wind-blown profile out at the border wall set hard against the road. Partly concrete panels, partly woven steel mesh, the twenty-foot-high line of separation extended for miles. More a show of strength than a deterrent, Jim thought, turning onto the long gravel drive toward his house. He slowed seeing a little car parked there, a compact box that didn't belong in this backcountry. A man leaned against it, thin and bespectacled in a short-sleeved dress shirt, thumbing a phone. Hearing the truck brake, he looked up and gave a wave. "Hey there. Mister James Hanson?"

"Easy, girl," Jim said to Jackson, a low growl rising from the dog, its eyes stuck on the man. Jim climbed from the truck and shut the door. "Who's asking?"

With a glance from Jackson to Jim, the man took a tentative step forward. "Carl Neeham. I'm from Merchants Bank. You're Mr. Hanson?"

"Yeah."

Neeham had been holding a document Jim hadn't noticed, which he extended now. Jim took it, staring at the block of words. "Sorry to be the one to tell you this, but the law requires that landowners be notified of a trustee sale," Neeham said.

Jim echoed it quietly. "Trustee sale?"

"Right. Well." The man adjusted his glasses.

"That means ninety days from today the ranch here will be sold at auction."

No need for that to be explained, Jim stood quiet, staring.

"I would've called but couldn't find a number for you, cell phone, nothing. Are you listed?" Neeham asked.

"Wait now. This—it can't be right. I was up to Merchants just a few weeks ago and met with Ned Fremont," Jim said. "I explained my situation to him. He promised we'd work it out."

"The bank made some changes recently. Ned's no longer with us. Not sure why he didn't follow up," Neeham frowned. "Regardless, it's bank policy to take action if there's been no payment in six months. In your case it's been eight. Of course you can avoid all of this if you get current on those missed payments within ninety days. But you should know, the bank has the option to sell the property before the auction if a reasonable offer comes in."

Jim glanced at the notice, looking through it, and then stared off into the distance.

"Mr. Hanson?" Neeham said.

"See that hill there?" Jim said, cocking his head. "The taller of the two?"

Neeham followed his gaze to the horizon.

"I spread my wife's ashes on top of that hill just last year."

With a nod Neeham said, "I'm sorry for your loss."

"I'm no deadbeat. Twenty-five years, I never missed a payment on this place, not until. Not since my Christine—" Jim said, stopping himself. "Listen. I need more time. A few months to sort things out, get back on track."

Neeham nodded. "I wish I could. You've got ninety days. Unless an offer comes in." His expression shifted, as if he were about to tell Jim to have a nice day but thought better of it. He climbed into his car, another wave, and drove off in a cone of dust. Jim watched him go and then went to the back of the truck, absently unloading tools. The shovel was in his hands when he looked at pink shadows spreading around the edge of twilight.

It was time for the flag to be lowered.

He went to the pole. Trudging over gravel, shovel in hand, Jim wondered why he raised and lowered the flag every day. Why he tended scrubby cattle that might not make it to market, broke his back out there fixing goddamn fences, and stopped in his tracks and threw down the shovel at the futility of it all, palming at his hot forehead.

Glancing over at that hill then, the taller of the two, he knew why he did it.

Jackson pushed her nose at his leg. Jim went down on one knee and touched his head to hers and laid arms around her neck and they stayed that way. After a while he stood. He gazed out at the land for a long time. A hundred and ten acres of red rock and brushy grass and baked sand, it was his and Christine's, the pinyon pines and spindle oak, white-tailed deer and warbler's morning song, all theirs. Turn around and he'd see the Mule Mountains streaked with gold. Rough and beautiful, bought with a VA loan, Jim drove Christine out here when they were courting. She'd explained it to him before: her short, unhappy marriage that ended five years earlier; her twelve-year-old daughter from that marriage, Sarah, the light of her life; how Sarah held out hope that her absentee father would appear one day and be everything he'd promised. Looking around the ranch then, Christine smiled at Jim and said, this, all of this, Sarah will love it because it's real. They were married shortly afterward. Jim said he'd build a better house than that old thing from the previous century. Christine said no, the house was as much part of the land as the red rock and limber pines. One thing for sure, Christine was right, Sarah loved the ranch. Jim taught her about the land, how to understand it. Sarah was respectful and friendly but stand-offish; maybe he didn't know how to be a father, maybe she didn't want him to be one. But they both had Christine, and they all had the ranch, and it was enough. It was where Jim cast off the bottle. After parking his truck sideways and stumbling toward his wife waiting on the porch, Christine listened to his slurring excuses and then laid a hand at the back of his hot neck and said she'd love him no matter what but she'd like him a hell of a lot more if he were sober. That was enough, too.

Under a white sun and fields of stars this land was where their two lives became one.

Where Christine now rested, and Jim persisted.

The sky's flame was nearly out as he pulled the rope hand over hand. When the flag was low he unclipped it, folded the cloth with stripes over stars, bottom edge to top, making alternate triangles so that it would be ready when he raised it the next morning. With Jackson at his heels, he moved toward the house. Then he slowed, and then he stopped. Call it a premonition, it rose up behind him as he turned and stared at the empty flagpole.

An itch at the back of his mind that tomorrow morning might never come.

4

Fear propelled her around the apartment as if she'd been injected with it, spinning from one closet to another with the red backpack that was nearly full of cash, shoving other things into it with a crunching sound like walking on dead leaves. Miguel stood motionless. The few objects he cared about most were in his own backpack, the one with the athletic swoosh Carlos had given him for school. His expression was trance-like, empty, but Rosa would deal with that later, make him whole again. Almost finished, she lifted a rosary from her bedroom mirror, brushed it with her lips, and took a scrap of paper from a dresser drawer. She stepped into the bathroom and looked at the digits printed on the paper and pressed them into her phone.

Two rings until a man's voice said, "*Taller mecánico Santana.*"

"*Carlos,*" she said, exhaling the name. "*Carlos me dijo que llamare questo número.*"

"*Quién? Carlos? No hay Carlos aqui,*" the man said. "There's no Carlos here."

"He told me to tell you, Chicago."

"Chicago."

"Yes. Please."

"You have money?"

"Yes."

"It's 5:15 now. Ten minutes. If you're late don't stop here, just go away, that's a warning." He gave Rosa an address and hung up.

Hands shaking, she threw the paper in the toilet and flushed. Miguel had moved to the kitchen and held the brown bag containing the *polverones.* For the second time that day she took the sugar cookies from him and set them

---

aside. Rosa instructed him to put on his backpack. She led him to the door and paused to wipe the soundless tears from his face, fixing her eyes on his and telling him that when the door closed behind them the apartment didn't exist anymore. When they left the neighborhood their street didn't exist anymore, and soon Nogales wouldn't either. They had to think forward. It was the only way they'd make it to her sister, Miguel's aunt in Chicago, *Tia Anna*, and when they could slow down and stop and rest then Rosa would explain everything to him. She promised, everything. But right now they had to fly. Did he hear her?

Miguel stared and nodded.

"*Mi querido,*" she said, giving him a little shake. "Be who you are. I need you."

And then they were in the hallway and Rosa locked the door behind her out of habit while the door across the hall opened to Mrs. Diaz who greeted them. Rosa said nothing, ignored the tears in her own eyes and kissed Mrs. Diaz on each cheek before leading Miguel to the stairs. He and the old woman stared at one another as his mother pulled him away. Mrs. Diaz raised a hand in goodbye but Miguel couldn't bring himself to wave back.

He knew this street. Not because he'd been in it before now but because it was similar to one where he grew up, identical to dozens of others in Nogales. Uneven sidewalks like broken piano keys running down the hill. Two- and three-story concrete apartment buildings veined and cracked and strewn with rigged wiring and satellite dishes, lines holding clothing baked stiff by the sun. A market sat at the end of the block, faded green with rusted awnings, a *lavanderia* next to it churning with lemony soap. Huge and peeling, a painted mural of Our Lady of Guadalupe dominated the wall of a tobacco shop, her expression so serene she looked asleep on her feet. Music from windows and voices down alleyways and shouted arguments created the background hum of people living shoulder-to-shoulder, unable to escape one another.

The black SUV pulled to a curb and cut the engine.

Mauricio climbed from the back while the block of flesh, Rigo, stepped from the passenger seat in front. On the sidewalk they looked up and down the street and traded a glance, knowing what had to be done here. The tall one, Hernando, crouched from the driver's side and met them on the sidewalk. He looked at the squat apartment building. "You sure this is it?" he said to Mauricio.

With a nod at the tooth hanging above the door of *Mejor Dental Ibarra,* Mauricio unwrapped a stick of gum, put it in his mouth, and led them toward the building entrance. It had taken him five minutes to get the information from one of the money counters whom Carlos had supervised. The skeletal guy, Hugo, shaking all over as he said yeah he knew who Rosa was, Carlos's sister, Perez maybe her last name, he wasn't sure, but he'd gone with Carlos for beers a couple times, Carlos stopping by his sister's building to drop off something on the way. A dentist on the ground floor, the sign, a tooth Hugo had said, and now Mauricio entered the building and stared at names on the mailboxes. No Perez but second floor rear: R. Lopez. He left Hernando at the entrance, and then he and Rigo were up the stairs quickly and quietly, past seven 7 p.m., the hall filled with dinner smells. Mauricio stopped at the apartment door and listened, then dialed Rosa's number on Carlos's phone. It didn't ring inside the apartment, only in his ear until a voice tight with hope said, "Carlos?"

An elastic moment, just long enough, Mauricio said, "I'm going to find you, Rosa."

The answer was a gasp, a *click*.

"Now?" Rigo said.

Mauricio said yes, and Rigo took his place at the door as the door across the hall opened. They turned to a small old woman wearing large eyeglasses with a chain dangling around her neck. The aroma of something sweet and freshly baked drifted from her apartment. Cinnamon bread or an iced cake, Mauricio thought, bringing up old memories. With a smile, he said, "*Hola, signora. Cóme estás?*"

"*Bien,*" she said coolly.

Eyes magnified behind lenses, and Mauricio knew she was someone's mother, *una madre mágica* who could see into his soul and knew what he was. He'd had a mother like her once, who'd baked for him and tried to save him.

Trying now to remember what she'd looked like but couldn't.

His mother's face disappeared with the rest of his childhood after he and his brother Rigo were taken away by the cartel as boys. Since then, every other magical mother had stared at him like this one, trying to see inside of him, find that lost boy. Mauricio let the mask slip for a few seconds, staring at her differently, as the lady's breath faltered.

"The woman who lives here. Is she at home?" he said.

Mrs. Diaz blinking, finding her voice. "They left."

"They? Who else? She has kids?"

She pursed her lips, regretting the slip, said nothing.

"Do you know where they went?" Mauricio asked.

Quiet a moment, looking at Rigo and back, she said, "Mexico City. They have a large family there. All policemen."

"Is that right? Well then, she should be nice and safe. Her husband is with her?"

"Yes. He's a police, too. Big fellow."

"Ah. Okay, now do me a favor? Go into your apartment, shut the door, and pay us no mind. Please mama."

Mrs. Diaz stood anchored to the spot, jaw set.

Mauricio held her gaze, let her see deeper inside of him, what would happen if she refused. The old woman paled. She stepped back, closed the door. A lock clicked, and Mauricio plucked the wad of gum from his mouth and pressed it over the peephole in her door. He turned to Rigo, said, "Open it." No need for force, kick down Rosa's door, Rigo was a natural with a pick, with tools and weapons. Mauricio was a natural too, in a way the cartel valued more than tools and weapons. Why he was a *teniente* with his own squad of *halcones* and *sicarios*.

A soft *click,* Rigo removed the pick and opened the door.

Mauricio stepped inside sensing the apartment was empty of people, telling Rigo to search for the money he believed was gone. In the kitchen a pot of stiff rice sat on the stove, another with congealing stew, hours old. A paper bag there, Mauricio opened it to *polverones*. Walking through the apartment eating cookies, he stopped at a memorial on top of a bookcase. A candle of the Virgin, a brass crucifix, snapshots of a man smiling with a woman who had to be Rosa. The two of them held a baby boy in one photo, another of the boy when he was older. Scribbled on the back, his ages and name: Miguel at two years old, Miguel at ten. Mauricio lifted a funeral card with an image of the man's face accompanied by a prayer for the dead. Inspecting the photos again, Mauricio's gaze went from the woman to the boy.

'They,' *la madre mágica* had said.

He lifted a photo and tore away the man, the dead husband-father so it was Rosa and Miguel alone, slid it into a pocket. Entered a bedroom to a dresser with its drawers pulled and a poster of Óscar Villa in the air kicking a leg over his head, a yellow-green banner of Club León with its lion's profile and soccer ball next to it. Mauricio moved to a shelf of bobbleheads, pro footballers, there was Villa again. A team photo of a group of boys in ragged jerseys, Miguel smiling on one knee holding a small trophy. Leaning in, looking closely, Mauricio felt it pierce a distant moment of sprinting down an alley, headed toward a makeshift goal pursued by boys who'd never catch him. He'd been in command of the ball at his feet, the mind-body lock of a real athlete, and wondered. If Miguel felt that same connection to the game. If his father's death had broken it, broken part of the boy, and glanced at a clean rectangle surrounded by dust. Maybe where that small trophy had stood. Important enough for Miguel to take with him, the thing he couldn't leave behind which meant they weren't coming back.

"Mauricio."

He followed Rigo's voice to Rosa's bedroom. His brother held a greeting card in one hand and a hundred-dollar bill in the other. "Found this in a drawer. The money was on the closet floor, she must've dropped it."

Mauricio took the card, signed by someone called Anna. Love and wishes that Rosa was recovering from Esteban's death, hard to believe a year had passed, she hoped they'd all be together soon. No mention of where. Mauricio tossed it aside and stared at the hundred-dollar bill. He turned it over to THE UNITED STATES OF AMERICA in capital letters proclaiming itself. Money generated by the cartel's drug sales in the U.S. was shipped to Mexico where the American currency was laundered for pesos. The first stop was a counting room like the one

Carlos had supervised. Inside a warehouse, a drug depot, on the outskirts of Nogales guarded 24/7 by Mauricio's men. Twice weekly a big rig that had driven tomatoes to California returned to Mexico and arrived at the depot carrying pallets of American twenties and hundreds in shrink-wrapped cubes. Each cube had been counted in the U.S. with the amount provided to Carlos. He counted it himself and then had one of his counters repeat the computation to verify the amount before the laundering began.

Only too late did Carlos realize he'd been tested and that he'd failed.

No overt suspicion, just the cartel's regular quality control. It sent a pallet with a stated amount of two million dollars but included an extra twenty-five grand, as if a cartel employee in the U.S. had made an error. Carlos counted it and discovered the overage and broke the cartel's cardinal rule, that its money was its money be it twenty-five thousand dollars or twenty-five *centavos*. Instead of informing his superiors that the pallet contained extra money, as they expected of him, Carlos placed the overage into a desk drawer. He gave his counter the paperwork stating the pallet amount as two million dollars. The counter computed the pallet and verified the two million and Carlos snuck the twenty-five grand to Rosa in a manila envelope. And then the cartel tested him again with an overage of a hundred and ten thousand, and once again to be sure, with seventy thousand, and by then Carlos had figured it out.

Mauricio folded the hundred, folded it again and slipped it in a pocket thinking of Carlos's corpse decorating the overpass, how the motherfucker believed he could steal and live.

How his fool of a sister thought she could escape with the cartel's money.

She'd be a fool to exchange it for pesos in Nogales or anywhere else in Mexico.

Mauricio left the bedroom and gazed around the apartment. He entered the bathroom and opened the medicine cabinet to aspirin, some tubes and jars, nothing useful. A card from a sister who-the-fuck-knew-where and a hundred-dollar bill, both useless in helping to find the woman and boy, and Mauricio closed the medicine cabinet. Stared into the mirror at the scar below his left eye earned when he was twelve years old, months after being taken by the cartel. Games, football, all of it done forever, he was working as a *halcone*, a lookout, before his real training began. Given a walkie-talkie, positioned on a city block, and ordered to radio the cartel if he spotted the military entering the area, he'd been sitting for hours, barely eaten in days, and nodded off. Missed the patrol that slipped past and although it had done no damage to the cartel, Mauricio's *teniente* taught him a lesson that stuck. Pushed the tip of a blade into the thin skin just below Mauricio's eye, the man told him if he ever again made the same mistake, missed any detail no matter how small, he'd pluck out both Mauricio's eyes; if you stop looking, stop listening and sniffing the air, even for a split second, he said, it puts the cartel at risk, and you'll pay for it.

Afterward Mauricio never missed a detail.

He looked past his reflection then, staring at the toilet. A slip of waterlogged paper stuck to the inside of the bowl. He turned and bent, peeled the paper free and inspected the digits printed there, runny but legible. No reason for a person to flush a phone number unless she didn't want it to be found or called, and he called it and listened.

One ring, a voice said, "*Taller mecánico Santana.*"

Mauricio knew then where Rosa had gone. Where she'd taken the boy. He knew that when this business was concluded both mother and son would no longer walk the earth and that

Mauricio would return to Nogales with the cartel's money.

It wasn't complicated.

It was how the world worked and why he was in the world.

5

Just over fifty head of cattle, all the backbreaking work Jim put into keeping them alive and now he had to nearly beg someone, anyone, to kill them.

Reps from the cattle brokerages came out to the ranch and inspected the bony herd. One named a price so low Jim chuckled, thinking at first the man was kidding, while another seemed offended at having the animals offered to him. But it was the slick old cattle dealer Jim had done business with for years, Everett Crawford, who stated it plainly: the malnourished cows were barely equal to the cost of slaughtering them. He'd go seventy cents a pound and that was being charitable. Jim did the math in his head. The selling price would barely put a dent in what he owed the bank and he told Everett he guessed he'd better think on it. Everett lit a cigarette. He looked beyond the herd to the sloping back of the mountains in the distance bathed in purple this time of day. "So you're getting out of the cow business, huh Jim?"

"Looks that way."

"How you plan on making a living?"

"Yet to be determined. Right now I just need money."

"What you got out here?" Everett said. "Hundred acres?"

"Hundred and ten."

"Why not sell some of it? You seen them mini-ranches out by Douglas? Fancy little spreads sitting on no more than fifteen, twenty acres. You could cut up some of this here and parcel it out that way."

Jim gazed up at the empty sky and then

down at his boots, Jackson there looking back. "Selling any of this land, even a single acre. It's not on the table at the moment."

"Well." Everett toed out the cigarette, picked up the butt, put it in a pocket. "You let me know about them cows." They shook hands then and Everett climbed into a new truck and Jim into his old one and they parted ways.

Jim arrived home to the flag up on the mailbox.

He removed three envelopes, a past due notice from Merchants Bank he tore in half without opening, a request from the hospice organization for a donation which he folded into a pocket, and his monthly benefit check from the Department of Veterans Affairs. The house inside was dusky in late afternoon, a contrast in light and shadow when Jim felt Christine was most present. He gazed at a rocker where she spent many hours dozing post-chemo, until the drugs quit working, until the hospice folks arrived to help ease her toward the end. An Arapaho blanket of desert oranges and blues lay over the back of the rocker. Sarah brought it to the house in those last weeks, came every day and tucked the blanket around Christine and sat close, mother and daughter with their eyes on one another. Christine was too tired to converse. Instead Sarah delivered quiet monologues on her most recent relationship, her challenges as a border patrol agent, a film she'd seen, a book she'd read. Jim stood back with empathy in his chest as Sarah threw out a narrative rope, hoping to tether her dying mother to her own living existence.

He still spoke to Christine each day, in his mind, often aloud.

The blanket situated that way over the rocker in those shadows, he held up the envelope from Veterans Affairs. "Three hundred and sixteen big ones. Problem solved."

You'll find a way, her voice said. *You'll fix this. You could always fix anything.*

"I couldn't fix you."

We did what the doctors told us to do, tried everything. It was just my time.

"Without you, my time," he said, shaking his head. "It moves in a hard way. The past won't leave me alone like it did when you were here, when you helped me push through it. Sometimes, you being gone, I can't help but think, well—" Jim sighed through his nose.

Say it.

"Losing you was payback for what I did in the war."

Cancer took me, not karma. You know that.

"What I got a medal for," he said, shaking his head.

You enlisted. You were special. They noticed.

By rote, recalling his commanding officer reading his shooting range evaluation aloud,

Jim said, "Unparalleled precision and efficiency. Extreme patience. Technical skill with a rifle."

You were doing your duty. Three tours, you did more than your duty.

"I know. I'm proud I went back, to protect my brothers. I'm a Marine forever."

But.

"But. A sniper's only purpose is to kill people."

Jim, she said in that tone he yearned for, reaching out to him.

"I don't regret my service. Yet, all those lives I took. How do I ever get right with that?"

What I urged you to do so many times, you know the answer.

He shook his head again. "It's not my way."

You need to talk to someone.

"I talked to you."

I'm gone now.

"And I worked. You and me together, we worked and brought this ranch to life."

I'm dead now.

Jim blinked at the chair, the blanket, and pulled a hand over his face. "I'll work."

When the sun rose the next morning he was already shaved and dressed. He sipped coffee leaning against the stove, waiting for the designated hour when people arrived at their jobs. With the flag hoisted and Jackson asleep in the house, Jim loaded the truck's toolbox. He drove toward the highway with the windows open, smelling the day heating up. A helicopter cut the clouds overhead in pursuit of drugs and guns and money, cartel bounty. The border wall flitted past on one side of the road and the desert like a long brown sea on the other.

Subtracting the years he figured Sarah had to be thirty-two now.

Twenty years past when she was a girl of twelve, whenever she and Christine and Jim drove this stretch Sarah always made the same

comment: how long until we reach civiliza-
tion? There'd been more truth in it back then.
A few other ranches had sat off in the distance,
nothing else. Sometimes they wouldn't see another vehicle until town. Jim gazed out at how
the world had shifted in two decades, passing
three, six, a dozen of the mini-ranches Everett
Crawford had spoken of, old west meets dude
resort, and then the first phase of a pricey res-
idential development. La Vista-something.
He once regarded such growth as encroach-
ment but worried now he'd been mistaken.
Opportunities he'd let pass by. Minutes later he
turned into the second phase of the development. Lines of wooden skeletons rose up, the
sound of hammers pounding down the block
as suburbia bloomed in the desert.

The door of a shiny pickup at the curb read
Frank Sims & Son Homebuilders.

Jim parked and got out with something in his
gut, nerves maybe, or desperation. He wouldn't

allow it, pressed it down, and walked the block quickly toward a construction site teeming with activity, men like ants on a sand hill.

"Jim? Hey, Hanson!"

He turned at his name. A familiar face smiled beneath a pearl Stetson, older now, young middle age. Jim said, "Randall. You're not a kid anymore."

"Pretty much running things since my dad retired." Randall extended a hand.

"Frank Sims, retired? Why can't I picture your old man on a golf course?"

"He still comes around, barking orders. Old habits, I guess," Randall said. "So what brings you out this way? In the market for a house, I can give you a deal on one of these beauts."

"Hoping to find your dad," Jim said. "Thing is. I could use some work."

A few seconds of questions in Randall's eyes and then that smile again. "Sorry Jim. I'm pretty much at capacity as far as employees go. Anyways, don't you have a ranch to run?"

Jim hated what he had to say, every time he said it. "Christine, my wife. She died—"

"Oh. Hell. I'm sorry to hear that," Randall said, slipping off his hat.

"—and with the medical bills and such, the insurance. It sort of left me in the hole." He squinted beyond the sun at men working on one of the wooden skeletons. "Put me up there with those boys. I'll have the whole thing framed out by day's end. Brought my own tools."

"That kind of work, up there? Well, look Jim. It's not really for—"

"Someone my age?" He met Randall's gaze, held it. "I can outlast any man here. Damn, Randall. I taught you to frame when I worked for your old man."

"You did, and taught me right. And if I had something for you I'd put you on it, but I don't. Listen, we have a new phase kicking off about two months from now. Come back then. I'll see if I can find something for you."

"Two months."

"I wish I could help you out. I really do."

A slow nod, moving away, Jim said, "You give Frank my regards."

"Sorry again about your wife, Jim. Take care of yourself, hear?"

A hand in the air, Jim waved over his back and climbed into the truck. At the crossroads he changed his mind and headed into town. He passed the border patrol station, sandstone and red brick built low to the ground surrounded by barbed wire fencing and satellite dishes twirling on the roof, the look of a high-tech penitentiary. A dozen SUVs sat in the lot, white with the green stripe. Thinking of what Randall said, Jim repeated it, "That kind of work, up there?" and answered it with, "Yeah that kind of work, goddamn it." An eighteen-wheeler blew past, a few cars, an RV. He crossed the town square and drove several blocks and found a space and parked there. Stared through the windshield feeling like a fool. How he'd brought along his tools, the truth on his shoulders now. That a herd of skinny cows and a daily wage combined wouldn't have earned nearly enough to satisfy eight months of overdue payments. He took off his hat. Threw it on the seat, palmed his eyes, and reached for it again looking through the windshield at the short commercial block across the street.

Acme Hardware sat next to Moe's Cantina sat next to Merchants Bank.

The pencil pusher in the short-sleeve dress shirt, Needham, Neeman, whatever the hell his name was, he was probably in there right now shuffling papers, ruining people's lives. A voice spoke at Jim then. Not Christine's but his own from the past, a younger Jim who dealt with problems differently. His eyes swept the block again as he thought of the ranch. How it was lost or had been taken from him, the same thing, his life ruined, and he answered himself, saying, "Fuck it. You're right," and climbed from the truck.

6

Her way, as it had always been when Sarah found herself in a tough situation, was not to complain or fold but to take it as a challenge. Be tougher than the situation and find a way to resolve it. The previous three years at the southern tip of the state, assigned to the border patrol family detention center, that inclination had been tested. A moral tightrope, no easy answers there, so she'd followed protocol while adhering to what her mother explained to her as a child, shown her by example. That strength didn't mean much on its own but add some intelligence and kindness to the mix, and a person could become useful.

Her mother could've taught Dalton McCarthy a lesson.

Sarah's direct report at her new assignment, *new* a relative term since she'd been there half a year. Her request to be transferred to the station close to where she'd grown up was granted due to her mother's illness, and Sarah returned and spent as much time as she could with her until she died. Three months together was all they got. Heartbroken, soul in little pieces, she'd wanted to talk to her stepfather about how she felt, but that had never been their way. Jim sealed himself up and headed out to the far edges of the ranch to work until he was numb. It was the PAIC, Patrol Agent In Charge, everyone's boss, Lee Hurst with his buzz cut and throat of gravel who told Sarah he understood her grief, that all these years later he still felt the loss of his own mother. Dalton was the Deputy Patrol Agent, second-in-command to Hurst.

All he said to Sarah was that she got two days of funeral leave, no more, and if she wanted additional time she'd have to take it without pay.

She sat now staring at a large screen with a live feed of the vehicle checkpoint.

Feeling nearly useless, aware that Dalton was marginalizing her, trapping her at a desk.

At first she assumed it was because she was a woman, how could she not? Seven years with the border patrol, sexism and harassment had been a constant. During her first assignment she got hit on so many times by other agents, single and married, she finally complained to the PAIC. As a result not one agent was disciplined while Sarah was transferred to the family detention center. Here though, she realized Dalton was an equal opportunity asshole toward all the agents, female and male, especially anyone who questioned an order or dared to ask for something. A month or so after her mother died, back from a patrol, Sarah reminded Dalton she was qualified to be a field supervisor and would appreciate the opportunity to lead a squad.

Weeks later he put her on desk duty in the control room with the screens and radios.

Each day she expected it to change but it didn't.

She was excluded from field patrols, strategic operations, the actual work of preventing the smuggling of humans and narcotics. All the reasons she became an agent. Lee Hurst was fair-minded and steady and seemed to like her but still, Sarah was wary of approaching him, of being branded a problem agent. What she needed was to draw Hurst's attention in a positive way. Be involved in some sort of action with consequences that made her necessary in the field. Which she realized was nearly impossible since she was trapped at a desk.

Her eyes flicked to the landline, its red light winking.

"Sarah Reynolds," she said into the receiver. A man's voice on the other end asked a question and she answered, "My stepfather, not my father." She listened some more. Sarah thanked the man and hung up and sat back with a sigh. "Shit," she said, standing, strapping on her service piece and heading for the parking lot.

One of those watering holes so daytime-dark that when the door opened to a rectangle of sunlight it was like a nuclear blast without goggles, drinkers squinting away from it, shielding their eyes. Sarah recalled Moe's Cantina by its potpourri of stale beer, burnt grease, and disinfectant. Last time she'd been in here, sixteen, seventeen years old, the same bartender had stood in the same spot behind the bar, difference now was he had less hair and more paunch. He glanced at her gun on one hip, badge on the other, and nodded as she went to him. "Sarah?" he said.

"That's right." She looked down the long bar to Jim sitting alone. He threw back a shot of something brown and placed the glass upside down among a group of other upside-down glasses. "How long has he been here?"

"Since I opened, noon. Thought I should call. His wife made me promise, she'd come and fetch him. That was years back."

"I came with her now and then." Sarah watched Jim's head dip to his chest. "How'd you know where to call me? How to find me?"

"Well, he told me about his wife passing, your mom. And that you were with the patrol now out at the station, bragging on you a bit."

"On me?"

"That was hours ago. Then he quit talking and started drinking to beat the band."

Sarah nodded, moved down the bar. Jim lifted his head toward her, half-mast eyes blinking in recognition. He slumped back and Sarah said, "Hey stranger."

"Sarah." Three full shot glasses sat in front of him. "Want something? A beer?"

"I'm on duty." She sat next to him, said, "Thanks by the way, for your radio to the station the other day. A few hours more and the guy you found would've been one for the coroner."

"I guess it was his lucky day." Jim threw back a shot, placed the glass upside down.

"Not sure he'd agree. Spent his savings on a coyote that left him for dead. All for nothing, he'll be sent back," Sarah said.

"World's cruel."

She paused, looking hard at Jim, but his eyes remained on the bar. "The pass near the ranch has been busy for months. The cartels are running everything through that area, drugs and weapons. People," she said.

"What else is new?" Jim said.

"I'm just saying. I worry about you, all alone

out there. Maybe it's time to join the modern world, get a cell phone."

"Don't need one. And I'm not alone. I have Jackson."

"You know what I'm saying."

"Well," Jim shrugged, turning to her with an effort to stay on the barstool. "You won't have to worry much longer. I lost the ranch."

Quiet a moment, Sarah said, "What do you mean, lost it?"

"I mean I missed a bunch of mortgage payments. Eight payments, and I'm broke." He killed a shot of whiskey, upended the glass, and explained it all. How the insurance stretched only so far, and then he'd used up his and Christine's savings covering the rest of her medical costs, and somewhere in that mournful blur of time he'd quit paying the mortgage, the money needed elsewhere. Jim told Sarah about the pencil pusher from Merchants. That the ranch would be auctioned in ninety days, counted at his fingers and said, no, wait, eighty-seven days now.

"Anyone to borrow from?" Sarah said. "How about that old Marine buddy of yours. Had a son about my age, they visited the ranch a couple times."

Jim shook his head. "Harold Richman. I haven't talked to him in a while. Besides, he doesn't have that kind of money. He taught school in Detroit."

"But. Why didn't you sell some of the land, Jim? My mother was sick for more than a year. When you saw the money running out, why?"

"We couldn't agree."

"She didn't want to sell?"

"I didn't." Jim circled a shot glass rim with a finger, gazing at it. "I thought she was going to live because I couldn't imagine her dead. I thought we'd get back to work, pay what we owed. Get old out there together." He lifted the glass, drained it, and set it upside down.

"Maybe there's a way to save the place."

He shook his head, a dizzy tilt. "It's gone. Like her. Wasn't right, her going out the way she did. Suffering like that."

Inhale, exhale, that quick, her mom's death as fresh as if it just occurred. "I'm sorry about the ranch. That it happened this way. I miss her every day. Some days, her not being here, it doesn't seem real," Sarah said, unsure when the tears began.

Jim stared, looked away, voice a quiet slur. "You're getting on though?"

Sarah nodded and thumbed at her face.

"Still seeing that fella, Mike was it?"

"Mark. No. I'm taking a break from seeing anyone. Need to concentrate on myself for a while, you know?"

"But work, the patrol. That's going good, right?"

"Sure. Right." She looked around the bar, a handful of people mostly alone at four in the afternoon, each bent over a glass or bottle. "Jim. What are you doing in here?"

"At the moment? Trying to get a drink." He waved at the bartender, who ignored him.

"You gave this up. What do you think it's going to do for you?"

"Can't say." Jim shrugged. "Maybe help me figure out how it is a man can work his whole life. Serve his country, pay his taxes, and end up without a pot to piss in."

"There aren't any answers here. You know that."

"What I know? Sarah, what I know?" His face tightened, eyes dark. "I lost her. Our home, our land, and she was the only thing that made any of it worthwhile." A hand slid over his brow, he whipped it away and pushed from the bar. "Fuck it, the man won't come to me, I'll go to him, get a damn drink." Jim took a step and stumbled, Sarah quick on her feet, holding him up. "I'm okay," he said, trying to find steady ground. "I'm okay."

"No, you're not." Sarah put his hat on his head, hooked his arm, and walked him out.

It was a day of returning to places.

The last time she'd been to the clapboard house was to select what her mother would wear in a casket. Jim would not do that, could not. After the funeral they spoke weekly, checking on one another, then every few weeks, then a month passed when they didn't speak at all. Jim withdrew to the desert. Sarah moved through the days like wakeful dreaming. The adage was true that life went on, shocking her that the world kept spinning despite the terrible event that had occurred. Another shock was the desire to talk to her father. Her real father, to tell him her mother was dead. Her mother had divorced him when Sarah was seven, and she'd barely seen or heard from him since. As a girl it had been worse than if he'd died, her father out there somewhere and didn't want her, and it made her resent Jim for not being the father she wanted.

"Goddamn it," he mumbled.

She watched Jim sway on the edge of the couch trying to pull off a boot, Jackson worrying at his feet. "Need some help?" she asked. Jim wagged his head. Yanked hard, knocked a side table covered in framed pictures onto the floor. He took a drag from the whiskey pint Sarah had bought for him, a tradeoff for agreeing to let her drive him to the ranch, and extended the bottle. "No thanks," she said. She righted the table, picking up photos.

"Sure?"

"Yeah," she said. While Jim tugged at the other boot, she paused to look at her mom and him on their wedding day, Sarah thirteen with a yellow poppy behind an ear. One of the happiest days of her life, seeing her mother so happy. The ranch felt strange at first, so different than town. But Sarah soon came to love how the desert was all things at once; desolate and bountiful, rocky and plush, sweltering and chillingly lovely. Jim knew every inch of the land. Watching him at work, listening to his quiet words, she came to understand that his knowledge and experience extended far beyond the border fences he planted and strung with wire. Yet when he tried to find ways to connect with her other than the ranch, Sarah rejected him. She was a child then, unable to put words to the internal conflict she felt. She'd liked Jim, even admired him, but the hope that her father would appear was ever present, the shadow of a possibility that he'd keep his word and reenter her life. Something about accepting Jim felt like betraying her father until her rejection became a habit. Still, Jim kept trying. Talking in his slow way about what the weather meant, showing her how to tie a rope in purposeful knots, how to behave around guns, how to point a telescope into the sky at stars like broken glass in a pond. She'd listened and participated but given no signs that she cared until finally he stopped trying as hard. She sorely wished now she could talk to herself when she had been that girl. Wished she could tell her what she was going to miss out on with Jim before she missed it.

"I—" he mumbled, dropping the other boot and reclining on the couch, "—have hit a damn wall." Jackson climbed up and tucked in at his feet, finding her place.

"I'll bring your truck back early," Sarah said. "Drive it up with one of the agents."

"Thanks. For bringing me home, too." Jim's voice drifted, nodding off when he said, "I was going through some things. Meaning to, for your mom. She left you a letter. Top drawer."

Sarah looked over at the roll top desk and

went to it. The drawer was a mess of paper clips and stamps and rubber bands, Jim's Silver Star medal lying among it like an afterthought. The envelope was on top, her name in her mother's precise hand. Sarah unsealed it and read a letter filled with things her mother wanted her to know and remember, about the past, about Jim. When she was done reading Sarah slid it into a pocket and went to him. Looked down at him fast asleep, his sun-creased brow, the age that had somehow crept into his face. The Arapaho blanket lay on the rocking chair. She spread it over him and went for the door, then turned back and looked at him. What her mother had written to her about Jim, a need to answer it rose up in Sarah, strong but reluctant, the words they'd never spoken aloud. A hand in her pocket, on the letter, she took a deep breath. "I love you too, okay?" she said quietly, careful not to wake him, and closed the door behind her.

7

Even with the slow hiss of voices around her, the soothing rhythm of tires creasing the road, Rosa felt as if her heart would never slow down.

Two hours earlier they'd made it to Taller Mecánico Santana with minutes to spare, the mechanic's shop on the west side of Nogales, a part of town Rosa avoided. Junked vehicles chopped for parts sat inside its chain-linked property, the building's facade darkened by soot. About to enter the shop, she'd remembered the instructions at the last second and hurried Miguel around back to a wooden fence trimmed with barbed wire. She'd knocked hard on the door and a teenage boy with a blank face peeked out at them, their backpacks. Locks moved and he'd opened it and led them to a shed where an obese man in a wheelchair and an older man who looked like him asked Rosa questions and demanded the fee. Carlos had cautioned her, have the amount set aside. Never open the backpack in front of anyone. She'd separated the money into an envelope and handed it to them then, seven thousand American. They were taken to a garage where other people waited. Rosa guessed fifteen others but she did not make eye contact. The van was emblazoned with *Caradides Católica Romana* *an*d an image of the Madonna and child. Everyone was aboard within minutes, the van heading east along the Mexican highway.

"*Cuanto tiempo hasta che lleguemos?*" Miguel asked. "How long until we get there?"

Lost in thought, Rosa looked from the van window with its unending desert backdrop to her son. "Very soon."

"You haven't told me where exactly."

"Someplace we have to stop first, sleep one night. Then it's like I said, we'll go on to Chicago and see your aunt."

Miguel nodded. "The place we're stopping first. Let me guess. Hmm," he said in that tone, how they teased each other. "Disneyland, right?" He glanced around the van at the other people. "This must be the Mickey Mouse Express."

Rosa looked at him seriously. "Someday, I promise. Let's get to Chicago first, okay?"

"Wait. So we're not getting our mouse ears?" He smiled.

That expression, grateful for it, she kissed Miguel's forehead. Turned back to the window and her thoughts, how she'd told him that his uncle had done something wrong, which made it necessary to leave in a hurry. She'd also lied to Miguel. Twice, the first based on a gut feeling, the second by omission. That Carlos would meet them in Chicago although Rosa was certain her brother was dead by now. She also didn't tell her son the cartel was surely looking for them, for the money, he didn't need that worry. Except that a wire ran between them, Miguel often able to feel what she felt without knowing the reason. She was tempted to look at him, what was in his eyes, but kept her own on the window and thought of what would happen next. How everyone in the van would spend the night at a motel in the tiny border town of Aqua Prieta. Early the next morning they'd be driven into the desert where the coyote would lead them on foot the rest of the way, across the border to a safe house on the Arizona side. After a day or two they'd be taken to Chicago by a different coyote in a different van.

Rosa's phone buzzed twice, making her jump.

The display, she stared at the name there with a rush of hope that everything would work out as he'd promised, and answered, "Carlos?"

A moment dragged until a voice said, "I'm going to find you, Rosa."

Not Carlos.

A stranger's voice, his tone like he knew her, like there was a smile in it.

Rosa gasped and hung up, tried to stick her gaze to the window but knew Miguel was looking at her. She couldn't help herself and turned to her son, whose smile was gone.

They'd left the apartment and sped to Taller Mecánico Santana where Mauricio asked that fat legless fuck Julian Santana a question: who owns the border? Julian had looked at his father, the two of them sharing one face, and back at Mauricio and answered, Ángel, and Mauricio asked another question: how much do you pay Ángel a month so you and your father can operate your human trafficking business, pretending to fix cars while you smuggle people over Ángel's border? Julian said twenty-five thousand and Mauricio reached into a pocket and threw the torn picture of Rosa and Miguel onto Julian's lap and said tell me where they went and when they're crossing the border or else your new monthly fee will be the amount that bitch stole from Ángel, two hundred thousand, and if you can't pay it I'll come back here and burn this fucking place to the ground with you and your wife and kids and father in it. Okay?

Okay.

Julian looked at the picture, showed it to his father. The old man flipped through a notebook and said the woman and boy left three hours earlier in the church van along with a dozen other people. They should be nearing Aqua Prieta by now, a motel there, the Mesa Inn. Then early the next morning everyone back in the van and into the desert to the wall, the place where they cross into the United States. Mauricio told

Julian to call the driver of the van, the *chequa-dor*, and tell him who Mauricio was. Julian did that in an urgent whisper. Mauricio took the phone and stepped away, a private talk with the driver whose voice was already quivering. Told the *chequador* that he and his men were heading to Aqua Prieta soon, to the Mesa Inn, and then explained how it would play out with the woman and boy. How the *chequador* would take the two of them into the desert in the morning, to that place where crossings happen. Keep them unaware, don't let them out of the van. Mauricio asked the *chequador* if he under-stood, the man saying yes, yes, yes, whatever you say, boss, whatever you say.

That was hours ago, the black SUV burning eastward now into the fading sun.

Hernando crouched behind the wheel like a praying mantis, Rigo asleep in the passenger seat with his shaved head against the window.

In the back seat, Mauricio felt the cold barrel of a gun nudge the base of his skull.

Imagining it, sometime in the future when the boy, Miguel, a boy no longer, would take revenge for his mother's murder. So of course he had to die along with Rosa. Maybe not as dramatically as his uncle, Carlos's corpse hung from the overpass, a promise sent to those inside the cartel and on the fringes: steal from us, a fortune or a peso, here's your fate. If Mauricio had caught the woman and boy back in Nogales he'd have hung them there too, shown how the cartel came for a transgressor's family. A place like Aqua Prieta, with no underlings or enemies to terrorize, was different. Bodies were a burden. Awkward, hard to dispose of, not like the movies, just dig a hole, bullshit. Besides, a murdered mother and child was a risk. Law enforcement paid to look the other way might get involved, cartel profits could suffer. Early evening at a motel with civilians around, there was nothing to gain from making corpses.

The SUV hit a pothole and Rigo sat up rubbing his eyes. He glanced out at twilight and then turned to Mauricio in the back seat. "We do it early tomorrow, yes?" Rigo yawned.

Mauricio nodded at what they knew from experience.

If this situation was a threat to the cartel or an outrageous sum of money, they'd do it as soon as they arrived at the motel, Mauricio first through the door, fuck the witnesses. But this, the smart move was to drive into the desert in the morning. The bodies could lay where they fell.

"Let the buzzards have them," Rigo said.

Another nod from Mauricio, the brothers aligned as always.

Raised by the cartel to think and function in the same ways. Obey its rules and honor its customs, he was in sync with Rigo, they balanced one another. And yet the thing alive inside Mauricio, it set them apart. A *teniente* with Rigo his right-hand man, Mauricio's reputation in the cartel was real and earned, but it was more than that. Deeper, it had always existed. An ability or desire, maybe a curse but surely a gift, no single word matched what he felt.

That if he decided someone would live or die, they would live or die.

Like fate, he was inescapable.

He removed the torn photo from his pocket. Stared at the woman and boy, examining their faces, their smiles. Air whistled past the SUV and Mauricio knew it didn't matter. He could speed up or drive slowly, hurry in when he arrived at the motel or take all the time in the world.

Rosa and Miguel were alive, but also dead. They just didn't know it yet.

***

What woke him, he was sure Lola had whispered his name. That she was perched at the end of the bed, but when Miguel sat up no one was there. The yellow buzz of security lights outside the motel room curtains was enough to cut the darkness, his mother motionless in the bed next to his. Thinking about it, feeling it in his stomach, Miguel realized it was hunger that woke him. Chunks of gray pork, the clammy plantains they'd been given for dinner, Miguel had ignored it all and chewed on a piece of bread.

A clock clicked with the time, 1:36 in the morning.

He put his feet on the floor and decided to disobey his mother.

Everyone in the van had been ushered into rooms and told to stay inside the motel. Be ready at 7:00 a.m. to avoid the U.S. Border

Patrol. On the way to their room Miguel had noticed a vending machine. Before leaving Nogales he'd stuffed what little money he had into his backpack. He crept to it now and unzipped the top, pushed aside his trophy and grabbed a handful of coins. Quietly, his mother would kill him if she caught him, the promise he'd made her that he would not leave the room no matter what. Well. She wouldn't have to kill him because he'd die of hunger if he didn't eat something. He lifted the brass key from a side table. Unlocked the door slowly, minimizing the click, it yawned and he shut it without a sound. Barefoot in shorts and a T-shirt, Miguel turned down the concrete walkway. Lights were on behind the shades in some of the motel rooms he passed, voices and low music coming from others, still others as dark and silent as his own. He turned a corner, crossed a courtyard. The vending machine was a bright rectangle at the end of a corridor and he went to it. Hoping against hope and, yes, right there, he peered through its glass face at a bag of *panditas*, all those colors sealed together like a burst of joy. He fed the machine and pushed the buttons and the bag uncoiled and dropped with a satisfying *thump*. Miguel slid a hand through the metal mouth, removed the candy. Headed back toward his room, opening the bag, he heard, "Hey little man."

Miguel turned, turned again to vehicles parked hard against the walkway.

A man leaned on a black SUV smoking a cigarette, boots crossed at the ankles, silver buckles winking. He pointed the butt at Miguel. "You into *fútbol*?"

The shirt Miguel wore, he looked down at the crest of the Mexican national soccer team. A golden eagle perched on the branch of a prickly pear, he said, "Yeah."

"Me too. Since I was your age, probably. How old are you?"

"Almost twelve."

"Late to be out here alone."

"I was hungry. I'm on my way back to my room."

The man nodded, exhaling smoke through his nose, dropped the cigarette and toed it into concrete. "Before you go, how about we make a bet?"

Miguel stared at him smiling there in black jeans, black jacket and T-shirt, plain-looking except for a scar over his left eyebrow. Couldn't remember if he'd been in the van. A pause and Miguel said, "What kind of bet?"

"That I can guess your favorite *fútbol* club. Not just that. Your favorite player."

"How?"

"I have an instinct," the man said. "Like I can read minds."

"If you win, what?"

"The *panditas*."

"What if you're wrong? What do I get?"

The man closed his eyes as if concentrating and then opened them and they looked different to Miguel. "A thing so valuable. A kid your age couldn't imagine losing it."

What his mother had taught him, Uncle Carlos too, but it was his father's voice he heard now. His *papá* who believed in superstitions and signs and the Virgin in a way Miguel's mom didn't, Miguel himself couldn't comprehend. He once told Miguel that when the facts in his head clashed with the feelings in his belly, heed his belly, the instinct there left over from when they were apes. Right now, the man's smile back in place, Miguel's belly told him to return to his room. "Thanks anyway. I'm too hungry to bet," he said, lifting the candy, moving away.

"Enjoy those. I mean it," the man said quietly.

Miguel walked down the corridor with eyes on his back, feeling a pull.

Turning him around to the SUV parked beneath a cone of light that was as empty as if the man had never been there at all.

* * *

Even when he slept he didn't sleep, not really. Through habit, caution, he was aware of what was happening around him, alert to noise and motion while drifting in place. Brief moments when he exited consciousness, Mauricio was quickly awakened by a voice. His own, unsure whom he'd been talking to, not caring to know. Whoever it was belonged back there, in the past, gone.

Sunlight made an arc outside the motel room, drawing his eye.

From the chair where he'd spent the rest of the night, positioned near the window, Mauricio looked across the courtyard at Rosa's room, gray and still behind the blinds. He glanced at his phone, the time, 6:50 a.m. In a few minutes the *chequador* would summon mother and son to the parking lot and drive them into the desert. He and Rigo and Hernando would follow soon after, time it so they could rush the van when it was near the wall. Get it done and retrieve the money, be back in Nogales before noon, back to more important business.

Blinds moved in Rosa's window. Miguel stood gazing into the parking lot.

Probably looking for the van, his expression the same as when he'd considered Mauricio's bet, some calculation happening there. The boy had to know crossing into the U.S. was dangerous. If he was scared it didn't show, and he left the window. Mauricio sat unmoving. The boy displayed little fear the previous evening, as well. Having a smoke, seeing Miguel approach the vending machine, Mauricio had slipped into a shadow and waited. It happened sometimes, rarely, a chance encounter with a target. Exchange a few words, ask a question or two, the person inevitably justifying their death. Mauricio wondered then, if Miguel had accepted the bet and won. If he'd named a *fútbol* player other than Óscar Villa as his favorite, would Mauricio have given the boy that invaluable thing, his life?

The van's horn sounded, calling mother and son.

Mauricio watched them leave the motel room, each with a backpack, the red one on Rosa's shoulder filled tight. A glance around the parking lot at a car nearby, a woman behind the wheel staring at her phone next to a pair of delivery guys unloading laundry bags from a truck. Walk outside with a nine-millimeter and put one in Miguel's head, one in Rosa's, lift that red backpack, then what? Kill the woman on her phone who saw it happen? The delivery guys? Everyone in the motel who heard shots and came running? Mauricio sat back, crossed his boots. Thinking of Hernando, his driver, clever and obedient, young enough that certain lessons still had to be learned. Why they waited until morning to take care of Rosa and Miguel.

Arriving at the motel yesterday, Rigo had explained the logic of it to Hernando, who'd listened quietly, and then Mauricio spoke. "We succeed most when we attract the fewest eyes. When we're invisible," he'd said, hearing traces of someone else's words, El General.

Outside an engine churned. Mauricio watched the van bump onto the highway.

A glance at his forearms, the tattoos not unlike those of the man who'd taught him the ways of the cartel. El General guided Mauricio to the thing alive inside him, helped him harness it, the memory sparking the question again: had Miguel won the bet, would he have let him live?

Kill the woman.

Take the boy.

As he and Rigo had been taken, Mauricio would teach Miguel as they'd been taught. Harness his calculations and lack of fear until his mother receded into the past. All he'd known and cared about would fade away with her, years would pass. Miguel would grow into a man not bent on avenging her but one eager to serve the cartel, his new family and identity.

There was more than one way to take a life.

Mauricio considered it. Rose from the chair and stretched and rejected it.

Miguel would die today, it was his fate, inescapable.

The clock clicked to 6:55 in the morning. Miguel lifted the blinds, peered out at the parking lot. No van, not yet. He turned and sat on his bed opposite his mother, both of them dressed with backpacks slung. She reached out and gave his hands a squeeze.

"Ready?" His mother's eyes were fixed and determined.

Miguel nodded.

"This is the hardest part, through the border

wall. There's a road on the other side, not too far. Another van will be waiting there. You understand?"

He nodded again.

"And then on to Chicago. We'll be driven there, across the country."

Outside their room the *beep-beep of* the van sounded. Rosa squeezed his hands again and they rose and left the room and crossed the parking lot to the van. The engine was running, the *chequador at* the wheel. He looked away as they climbed into the empty vehicle, the first two aboard, Miguel sitting behind him. Rosa next to her son, she snapped on her seat belt as the *chequador re*ached over and shut the door and put the van into gear. He crossed the parking lot and turned onto the highway, Rosa looking around. *"Donde estan los todos?"* she said. "Where are the others?"

"Es más seguro, ustedes dos solos. Los todos más tarde, en grupos más pequeños," the driver said.

"It's safer, you two alone. The others later, in smaller groups."

"How is it safer?" she asked.

The man's eyes went to hers in the rearview mirror. "Trust me, okay? I've done this a million times. It's best this way."

Rosa sat back and exhaled, bit at a thumbnail. Miguel wanted to ask her a question but remained silent. Soon they left the highway for a rural road, the pavement fading to dirt tracks. The van passed a boarded-up house, the belly of its septic tank rusted away, and then Miguel saw no more buildings. Up and over small hills and around bends that dipped, they followed the contour of a red rock mountain that unwound into a valley until they were crossing the desert floor with a funnel of dust in their wake. For the first time Miguel noticed the wall, a long dark line extending in both directions until disappearing over the edges of the Earth. As they approached he watched it become a fence of thick interwoven steel wire. Maybe fifty yards away now, a small rise on the Arizona side with a road running over it. The *chequador* pulled behind a rocky outcropping and looked at his phone as Rosa said, "Is this it? Where we cross?"

He nodded, eyes on the screen.

"How?" Rosa said with an edge to her voice, it made him look at her in the mirror. "Where are you taking us through?" she asked.

A pause and the man said, "You're crossing by yourself."

"What do you mean?"

"I mean like I said, it's safer." He pointed through the windshield at the fence, twenty-five feet high planted in a concrete trench. "At that corner, you see? The orange paint sprayed there, the X? The wire's cut loose, you pull that back and slide around it. The road is just up there, where the other van will meet you."

"When do we go?"

"A few minutes. We have to wait."

"Why not now?" Rosa said.

"The van isn't there yet," the man said, glancing at his phone again, studying it, and then flicking his eyes at the rearview mirror.

A slow turn in his seat, Miguel looked through the back window. In the near distance a dark whirlwind approached, a zephyr speeding toward them. Surprised to hear his own voice, an intuition spoken aloud as he said, "It's coming for us."

Rosa spun and looked back, then twisted toward the driver. "We're going, now!"

"No. You have to wait," the *chequador* said.

Pulling at Miguel, rushing him to the door, Rosa said, "Open it!"

"Sit the fuck down. You're not going anywhere," the man said, rising from his seat.

"Open it!" Rosa screamed, pushing at the door as the man lunged for her, grabbing her arm while she swiped at his face, nails across his cheek and he backhanded her and she hit the door. Going for her again when Miguel reached into his backpack, grabbed at his trophy and swung it without thinking, cracking it against the *chequador's* head in a detonation of tin and sharp plastic, the man grunting, losing his feet. Rosa pushed Miguel through the van's open door and they were out beneath the morning sun, running hard for the wall.

Not far off an engine roared.

Miguel glanced over his shoulder watching it emerge from a gritty cloud, the black SUV from the motel slicing the desert like an arrow shot in their direction. The man, the scar, the *fútbol* bet, Miguel frozen in place until his mother screamed, "Keep going, *mijo*! As fast as you can, run!" And Miguel was gone, sprinting for the wall. He got there first, went to his knees at the orange X spray-painted at the base. A triangular section of wire was loose, the *chequador* hadn't lied, no reason to, he hadn't expected them to escape the van. Miguel strained, bending it back for his mother but she grabbed it and shoved him at the opening instead. He wriggled through and pushed at the section for her, the sharp metallic squares hot in his hands. Miguel watched the approaching SUV, heard a yelp and a curse as his mother dragged herself through the opening holding her calf. A snaking wire had cut her, gaping flesh visible through her pant leg stained with blood. She tried to stand and gasped and fell with pain reddening her face. "Go, Miguel!" she said, pointing up a sandy rise. "Up there, go, right now!"

Jittering all over he could only say, "No, no, no."

Their heads turned at the growl of the SUV closing in and Rosa spoke her son's name again in an electric way that got his feet moving. Miguel spun and scrambled up the short hill, fingers digging dirt, leaving his mother behind.

8

The hangover receded after a couple days and it taught Jim a lesson. Or re-taught it, as he'd forgotten after so many dry years that flooding himself with alcohol would end only in pain. To avoid such a thing happening he had to keep it going, a slow, steady drip, and tipped a bottle of whiskey into his coffee cup and carried it to the rocking chair.

He sat and sipped in the silent house feeling like he'd been sitting there a thousand years.

Waiting for the end to come, the sensation of being powerless, his whole life he'd never experienced such a thing and it made him ashamed. Aware that Christine would not let him do it, just sit. That she'd say to him what she'd said to Sarah as a girl, and what she told herself on occasion, make yourself useful. Not an admonition, she'd meant it as a tonic. That when a soul was feeling poorly about something or suffering a case of the blues, the best way out of it was to rise up and do something for someone else. It made problems shrink.

A growing pile of unopened mail sat on the desk.

It got Jim out of the chair and he picked up one letter in particular, from the hospice organization that helped Christine at the end, a solicitation for a donation. He thought of the people who'd visited the ranch those last days. Wendy, who had just become a grandmother, and the younger fellow, Jim couldn't recall his name now. But then, the man's soothing voice and Wendy's warm gaze were as necessary for Christine as the morphine. Jim remembered his cows then, that he hadn't tended to them in a few days, and of Everett Crawford's offer, seventy cents a pound. Come what may Jim still needed money, some to live on, some for the hospice folks, which felt just as important. Maybe get that old rustler Crawford up to seventy-five cents. He dressed without shaving, found his hat, slid a pint bottle into a pocket, and whistled for Jackson. After loading his gear, several bales of hay, he made sure the M21 was there in case of coyotes.

Jim started the truck and then paused behind the wheel, gazing up at the empty flagpole.

Over the past week the ritual of raising and lowering the flag had come to seem futile. Jim took the pint from his pocket. He drank and glanced at Jackson, the dog's eyes pinned to his.

"Don't look at me like that," he said, heading off into the desert.

Just past seven a.m., the sun a blazing silver disc, Jim left the cutoff at Moss Road and began descending to the floor with the border wall outside Jackson's window. A mental bump, like a hiccup, something of a dream he'd had the previous night came to him. Back in the war walking a bombed-out village street, being watched from shuttered windows, Harold Richman at his side. Fatigues and flak jackets, locked and loaded, Harold with that smile trying to calm both their nerves, referring to the pair of them as the TFA, man, Team Fucking America, a Black dude with Detroit street smarts, white dude with Arizona desert skills, both determined to stay the fuck alive in Viet Fucking Nam, and goddamn, hadn't Jim kept Harold alive? Harold nudging Jim as they walked, saying, I owe you man, how can I keep you alive?

Sarah put Harold in his head, wondering if Jim could borrow money from his old friend.

Not money but maybe his ear, maybe call Harold and talk to him, tell him about Christine, the ranch, Jim reached for the pint bottle and unscrewed the top and was tipping it back when Jackson gave two sharp alarm barks and Jim blinked through the windshield at something in the road, an animal or, no, Jesus, a person! Slammed on the brakes, the truck skidded sideways as he fumbled the bottle. Hearing it gurgle at his feet. The dust cleared and he stared out at a kid who stared back with eyes wide, face blank. Jim climbed from the truck, hadn't closed the door when the boy turned and a woman reached the top of the rise and they embraced. Her ankle soaked through, blood in the dirt. She looked at Jim, looked back from where she'd come. With an arm at the boy's shoulder she aimed him down the road and began moving off in a rapid hobble.

"Hey. There's nothing that way you can walk to," Jim said. "Except more of this."

The woman turned, stared at Jim as if seeing him for the first time. "Help us, please, I'll pay,

I have money," she said, her English fast and stumbling with urgency.

"Money? Uh-uh, I'm no smuggler, lady." He reached into the truck for the walkie-talkie. "Border patrol will take you out of here, get you to a doctor for that leg."

"No, please! We have to go now!"

Jim looked from her to the boy, some cold fear there that made him hesitate before he pushed a button, said, "Border patrol dispatch it's Jim Hanson, over."

Static, a voice behind it saying, "Jim, Sarah here, come back."

"Sarah. I got two illegals about a mile south of the Moss Road, over."

"Please," the woman said, bringing the boy closer.

"One's hurt, over," Jim said, listening to the crackle of air. "Sarah, over."

"No agents in the area now Jim, we're spread

a little thin. I'll put out the alert, it shouldn't be too long until—"

Sarah's voice faded to a buzz as a louder noise turned Jim's attention to the wall. Not twenty-five feet away, the bite of tires on the other side of the wire fencing. A black SUV there, three doors opening. Three men got out, one tall, another thick and flushed. The third moved slow and ready, clearly in charge. He led the other two toward the fence in a way that made Jim reach for his rifle. Took a step with it on his hip. In black from T-shirt to jeans, the one in charge smiled and said over his shoulder, "*El viejo tiene un rifle. De medio!*" and the men laughed.

"I'm not that old," Jim said.

The laughter dried up, the man still smiling, he said, "*Vengo por la mujer y el niño.*"

The only sound was the wind, a hot burst that made Jim squint. "Talking to me, speak English."

With a nod the man said, "The boy and his mother. Give them to me. Right now."

Jim glanced at the pair, his gut telling him he had a choice to make, he said, "Uh-uh. Sorry, friend. We got laws here. These two are mine now."

"You are border patrol?"

"Marine Corps."

"Yeah? You guarding the border, you and your rifle?"

"Something like that."

"Then you know they don't belong on that side. You don't want them in your country, taking your jobs, eh Marine Corps?" the man said. "Listen. I'm a soldier, too. My orders are to bring them back. Give them to me and you won't get hurt."

"You're no soldier. And I don't scare easy." Jim adjusted the grip on the rifle. "Border Patrol's on the way. I suggest you turn around, go back where you came from."

His smile died, the man's face became something else as his shoulders tensed and fingers played the air. "I'm done asking," he said, the other men fanning out in careful, sideways steps. The tall one on the man's left, the thick one on the right, seconds uncoiling.

"It's not worth it, boys," Jim said, words distant to his own ears because his mind had left them behind and was doing the calculus of the thick one's hand coming up with a nine millimeter behind wire fencing that created a grid of squares large enough for bullets to pass through and Jim's eye went to the rifle scope, to one of the squares, to the thick one's heart behind that square like a target and he pulled the trigger twice, *blam-blam*, the thick one's gun spraying the air as he collapsed into dust and the world started spinning again.

Jim knew enough to leap.

Behind the truck as a storm of bullets pounded metal, blew out the passenger window,

Jackson curled tightly behind the seat while the woman and boy huddled against a white boulder ten feet away. Jim counted his breath knowing to the second how long it took to pop and replace a pistol clip, knew that he himself had eighteen rounds left, and stood and cracked off four more watching the tall one scatter for the SUV, the one in charge drop to the ground, and Jim called to the woman, "Now! Get over here, now!" She dragged the boy and Jim shoved them into the truck's cab, pushed their heads down, slid behind the wheel seeing the tall one lift a hand cannon, a pistol grip AK-47, the one in charge on his knees at the corner of the fence. Jim cranked the ignition. The engine screamed to life. A barrage from the AK chased the truck as he fishtailed along the stony rise with a *thunk* sounding from the back, the bed, he hoped to Christ he hadn't blown a tire, and sped on.

"*Mamá?*" The boy's voice small and shocked.

The woman was heaving air, tilted against the passenger door with a dark stain spread over her stomach. Jackson behind the seat barking at the rear window, Jim knew what gut-shot looked like, he found the walkie-talkie and said, "Patrol, dispatch, it's Jim Hanson, over!" Sarah said his name and he cut her off, Jackson roiling with fury as he shouted, "I took heavy fire, armed men, got a woman here bleeding, she's shot! Headed east toward Table Rock, that's east toward—!" and then his breath went away and he was choking. A black steel snake around Jim's neck, an arm in a black jacket, the one in charge having made it through the fence and into the truck bed, and was now balanced on the running board leaning in the window trying to kill him. Jim punched the gas barreling over the rise, the woman screaming, boy frozen. Jim felt as if his head would burst, the pain of creeping unconsciousness, and whipped the steering wheel trying to shake off the one in charge, hearing a voice at his ear.

"This is the day you die, old man! You'll never—"

Jackson was bellowing now, straining from behind the seat in a frenzy of snapping jaws and lunged at the man's arm, loosening his grip, the man falling backward but grabbing the door-frame. Jim inhaled and cranked the wheel. Into a ravine rocketing downward, he stood on the brakes with the broken momentum throwing the man free. On his back, then he rolled to his feet and started toward the truck, a red gash over his cheekbone. Jim put it in reverse, churning dirt, downshifted, and climbed the short hill and fled down the road. A glance in the rearview, he saw the man standing as still as a hawk on a fence post watching them go. Up and around a bend, and another, putting distance behind what had just occurred, an extended moment of unreality, of deadly gun-play; his aching neck and a boy in his truck, a woman bleeding against the door, and Jim came back to himself. Leaning there, she was as pale as salt, the intensity of her eyes the most alive thing about her. "Hang on," he said. "I'll get you to a doctor."

"Please. You must. Help my son. If he goes back they kill him."

Jim looked at the boy shaking all over staring at his mother, and back at the woman. "No one's killing anyone. Like I said, we got laws here."

"He can't go back. Please." Her voice was spiky, agonized, blood bubbling from the wound like ground oil. What happened to Harold Richman so long ago, what Jim had done to keep his friend alive. He pulled to the side of the road, eased to a stop. The woman shrieked when he lifted and laid her gently on the ground, propped up her head. On his knees beside her, the boy still shaking but saying things in soft, determined tones. Jim turned him away, quickly cut back the woman's shirt, and eyed the wound, the torn depth of it. The boy pleading at Jim in Spanish while Jim ignored what he knew about the gut-shot, all of that blood, and applied pressure to it anyway. The woman swallowed her screams, turned them into whispers. "Everything. I have. Yours. Just please help him. Save him."

"The patrol's coming," Jim said, looking down the empty road.

"Everything I have. My boy, those men will take and kill him." She opened a hand at Jim. A crumpled slip of paper there had words and numbers on it. "*Es mi—*" she said, stopped, continued in English. "My sister. His aunt. Get him to her. Please."

"No, now. You're gonna make it."

"Promise me," she said.

A pause, and then Jim nodded and took the slip of paper, unsure what else to do.

"*Miguel,*" she said searchingly.

The boy went quickly to her and she touched his face and they said nothing, exchanging thoughts in that long silence until he spoke. "*Mamá, por favor, no.*"

"*Quédate con el Señor mijo. Él te. Va a ayudar,*" she said, her gaze shifting to Jim, holding it. "He's a good man. I can see it. He'll help you."

Something at the back of his throat, Jim wanted to look away but couldn't.

"*Mamá,*" *the* boy said as she struggled, removed a small wooden cross from her neck and folded the rosary into his hand, he went nearer to her and pled with her while that intensity in her eyes cooled and drained off. The boy locked himself to her then, arms beneath her shoulders, lifting her a few inches from the ground. Jim could only stare, feeling the weight of the boy's agony. In the near distance, the sound of an approaching vehicle; it moved Jim to the truck, the rifle, watching a Border Patrol SUV crease the bend with another behind it leading an ambulance. He turned back to mother and son, as intertwined as statuary, and then opened his hand to the slip of paper. No name, just an address in a city across the country, the word *Chicago* marked with a bloody thumbprint like a wax seal.

Nearly every resident of the Miracle Valley knew some Spanish, border agents mostly fluent with a pair of them talking to the boy now, making sure to draw his attention from the scene as his mother's covered body was lifted and slid into the ambulance.

Standing off with Sarah, Jim said, "Makes no sense. Dead, just like that. Why do you think they wanted her and the kid so bad?"

"Maybe he'll tell us, maybe not. You know

how it is," Sarah said. "Cartels run on their own logic. Wicked mix of drugs, money, and violence."

"I wasn't looking for this. Nothing like it."

"I know you weren't." Sarah inspected him for a few seconds. "You encountered the woman and boy on the road. The men demanded you give them up and when you refused they threatened you. You took the woman and boy and fled and the men fired on your truck."

"That's right."

"And you didn't return fire."

"No." A pause and he said, "I fired first."

Sarah sighed, her expression tightening. She nodded at a group of agents, one in particular, the guy too starched and tucked-in for the field. "Him, Dalton, you know he's the deputy patrol agent, right? He already has it in for me and knows you're my stepfather. I stood right there while he questioned you about the incident. You fired first, why didn't you tell him?"

"He didn't ask."

"Jim."

He faced her with righteous eyes. "One of them lifted a gun and I knew. If I didn't make a move it would've been them or us. To be honest I didn't feel like dying today." He took off his hat, palmed his brow. "Also didn't feel like wading into all the government bullshit about how I fired across the border."

Sarah looked around and back. "You hit the guy?"

Jim nodded.

"Is he dead?"

"Be surprised if he weren't."

"Jesus," she said, shaking her head. "This isn't good. Not the law, Dalton, I don't mean any of that. I mean for you. The cartel."

"I'll be fine." Jim glanced over at the boy who was pointing at him, saying something to the agents. "What happens to the kid now?"

"Placed in holding and then sent west to

the regional station where he'll be processed. The agency will try to find a relative to claim him but either way, he'll be sent back," Sarah said. "If not to a family member then to foster care there."

"His mother didn't want him to go back," Jim said. He watched an agent approach, one who had been talking to the boy. "Hey. What was he saying about me?"

Behind sunglasses the agent glanced at Sarah, who gave a slight nod. Sunglasses faced Jim, said, "He told us if you hadn't stopped them from walking into the desert, away from the wall, his mother would still be alive."

Jim was quiet, looked into the distance as the agent moved off. Sarah said, "He's a kid. What happened, whatever it was all about? All he knows is that his mom is dead."

"She sure is," Jim said slowly.

Things Sarah wanted to tell Jim, reassuring things, unsure how. Instead she said, "You have to come to the station and sign a statement. Tomorrow morning, okay? Ten o'clock."

Jim nodded and went to the truck, looking at the boy, who turned away. Jackson waited at the window. Jim climbed inside and made a U-turn and thought of the woman going cold in the back of the ambulance, and asked himself questions: Why did I stop them, why didn't I just let them go, would she still be alive?

Death caused by bullets sometimes had a burnt-sugary odor to it, like strong incense. Hernando put down a window and Mauricio ordered him to shut it and not open it again. The tall young man did as he was told, gripping the steering wheel in silence as they cut a line across the Mexican highway aimed toward Nogales.

In the rear of the SUV the body lay covered with its chest blown open.

Mauricio trying to contain what was left of Rigo in this rolling tomb. A presence, a density, a smell, yet he was most aware of his brother's absence. Something that depended on Rigo being alive, a slim, crystalline connection running through his brother to the outside world, linking Mauricio to it, as well. That link was breaking down now, mile by mile, and at the end Mauricio would be alone, and Hernando said his name again with, "Ángel wants you."

Mauricio glanced over at the phone. He took it, spoke, and then listened to Ángel say, "Hernando tells me Rigo was shot dead by a gringo."

"Yes, he's dead."

"You have him?"

"Yes, I have him."

"Bringing him back to Nogales."

"Yes."

"And what of my money? What of the woman and boy?"

Mauricio said he would return tomorrow with more men and take care of them, and said nothing more about his brother or how he'd soon put him in the ground beneath a carved headstone because the only things Ángel cared about were his money, and the woman and boy dead, as it should be. Mauricio hung up then, shifted around, and looked at the body.

Since boyhood he'd felt the threat of losing Rigo.

The life they shared was too voracious, it demanded sacrifices, and couldn't take Mauricio, so it would have to be his brother. The old man who'd made it a reality was a soldier, not a gringo as Ángel said. The cartel flourished because of cowardly gringos and crooked law enforcement and fearful citizens who looked away or were paid off, who hesitated in the face of death and died because of it. The old man, Marine Corps, was not one of those people.

Mauricio touched at raw skin on his cheek-bone where a bullet had cut him.

A couple inches higher and it would've gone through his eye.

It was miles until Nogales and he settled back thinking about Marine Corps. Cold and fast, not a moment's hesitation in pulling the trigger, he'd kept firing and moving until finding a way out, and Mauricio knew one thing for certain: The only way for a man to earn those skills, become dangerous with them, was by killing scores of other men.

9

Jim sat on the middle of the couch with his left hand on Jackson and his right on a whiskey bottle, boots on, head back, eyes closed at four in the morning, waiting. For daylight so he could go down to the patrol station and sign a statement. So he could quit talking to the man in his head. Not God, but the son of a bitch he'd killed, who'd only halfway drawn on Jim before Jim split his heart like an apple on a tree stump. A thing he hadn't wanted to do and sorely regretted. He'd told Sarah the truth, that he didn't want to die, didn't want the woman and boy to die, so he'd given over to himself. Now the son of a bitch said, *You got the woman killed,* and Jim rolled his head over the back of the couch and said, *No, someone on your side of the fence shot her, the tall one with the hand cannon,* and the son of a bitch said, *If you hadn't shot me none of it would've happened, you started it all,* and Jim said, *Bullshit, it started when the one in charge demanded the woman and boy, and I couldn't do it, hand them over, the one in charge had blood in his voice,* and Jim drank deeply while the son of a bitch said, *So you're a do-gooder out there saving the world,* and Jim said, *It's not that, no, might've been my wife Christine reminding me to do for others in order to shrink my problems,* and the son of a bitch grinned and said, *Oh yeah? How'd that work out for you? You killed me, nearly was killed yourself, the woman's gut-shot dead, and her son will be sent back to wherever. Maybe you shrunk your problems but you made some damn big new ones along the way,* and Jim blinked his eyes at the ceiling as morning sun floated through windowpanes and could not disagree.

The phone alarm jangled before dawn, as loud as church bells, Hernando fumbling to quiet it.

"*Porque tan temprano,*" his girlfriend yawned next to him. "Why so early?"

"Have to get on the road." Hernando swung his long legs over the side of the bed.

"I'm not even going to ask where."

"Same place I was yesterday," he said, dressing quickly.

"I don't know where you were yesterday."

"That's the point." Hernando crossed the room and entered the tiny bathroom and pissed and shaved and brushed his teeth and returned to the bedroom where she was sitting up, Juana showing those gorgeous *tetas*, warm sleepy eyes focused on his, and Hernando said, "I can't."

"You sure?" she said, pushing her hands through her hair.

"Mauricio," he said, the name a word she understood without needing explanation. He strapped on a nine millimeter and went to her, kissed her, and turned for the door with Juana telling him to be careful. The street was gray and chilly as he walked to the SUV, Nogales before sunrise like the dark side of the moon. After he and Mauricio delivered Rigo to *la casa funeraria* the previous evening, after he'd listened to Mauricio's orders and dropped him off, Hernando scrubbed the vehicle until his arms ached. He opened the rear door of the SUV now to check. The death stink was still there, circling his nostrils, and he cursed under his breath and slammed the door and climbed behind the wheel. Rumbling down the narrow street then with all the windows open, he texted first one and then the other, telling them to be ready. Isidro, missing an eye, always in sunglasses, guys called him Cyclops. And the kid, Jorge, maybe twenty with a face like a cherub, deadly with a rifle. About to call Mauricio, let him know he was en route, Hernando paused because he hadn't made up his mind.

Should he tell Mauricio about the phone call last night or not?

Ángel did not tell Hernando to keep their talk a secret, but then, that was Ángel's way. The *capo*, the cartel's boss of bosses operated with a calculated vagueness meant to keep his men off-balance. Had he been gleaning information or testing loyalties? If Hernando told Mauricio about the call would it anger Ángel? If he didn't, was it a betrayal of Mauricio?

He'd been cleaning the SUV with a bandanna over his nose when his phone buzzed.

Ángel started in about the incident at the border wall, Hernando aware of being grilled outside Mauricio's presence. Trying to discern if Ángel expected him to criticize Mauricio or was daring him to. But it was Mauricio he took daily orders from and carried weapons with, so he'd told Ángel that Mauricio had done everything possible to retrieve the money and to kill the woman and boy. Even crossed into

Arizona and almost killed that *gringo* with his bare hands.

Ángel had said, "He's your leader. You trust him."

"Yes, absolutely."

"My money gone, the woman and her son alive and Rigo dead. His own brother gunned down in broad daylight, and the man got away, too," Ángel said. "You call that leadership?"

In a corner, it felt that way, Hernando said, "Well. Maybe—"

"What?"

"He. Maybe there was something more he could've done."

"So. Now you're telling me Mauricio isn't a leader," Ángel said. "One of my finest *tenientes*, the most relentless of them all, and you have the balls to claim he didn't do enough. You say it to me, you'd say it to his face?"

"I. Misspoke, capo. What I meant was,

maybe we, there was something more we could have done. Mauricio did so much—"

With the sigh of a disappointed father Ángel said, "Then it was you who failed me. You and that dead fuck, Rigo." Hernando didn't reply, unable to muster one, and Ángel said, "Your absolute trust in Mauricio? It means you believe his leadership is perfect and you'll carry out his orders perfectly and I'll get my money back, the woman and boy will be taken care of, and there will be no more mess. I think that's what you've expressed to me, yes?"

Hernando swallowed what felt like charcoal. "Yes, capo."

"Keep me informed," Ángel had said, and hung up.

Even those three words had been woven with vagueness. Ángel was an octopus of information, consuming multiple reports, rumors, data, leaks, surveillance, and whispers every day, all day long. Hernando knew Mauricio constantly updated Ángel regarding his operations, often communicating to the *capo* through Hernando as all *tenientes* did with their soldiers, so what had Ángel meant by 'Keep me informed?' A moment-by-moment report of their activities, or to monitor Mauricio, or had he meant something Hernando didn't comprehend?

He saw Isidro and Jorge just ahead on the sidewalk and told himself, Fuck it.

Just do your job, keep your head down. Get your ass back to Juana in one piece.

Jackson knew when Jim intended to leave her behind, showing her displeasure by burrowing under the couch, where she was now. "I'll be back as soon as I can, girl, just have to give a statement. Be done with this damn thing once and for all," he said, going for the front door. She didn't respond, not even a whine, and he sighed and left the house. Stood a moment looking at his truck. The blown-out window he'd replaced, stopped yesterday and bought a pane and slid it in easy enough, he'd been doing surgery on the old machine for years. It was the bullet holes that got him, the metal rips and tears making him sigh again.

In the truck, nerves jangly from whiskey and little sleep, Jim reached for more whiskey.

The interstate was empty. He sped into dusty sunlight knowing he'd be at the Border Patrol station early. Not yet eight a.m. but maybe Sarah would be there. He'd have to repeat it again, what happened at the wall, and then put his name to it, and afterward he wouldn't think of it again, at least not on purpose. He could do that. Had the ability to place memories in boxes and pack them away. Except now and then one popped open and its contents would drag him down, bring him low, things in there Christine encouraged him to talk to her about, talk to someone. In this case a box would have to do, he'd make sure to seal it up tight.

Jim cut across the valley so fast he barely remembered driving it, the station just there.

Slowing, he sipped and turned into the parking lot and called out, "Shit!" Juddered to a stop nearly sideswiping a patrol SUV, the agent at the wheel shooting him a death glare. Jim gave a my-fault wave and pulled ahead, found a spot, and noticed the backpack on the floor.

Red nylon, a smear of bloody fingerprints gone brown, the woman had been carrying it.

The thing must've been under the seat, forgotten until he jammed on the brakes.

He hesitated a moment before lifting and unzipping it and pushing aside socks and underwear, and froze. Blinking down at tight bricks of banded U.S. currency. Ben Franklin with that smirk looking back, Jim's eyes felt hot. He scanned the parking lot. No one. Behind the high chain-link fence vehicles inched from the

Mexican border to the American checkpoint stations. The parking lot on the Mexican side was empty. With his breath in his chest, Jim counted the money, each brick ten grand, figuring about two hundred thousand dollars, Jesus. Remembering the woman on the ground, applying pressure to her wound, knowing it was useless while she bled out, pleading with him. All she had, everything, if he'd take her son, get him somewhere. Jim touched at his breast pocket. Same shirt as yesterday, the crinkle of paper there, an address in Chicago scribbled on it.

Two hundred grand at his feet, Jim pictured it in his mind's eye.

Walking into the Merchants Bank, to that pencil pusher's desk where he'd stack handfuls of paper bricks. The heat of it spread over his head, the ranch and his cattle and that rough old beautiful land, and Christine's ashes spread atop the highest hill, he had only to start the truck and drive into town and enter the bank and apply his signature there, and there, and then cross the valley to home, to Jackson, to work, while putting all this behind him, what happened at the border wall, that dead son of a bitch, where the money had come from, all of it into a tightly sealed box, his hand moving toward the key in the ignition when Jim glanced up. On the Mexican side, the parking lot. A black SUV eased to a halt, and Jim checked his memory, what the woman said. Not just take her son, but.

Save him from those men.

If he's sent back they'll kill him.

Jim squinted at the SUV. The one in charge was in the front passenger seat on the phone, the tall one behind the wheel. Another guy in sunglasses climbed from the back and lit a cigarette. Someone else back there too, all of it swirling into an answer now, why they'd wanted the woman and boy so badly, the red backpack, willing to kill for it and keep on killing. As Sarah had said, it was cartel logic.

Sarah. He had to tell her about the SUV, the men.

Jim left the truck and hurried across the lot. The patrol station was glassy and secure, a rectangle of windows looking out on the checkpoint stations in one direction, the desert in the other, cameras pointed everywhere, doors to offices and meeting rooms requiring a magnetic badge to enter and exit. A clock above the reception desk said 8:19 a.m. An agent seated there pinched at her eyes, finishing the night shift, as Jim said, "Sarah Reynolds in yet?"

"Not for a bit," the agent said, glancing at a screen. "About forty minutes."

Considered asking for a phone to call Sarah, but no, Jim wanted to talk to her in person. He told the agent he'd wait, paced a few steps and stopped in front of a glass door marked

HOLDING. He wondered, seeing an agent at an open file cabinet, a fellow he'd known for years, that handlebar mustache gone gray, and tapped on the door. The agent looked around and smiled, buzzed Jim inside and said, "Hanson, you old so and so. How are you?"

"Good Denny. You?"

"Can't complain. Some excitement yesterday, huh? Out your way?"

"Guess so. How's the boy?" Jim said, nodding at a metal door, a short hallway behind it lined with rooms, cots, sinks.

"About like you'd expect, with a dead mom and all. Tough night for him," Denny said. "At least he's got people."

"Relatives?"

"Being turned over to them today. This morning."

It stopped Jim. "Wasn't he supposed to be processed through the regional station?"

"Word came down overnight," Denny

shrugged. "An uncle made himself known. Be here anytime now. The kid's luckier than most."

In a few seconds of nodding his head Jim sifted probabilities and possibilities.

That the one in charge had an informant inside border patrol, probably knew the woman was dead, and thought the boy had the money or knew where it was. If he'd been willing to crawl under a border fence to try and choke a man to death in a moving vehicle, there was a hell of a lot more the one in charge would do to the boy to make him talk. Jim could drive away with the money right now, it wouldn't matter, the boy was dead whether he was released to the one in charge or somehow made it back to Mexico; foster care wouldn't protect him from a cartel. Unless Jim did what the woman had asked of him. Drive away with both the money and the boy, and he quit thinking and said, "Denny, a favor?"

"What's that?"

Settling into a chair with a grimace, Jim removed his hat and pushed a hand through his hair. "I have to give Sarah a statement soon, and to be honest? A dog bit me last night. Hard, if you get my drift."

"Ouch. How'd it get you?" Denny winked. "Straight or on the rocks?"

"Tell you what, some black coffee sure would help. You mind?"

"I'm sure there's a pot somewhere. Sit tight," Denny said, leaving the office.

On his feet, Jim went to the metal door and tried it, locked. Guessing where agents in a hurry would put it and pulled the top drawer of the nearest desk to a magnetic badge there. He grabbed it and buzzed through the door. First room on the left sitting on a cot fully dressed plus a ball cap, Jim saw him through a square of glass, opened the door and said, "Let's go." The boy's head turned like an owl's. He stared, thumbing a rosary, expression blank. "You're in danger, understand? Wait here, you're dead," Jim said. Still unmoving, Jim lifted him by an arm. "*Andale* goddamn it. Come on." He hauled the boy to the office, pausing at the door. Hallway empty, Jim rushed them toward the exit hearing a voice ahead. He put an eye to the corner seeing the guy with the hair and starched uniform, Dalton, Sarah's direct report. Hectoring the agent at reception about something and then Dalton stalked away as the receptionist swiveled back to a screen and Jim walked the boy through the exit. Aware of the black SUV on the other side of the fence, he resisted the urge to look back. The patrol shift was about to end. Agents would be coming and going soon, Sarah among them. She was dedicated, a first-rate agent, that was the problem. Following protocol seemed to Jim the quickest way to get the boy killed. Then there was the money, all that cash. He couldn't explain it to Sarah, not yet, and opened the truck door and pushed the boy inside, the boy's eyes darting from the red backpack with the dried bloody handprint to Jim. "Your mom," Jim said. "Told me I could have it. If I got you to Chicago."

Not a blink, not a word, the boy just stared.

"English, *ingles*, you speak it? Whether you understand or not," Jim said, cranking the engine, wheeling from the parking lot, "—this is for your own good." On the interstate speeding toward the ranch he glanced into the rearview, looking for the black SUV. He knew it was on the other side of the fence in Mexico, which didn't stop him from glancing again. Gravel flew as he roared up the long drive to the clapboard house feeling an internal clock ticking. Anytime now the boy would be found missing. Denny would put it together. Sarah would be called in. Jim braked and pointed a finger and said, "Stay here," and left the truck with the boy gazing after him. Inside the house he moved quickly, Jackson catching his mood, alert at the front door. Jim pulled a duffel bag from under the bed, kicked back a rug to a floor safe. He spun it open and removed a .45 and three boxes of bullets, threw it in the bag, threw in some clothes, plucked a picture of Christine from the bureau and dropped it in, too. The rifle was in the truck, whiskey in the kitchen, he grabbed two bottles and remembered his cattle. Punched at the landline and told Everett Crawford the price was okay, come take the cows and hold his money for him and hung up the phone because Jackson was baying at the window. Jim reached for the .45. He went to the curtains and carefully moved them, seeing the boy out of the truck.

Looked left and right and then the kid sprinted down a path into the desert.

"Dammit," Jim said, grabbing the duffel bag, Jackson at his heels. On the porch he said, "Go on girl, get him," and the dog whirled down the stony path. Jim went the other way.

Slid through brush, stickers biting his arms, he ran to where a line of shale turned the path into a maze. He heard the bounce of Jackson's bark and pressed against a tall slab. Footsteps approached on the run and he spun out and grabbed the boy who shrieked and tried to fight free, yelling Spanish into Jim's face, Jackson coming up from behind. Jim gave the boy a shake, stilling him, holding his eyes. "Listen to me now. Return to that station, you'll get sent back to Mexico. Either way those men will be waiting for you. You'll be dead, quick."

The kid stared hard, breathing harder with his jaw quaking.

"Move it," Jim said, pushing him up the path and into the truck with Jackson at his side. He threw the duffel in back. Locked the backpack full of money in the truck's equipment box, and paused, staring at the flagpole. Empty, stripped of meaning, it was hard to abide. Jim hurried to fetch the flag. He unfolded and raised it to the top, watching it snap in the heat, and then climbed into the truck and aimed for the interstate. He'd settle on the most direct route later, the point now to get the hell out of Dodge. Churning along, the realization of what he'd done settled over his shoulders like grit on the windshield. At least two or three laws he might've broke, and what about Sarah? What the hell would she think? He reached over and found the whiskey pint, dog and boy watching as he took a long drink. When the boy didn't look away, Jim said, "I got an address but no name. Your mom said an aunt. Your family, *familia*, any idea?"

The boy's gaze knit together from confusion and fear but mostly rage.

"I'm doing what your mother asked me. Taking you to Chicago, if you don't like it, like me, tough shit."

Turning his head, the boy clutched the rosary cross like a dagger.

"Don't understand a damn thing I'm saying, do you?" Jim drank again, wiped his mouth on his sleeve. "It's going to be a quiet ride to Chicago."

For the second time in twenty-four hours Mauricio watched from one side of a fence while Marine Corps hurried the boy into the truck and drove him away on the other side.

"*No era ese el niño? El Viejo?*" Hernando had said. "Isn't that the kid? The old man?"

Mauricio nodded, fury gathering behind his eyes as he'd stared at the license plate, memorizing the letters and numbers. He'd opened the glove box then to a roll of cash, five grand American, a U.S. passport. "*Vámos a cruzar,*" he had said. "We're crossing."

That was forty-five minutes ago.

Now they moved in a queue of vehicles

toward the American checkpoint stations, taking forever to get into Arizona a hundred yards away. Isidro and Jorge in back, Isidro as chill behind sunglasses as a mannequin, Jorge with an expectant look on his chubby face like it was some kind of adventure. Hernando bent over the steering wheel while Mauricio stared out the window waiting for information from his contact. Cars and trucks out there trying to get over the border, some from Mexico, it seemed like more from the U.S. returning to their own country. Mauricio thought, probably coming back from vacations, wondering what it was like, a vacation, hearing Hernando say, "Your phone."

Buzzing in Mauricio's hand, his mind elsewhere, his contact trying to reach him.

Mauricio said, "Bueno," and the voice gave out Jim's address, obtained from the truck's plate. The SUV moved toward two lanes, each with its own customs officer. Mauricio asked his contact which lane, listened to the answer, and pointed Hernando left and hung up.

Soon Hernando put down the window and the customs officer said, "Passports or visas."

Hernando held out a passport Mauricio had given him so that the tattoo on his forearm was visible. Same skull and bloody knives as the tattoo Mauricio wore, as Isidro and Jorge, all the other soldiers on Mauricio's crew. The officer's gaze went from Hernando's forearm to Mauricio's face like a stone mask, and then he glanced at a nearby K-9 officer with a German shepherd straining at its leash. The customs officer plucked the passport from Hernando. He opened it and inspected an ID picture that looked nothing like Hernando, with some name other than Hernando's, and turned to his computer and began quickly processing the information. The K9 officer approached and ordered the back of the SUV to be opened.

"No problem," Hernando said, popping the rear door.

"What brings you to the U.S.?" the customs officer asked, tapping at the computer.

"Business."

The customs officer looked past the vehicle full of men to the K9 officer at the back, the dog energetically nosing around near the odor-proof side panels where their pistols had been concealed. The officer's gaze shifted to Hernando. "Any weapons or narcotics in the vehicle?"

"No, sir. Of course not," Hernando smiled.

"Clear here," the K9 officer said, leading the dog from the SUV.

The customs officer closed the passport, handed it to Hernando. "Adelante. Bienvenido a los Estado Unidos," he said quietly. "Welcome to the United States."

* * *

Mauricio stared at the wooden house at the end of the long pebbly drive near the desert's edge. With the mountains pale yellow behind it and not another building in sight, it looked like a scene out of some old movie. A western, huffing horses, and cowboys with their jangling spurs.

He approached the porch with a nod as the other three fanned out, guns drawn.

Up the steps, Mauricio put an ear to the front door, then opened it and stepped inside. He ignored the silence, going room to room kicking doors and looking under beds, listening for a muffled cough or skittering feet. At a window he watched Isidro step from an outbuilding brushing hay from his sleeves, shaking his head at Hernando. Jorge emerged from the back of the house and shook his head, too.

Entering the living room, Mauricio drew it in, trying to feel Marine Corps there.

He went to a side table holding framed photos, the same woman in every one, slim and fair-haired. She and Marine Corps smiled on horseback. Stood near a bonfire under a slate night sky. The two with a young girl, all dressed up. More pictures, the girl grown, wearing a Border Patrol uniform, the years accumulating to a more recent photo of Marine Corps and the fair-haired woman with their arms around one another. Mauricio crossed to a desk in the corner, pushed a stack of mail around until finding an unpaid bill, and folded it into a pocket. Pulled the desk drawer and stopped, looking down at a military medal. He lifted it, the five-pointed gold star holding a smaller silver star at its center, its worn ribbon striped with blue, white, and red. Mauricio dug deeper into the desk to a document shoved at the back. He unfolded it and read:

This is to certify that the President of the United States of America has awarded the SILVER STAR MEDAL to James L. Hanson for Gallantry in Action.

"James L. Hanson," he whispered. A real man who'd done things to earn a medal. Mauricio slipped it into a pocket, the medal feeling like a compass or amulet that would guide him to Marine Corps. He looked around the room then, a presence woven into the house. Knowing words for it but not the reality of them: love and pride in the air, in the walls, the framed photos and grain of the wooden floor and blanket folded over a rocking chair. Jealousy scraped at sorrow, sparked inside him, Mauricio going to the door and calling out to Hernando. Told him what he wanted. Hernando entered the outbuilding and exited soon after carrying two sloshing metal cans.

Mauricio sent him away and did it himself, bathing the house in gasoline.

He stepped onto the porch and dropped a match, a blue flash jumping quickly, and faced his men. Hernando and Isidro and Jorge stared at him, Mauricio feeling their confusion, their temptation to ask him questions. He passed among them and went to the flagpole, stared up at the stars and stripes hanging limply in the sky, then turned back to the house and watched as it was overtaken, flames a riot behind popping windowpanes. When he'd had his fill, he said, "Let's go." They climbed into the vehicle. Mauricio gave Hernando an address, and Hernando put it in his phone. They crunched down the long drive, the SUV silent. In the rearview mirror Mauricio watched the house turn orange and was touched by a suspicion that he'd left something behind, and made himself look away, not wanting to know what.

10

Miguel couldn't help it, when they passed the billboard shouting UNCLE BUDDY'S FAMOUS FLAME COOKED BURGERS! with juicy images of grilled meats and thick swirled ice creams, his stomach growled.

Without looking from the road, the man said, "You hungry? Uh—*comida*?"

Miguel was silent. Jackson was lying on the seat next to him. He spread his fingers along the back of the dog's neck.

"Thirsty?"

Throat dry, they'd been on the road for hours, but Miguel did not react.

"Suit yourself," the man said, exiting the

highway at a place called Las Cruces, bumping into the parking lot of a drive-through restaurant. Food smells, fresh and salty, drifted in the truck's open windows, reminding Miguel of his apartment kitchen. Of opening the front door to his mother preparing a meal, the warmth of that little space meant safety and joy and comfort, all of it gone forever. Miguel was being crushed from the inside out. All he wanted was to cry, he'd felt the need since passing the sign that welcomed them to New Mexico, that word, his home, Mexico. He wouldn't allow himself to shed a single tear. Not in front of the man responsible for his mother's death. He turned to the window and felt the dog's steady breathing beneath his hand and tried to breathe along with it while the man talked to a speaker. It asked if that was all he wanted. Miguel listened to the man pause before saying, "Better give me another hamburger and fries. One of those chocolate shakes, too." The food came out of a window in two bags and the man left the parking lot eating as he drove. After a short stretch of road, he pulled into a service station and climbed out, went around and unscrewed the tank.

The other bag with its top tightly folded rested on the dashboard.

As soon as the man was out of sight Miguel grabbed the bag. He peeled it open and stared at the food, hit by a wave of guilt. That he was alive and his mother wasn't, how could he possibly be hungry? It felt shameful, even sinful, but his stomach was complaining again, and he began to eat in a way that made him want to cry even more.

Jim swiped a credit card. He pumped gas and watched through the back window as the kid opened the bag and took a few bites, chewing slowly. Understanding, yeah, of course, he was suffering his mother's death. At the same time, he could try to help himself by helping Jim get where they had to go. With a sigh, Jim gazed around at a towering sign that said Red Rock Gas Mart, fuel prices, beer and liquor, lotto. He holstered the pump and entered the station, door jingling after him. The clerk a young woman behind the counter with long dark hair pulled into a braid, she looked up with a smile. "Hey there," Jim said. "I need an atlas."

The clerk's eyes were confused.

"An atlas. A book with maps in it, you know. Maps of all the states."

"Maybe check the rack there. We don't sell many maps. Wherever you're headed, why not just put it in your phone?"

Jim went to a circular rack, creaking past postcards, and said, "Here we go."

"I'll be darned," the clerk said as Jim laid the atlas on the counter. "Road trip?"

"That's right. One of those too, if you please,"

he said, pointing at a pint of whiskey on the shelf behind her.

She reached for it, rang it up, and turned over the atlas. "No price on this thing, it's been here so long." That bright smile again, she said, "Take it. It's on the house."

"Nice of you, thanks," Jim said, paying for the whiskey, moving toward the door.

"Hope it gets you where you want to go!"

Jim cut across the parking lot, glancing up at the service station sign. A digital clock showed a few minutes after one p.m. At the back of his gut then, a twist of guilt. He eyed an old payphone at the corner of the lot and went to it, fed it coins, punched a number. A voice answered. Jim spoke a name and after a few seconds of silence Sarah said, "Agent Reynolds."

"Sarah. It's me."

A pause on her side and she said, "Oh my God. Are you okay?"

"I'm fine. Just called to tell you not to worry."

"Not to worry? What the hell were you thinking, taking that kid?"

"Listen. They were going to kill him, same ones who killed his mother. They were at the station, waiting for him on the Mexican side," Jim said. "The one supposed to be his uncle, that was him, the cartel guy. There were four of them."

"So instead of telling me, telling any agent on duty, you just snatched the kid?" Sarah took a breath, slowed her voice. "Besides every other stupid thing you did today, you also put my ass on the line. You have to bring that kid back. Right now."

Jim shook his head at the ground. "Can't do that. His mother, while she was dying. I promised her."

"Promised her? What?"

"That I'd get the boy to safety."

"Get the boy to safety," Sarah echoed. "What the hell does that mean?"

"It means we made a deal and she paid me."

Quiet a beat, Sarah said, "She paid you. How much?"

"Around two hundred thousand dollars."

"Two hundred—Jesus. In cash? Cartel cash?"

"Listen. I made a promise—"

"Jim," she said sharply, cutting him off. "We sent agents out to the ranch looking for you. They found the house burnt to the ground. There's nothing left."

Silent, he held the receiver feeling like he'd been punched in the heart, deeper.

"It means those guys at the wall, at the border today, they're here in the States. If you'd been home when they came to the ranch you'd be dead now, you and the boy. We have no idea who they are or where they are," she said. "So whatever promise you made, whatever deal, it doesn't matter. Give me your location. I'll send agents."

That heart-punch, the grievous sensation burnt off to quiet rage, he said, "No."

"Jim. These guys aren't fucking around. Come back, now. Please."

"Call you later," he said, jamming the receiver back with a fist, turning to the truck, seeing but not seeing a green trickle of radiator fluid there. His mind's eye filled with flames and blackened timbers, ashes and debris all that was left of two lives intertwined. In the truck then, he banged the door shut in a way that made the boy jump and Jackson protest. "Quiet, girl," he said, opening the pint, knocking back a drink. He flipped the atlas and traced a finger over New Mexico. Roared away from the gas station and onto the highway. Traffic was light, mainly wind-rattled big rigs and muddy pickups as Jim drove on with fury stuck hard in his throat.

* * *

Something different about the man when he returned to the truck, like the end of a blazing day in Nogales when the sun left suddenly and shadows came out and took over the streets. Angry and cool at the same time, his taut silence made Miguel want to bury his face in the dog and mute the presence of his mother that wouldn't leave his head and chest. An hour on the road passed, maybe more, with her insistent spirit saying things to Miguel only she could say. She loved her *mijo* and trusted his smart brain and strong guts. He had to keep going and not give up, but she couldn't travel with him anymore, she was gone and would never leave him but would never return, and then tears flooded his eyes and nose and he couldn't hold them back any longer, shaking all over. The dog woke and lifted her head. Gently nosed at Miguel's face and he felt the man looking at him but couldn't stop crying.

"Goddamn it," the man said. "Why'd you have to cross my property?"

"I don't even want to be in your stupid country!" Miguel blurted behind tears.

The man stared a moment before looking through the windshield. His words were steady but streaked with anger, the cold tone of having been lied to, when he said, "He speaks English."

Miguel palmed at his face. "I want to go home."

"It's not safe there. Probably never will be again."

"Why are you doing this, driving me?"

"You were there when she asked, your mother," the man said. "Take my boy or those men will kill him, and she was right, they almost got you this morning."

"You're doing it for money."

176

"That's not . . ." the man shook his head. "Listen here, you think any of this is fun for me? Christ, you ought to thank me. I'm doing it to help you."

"Wouldn't need your help if you hadn't stopped us."

"The desert, that land out there, you would've died."

"We did," Miguel said to himself, to his drifting mother. "I'm alone and she's dead, because of you."

The man squinted at the horizon, said nothing.

"Take me back. I'll find my own way home," Miguel said.

"You're going to Chicago."

"I don't want that." Miguel tumbled again, tears lighting up his face, he said, "My mother. I want her to come back. I want us to go home."

It was quiet until the man said, "This is for the best. After, you want to blame me? Okay. At least you'll—" and the man went silent, staring at a flashing red light on the dashboard, and cursed and sighed and steered the truck toward the nearest exit.

The background noise a hypnotic buzz like thousands of well-fed cicadas, it gave Mauricio the uneasy sense of being immersed in lazy prosperity. In a manicured Arizona suburb where everyone minded their own business, the four-bedroom home's exterior resembled those of its neighbors while the interior had been cut up and reconfigured as a cartel safe house. Mauricio stood at a window staring out at a squad of landscapers armed with leaf blowers and lawnmowers. Like he'd seen on television as a boy, American shows with perfect families living in perfect neighborhoods, versus his world, his headspace, where he was a master of navigating chaos. A place like that with its aura of secure calmness, it set him on edge, made him feel vulnerable, a jumpiness he hated.

"That's it?"

Mauricio glanced at the blob sitting at a table behind a row of computers. Emilio, one of the cartel's hackers, the guy like an unshaven toad on a log holding up the credit card bill Mauricio had taken from Marine Corps's desk. Mauricio said, "Should be enough."

"Let's hope so," Emilio said in the put-upon tone of someone who made a big deal out of things so he could resolve them, be the hero. He tapped at a keyboard exhaling annoyed little huffs through his nose, Mauricio tempted to crack him on the back of his fat head with a pistol butt. Instead he turned to the window and looked into that other world. Across the street a postal truck moved down the block while a woman took letters from a mailbox. Maybe thirty years old, maybe younger, her back was to Mauricio, he couldn't see her face, and he felt the old bump of unease. That he could not remember what his mother looked like. His father had been an addict who'd drifted in and out, finally leaving for good when Mauricio was ten. The cartel men arrived shortly afterward and told Mauricio's mother her sons would be better off with them. Poor and alone, she begged the men not to take away Mauricio and Rigo, just eight years old, weeping and tearing at her hair and at the men's sleeves, her face a permanent blur. Mauricio tried to will away that memory of his non-memory but gazed through the window, knowing.

That any backtrack into the past always found its way to *el campamento.*

Where the cartel men told the boys they were going to camp, and Mauricio looked hard at the manicured lawns but his mind's eye went into the jungle. A month into training, he and Rigo standing in formation with a dozen other boys while the one called El General, cuffed with tattoos of *Santa Muerta*, told them they were descendants of the Aztec warriors who'd once ruled Mexico. Soldiering was in their bones, the cartel had recognized it and taken them into its family, they should be grateful. And Mauricio was, having been praised by El General for his skill with the AK-15s; it shocked him how badly he wanted to be part of that family. El General saying it was built on obedience and loyalty, the boys would learn now what that meant. Mauricio watched as a pair of cartel men pushed another man from the trees, wrists bound and face swollen, his mumbled pleas for mercy spilling out like the rosary. Nothing worse than a coward, a turncoat, El General told the boys, removing a knife from a sheath on his hip, the crunch of his boots stopping in front of Rigo as he asked the boy if he was a soldier. Gave Rigo the knife and ordered him to kill the man, prove his obedience and loyalty, but Rigo seemed frozen. El General reached to his other hip and came back with a pistol. He pressed it to Rigo's head, telling the boy to kill the man or he'd die with him. Mauricio's heart was hammering, he was barely aware of himself as he stepped forward, took the knife from his brother, said he'd do it. A pause with El General's cold black eyes stuck to Mauricio, and then he said, "So do it."

Outside the window a man yanked at a lawnmower, Mauricio looking through him.

Instead watching his ten-year-old self, the heft of the knife in his grip as he moved toward the man whose pleas became one continuous plea, a desperate stream of mercy-mercy-please-mercy-oh-god-please-mercy, and Mauricio froze too. Flooded with horror at what he was about to do, wanting to drop the knife and take Rigo's hand and flee into the jungle but

El General held the pistol to his brother's head and said, "What the fuck you waiting for, it's time, right the fuck now," and Mauricio felt the seconds dissolving, no choice left, he closed his eyes and lifted his arm and thrust the knife into the man's chest. The scream had blood in it, sending birds from the treetops. Mauricio stabbed again and again trying to quiet the man, growing angry that he wouldn't shut up and collapse and be still, and stabbed him to save Rigo, to please El General, because he was a soldier, and because something inside him knew he could do it.

The lawnmower roared to life behind glass, making Mauricio flinch.

Gazing down at the tattoos on his forearms, inked knives like the one he'd used that day carved into his skin, deeper, he heard his name and turned to Emilio who said, "I got something."

Mauricio blinked into the present, went to the computer. "Show me."

"The card was used at a station in New Mexico. Red Rock Gas Mart in Las Cruces, just off Highway 160." Emilio nodded at the screen. "He was there like half an hour ago."

"How far away is that?"

"From here? Three, four hours depending on traffic."

Mauricio took a screenshot with his phone and went for Hernando, the house alive with activity. An overlarge kitchen used as a drug depot with a dozen people following digital spreadsheets, filling orders: baggies, vials, bottles readied for dealers, the items being packaged for on-time delivery. Down a hallway the *chik-chik-chik* of currency-counting machines came from the master bedroom. Three solemn women there tabulating and banding cash with a red-faced older man smoking and watching, he nodded at Mauricio as he passed by, so did a goateed gargoyle slinging an AK just inside the room. Other bedroom doors padlocked on the outside, Mauricio approached the rear of the house, the armory, where Isidro and Jorge held assault rifles, a heavy Kalashnikov, a Colt, speaking quietly with Hernando. "Four of those," Mauricio said, nodding at the weapons. "Extra ammunition, too. Load it up."

Hernando said, "Boss. It's a lot of firepower."

"So?"

"For one old man and a boy?" Hernando said. "Maybe we should check with Ángel, see what he—"

A heartbeat of staring into Hernando, Mauricio said, "Who?"

Eyes darting to Isidro, Jorge, back to Mauricio, Hernando said, "I just thought—"

"Right now, you're either my soldier or Ángel's." His tone of voice quiet, packed with threats and promises, Mauricio said, "Which is it?"

Knowing not to hesitate, Hernando said, "Yours, boss. I'm yours."

"Then gather up the guns and ammo, what the fuck are you waiting for?" Mauricio said. "It's time. Right the fuck now."

11

Jim got the joke, didn't think much of it, *Otto's Autos*, just because the old guy was called Otto didn't mean he had to use it for the name of the repair shop. Not to mention he dipped his shaggy head and looked over the top of his glasses when he spoke, to Jim one of those things certain people did when taking note of other people's stupidity. Fact was he did feel stupid standing there in the mechanic's garage while Otto looked up from the truck's radiator and said, "It's near bone dry. You didn't see any fluid leaking out?"

"I guess not. I was preoccupied, back in Las Cruces—" Jim said.

"You telling me you drove all the way up

here to San Pablo with an empty radiator?" Otto peered over the glasses. "You realize the block could've cracked?"

"Like I said, until the engine light came on—"

"Think you would've noticed with fluid all over the place," Otto said, holding a light over the radiator. "See there, it's leaking from the core." He looked more closely, then reached inside. "There's something loose here," he said, removing his hand, opening it to a slick metal slug. Took a step back and inspected the bullet holes zigzagging the truck's side panels, dipped his head at Jim. "Somebody using this thing for target practice?"

"Long story. Can you fix the radiator?"

"Yeah, sure. Take a few days to get the parts. Don't have them in stock."

Jim shook his head. "We can't wait around that long."

"Well, you can't drive it the way it is, you'll blow the engine." Otto wiped his hands with

a rag, said, "I could patch it for you, tempo-
rary. Should hold long enough until you get
it fixed."

"Okay. Do that."

"No problem. Cost you a hundred. First
thing tomorrow."

"What? Why not now?" Jim said.

With a thumb over his shoulder at the clock,
Otto said, "It's six. I'm closed."

"Make an exception, I'll pay extra."

"If you knew the missus and her belief in
the sanctity of dinnertime you'd not have
made that offer," Otto said. "I open at eight in
the morning."

"Two hundred dollars if you do it now."

"That right? Well. I guess dinner can wait—"

"Thanks."

"—for three hundred." Otto smiled. "Cash."

Guy looking at Jim over the top of his glasses, Jim said, "Fine."

"Pay first."

Jim reached for his wallet, counted out most of what he'd brought along and Otto took it and said, "All right then. Give me about an hour and you'll be good to go."

"Guess we'll get something to eat." Jim gestured to the boy out of the truck. "Okay if my dog stays in the cab?"

"Sure thing. Now listen, you're not back in time, I'll leave the truck in the lot and hide the keys in the wheel well. Should be fine but still, this town has its share of knuckleheads," Otto said. "Food-wise, just down the street, Dusty's does a decent job with a piece of cow. I'm sure your son will find something he likes."

It reminded Jim, hearing the boy referred to that way. Of when Sarah was a girl, someone would call her his daughter. He'd liked the idea of being important to her, necessary, but there'd been a distance between them. He looked at the boy. His mother's last thoughts were of his survival. Saying Jim was a good man, she could see it, that everything she had was his if he'd save her son, his mind shifting to the red backpack locked in the truck's equipment box. A phone call he had to make. Jim led the boy down the block, a dingy street in a dingy little town, he wanted to get back on the road, get that thing done, a neon sign just ahead, DUSTY'S OUTPOST GRILL. With a plank sidewalk and swinging doors, Jim couldn't tell if it was an old joint or made to look that way. As if he had a nose for the last payphones in the southwest, one waited on a wall just inside the restaurant. A hostess asked how many for dinner and Jim said just the two of them, pointed the boy at a booth and told him to sit there, don't move. Rummaged his wallet for a business card. Ned Fremont, his former loan officer at Merchants Bank, it was after hours but Jim dialed the number, found his way to the pencil pusher's voicemail, Carl Neeham, and left a message that he needed a few days and would be into the bank to make the loan current. Jim hung up with his mind on the backpack full of cash. A dried handprint, a smear of brown, the words perched on his mind, he couldn't shoo them away: blood money.

Miguel sat inspecting the menu, a large plastic tri-fold with an endless number of choices, wondering how one place could offer so much food. He looked up as the man approached, wearing a heavy expression as if he'd heard bad news, but when he sat and faced Miguel he smiled a bit. "What did you decide on?" the man asked.

"Same as today," Miguel said, setting aside the menu.

The man nodded, and when the waitress arrived he said a double whiskey and a steak, medium rare, and then the waitress smiled at Miguel and Miguel said, "Hamburger, please."

She asked him about jack, cheddar, American. He thought she meant cheese but wasn't sure so he said no thank you, and then she said rare, medium, or well, and he repeated what the man had said, medium rare, and said yes to fries when she asked and yes, a Coke, and then she took the menus and left. Soon the drinks arrived. Miguel tapped a straw from paper. The man sipped and said, "Where'd you learn to speak English?"

"School mostly."

"Must be a good student, huh?"

"It was my mother. She made me study, all the time."

The man took another drink, said, "Those men at the border. You know why they were after you and your mom?"

"She said my uncle did something to make the cartel mad. I think it's probably the money. In the backpack."

"Probably," the man said.

"My uncle told my mother they would come for us so we had to leave in a hurry."

"How about your father?"

Pushing the straw at the soda, moving ice, Miguel said, "He died when I was nine. He had cancer."

"Mm. That's too bad. My wife, too, cancer."

"She died?"

The man nodded and finished the drink, wiped his mouth. "Your name is Miguel."

"Yes."

"I guess this is overdue. I'm Jim. Can I ask your mother's name?"

From his chest, quietly, Miguel said, "Rosa."

"Nice name," Jim said, turning his glass in a circle.

"What about your wife?"

"Her name? Christine."

"That's nice, too," Miguel said.

The food arrived and Jim ordered another drink and drank it. Miguel ate and Jim indicated his cap, the lion's head and soccer ball there, asked if he liked the sport. Miguel told him about Óscar Villa and Club León while Jim held up his empty glass to the waitress who brought him another full one and he worked on it without touching the steak. Later when the waitress asked, Miguel said yes please, chocolate cake, and Jim said another double, and squinted at Miguel and said, "My house, my wife's house, ours, it's gone. They burned it down."

Miguel held his fork, said, "Who?"

"The men who killed your mother."

Fork on the plate now, Miguel said, "They're in the United States?"

Jim nodded as the waitress placed the drink in front of him and asked if there'd be anything else and he wagged his head. He handed her a credit card and she walked off and he sipped at the glass saying, "Don't worry, they don't know where we are. Got no idea where we're going. Just got to keep moving, get you to Chicago."

A flicker of nausea, Miguel pushed back from the table.

"What you said earlier, you want to go home? Me too. Wish I could. Just drive the hell back home," Jim said.

Miguel stood, said, "I have to use the restroom," and Jim toasted him. Miguel crossed the restaurant to the men's where he looked at himself in the mirror trying to get his mother to talk to him. Tell him what to do, stay with this man and trust him or run away, try to get back to Nogales. But then what? The nausea crept to his head. He splashed water on his face and left the restroom and returned to the table. Jim's last drink, the empty glass, sat upside down on the tabletop, Jim nowhere to be seen. Miguel hurried from the restaurant, streetlights beginning to flicker. He looked right and left, saw Jim down the block at Otto's Autos climbing into the truck, fumbling behind the wheel, brake lights popping on. Starting the engine?

Driving home? Miguel began to run. He waved his hands saying, "Wait! Don't leave me!" and the brake lights dimmed and he looked in at Jim's head back, hat down and mouth open, asleep that fast. Miguel opened the passenger side to Jackson. The dog jumped down. She did her business and jumped back in and Miguel curled up next to her and they slept.

Not the glowing blue moonlight but it was the dream that woke him.

He sat up slowly hearing Jim's snore, Jackson's measured breathing. Feeling that only moments earlier he'd been sitting at the kitchen table before school where his mother said yes, your favorite breakfast today, a treat Miguel loved, she took it from the toaster and set it in front of him. He'd placed a hand above the plate feeling the warmth of it, the warmth of his mother, the kitchen and home and wanted it, right then.

The dashboard clock said 6:05 in the morning.

Jim's wallet lay on the seat.

Miguel reached for it and Jackson stirred without making a sound. The highway ramp was up there, San Pablo spread out behind the truck. He opened the wallet. The currency was soft in Miguel's hand, three bills. When he opened the door and slipped outside Jackson whined after him. Glancing from Jim to the dog he whispered, "Okay. Let's go together," and Jackson jumped down. Miguel shut the door softly. He tapped the dog's head and then they moved down the street side by side.

Harold wasn't dead, which didn't mean he wouldn't die any second.

Shot multiple times, the leg, the shoulder, but what scared Jim was his friend's breath coming in short, wet gasps like gut-shot, bleeding out. Jim couldn't stop to check, could only drag Harold through the jungle trying to escape the Viet Cong, voices in the near distance, footsteps crashing through underbrush. Jim stopped, scouted the area, found a spot. Dragged Harold up a short rise and sat him behind a tree, Harold asking Jim in a rutted voice not to let him die as a scarlet shadow colored his shirt. Jim used a bayonet to shred cloth from Harold's pant leg, pressed it to his chest and told him to hold it there, and then turned to his M21. There were bullets left in the twenty-round magazine. He hoped to Christ it was enough, crouching into position, the jungle gone quiet. Jim had been trained to listen through the stillness. He narrowed his eyes, scanning the trees. Heard a crush of leaves and saw someone rise up, had to be five hundred feet away when Jim pulled the trigger and watched the figure collapse, and then the barrage of bullets started. One struck Jim's helmet and spun it from his head, his throat filled with fear but he had to swallow it because men were running at him from the trees. He shot the closest one without thinking, letting his mind turn cold and mechanical, finger on the trigger, lungs filling with air, then numbers as he shot the second man, the third and fourth, and then stopped counting until it was over. He stood breathing hard. About to turn away when he heard the *thump-thump* of a man on the run who emerged from the jungle lifting a rifle. Jim lifted his, squeezing the trigger, but there were no more bullets, the man ten feet off, less when Jim pulled his sidepiece and fired twice. The man stopped like he'd hit an invisible wall, eyes hooked to Jim's with a question there, and fell dead. Jim went to him and looked down, saw he wasn't a man but an older boy, maybe sixteen, and then turned to Harold. His buddy was unmoving beneath the tree. Jim spoke his name. Spoke it again and Harold's head swiveled. Jim said we got to move, lifted Harold and pushed off through the jungle feeling like he might throw up, unsure if it was from the question frozen in the boy's eyes or from all of the whiskey he'd drunk at dinner.

He sat forward with a woolen tongue, a face hot with sweat.

It took seconds to separate himself from the old memory that came at him like a nightmare, figure out why the hell he was parked in his truck with the sun rising. Years of fighting whiskey had taught Jim the difference between waking up and coming to, and this was the latter. His squint moved from a digital 6:24 a.m. to the empty seat beside him. No Jackson, no boy, his wallet on the seat. He opened it to money missing. What to do, he began to start the truck, but to go where? He slumped back, pain needling his head as he tried to think. Maybe the kid made it to the highway and hitched and was gone, Jackson gone with him. Or maybe someone had come along and taken them both, Jesus, driven off somewhere. Maybe they were still nearby. Jim sat forward and rolled down the windows and cranked the engine and drove slowly, scanning the streets and sidewalks of San Pablo, listening through the stillness.

Jackson had spotted it in the vacant lot, in the tall desert grass, a watchful brown rabbit that sprung up at the dog's first bark. It ran and Jackson ran after it, and Miguel ran after them both. Calling out the dog's name, it was scary and thrilling, the chase, out of the vacant lot and across an empty street and another until the rabbit squeezed under a fence and disappeared with Jackson sniffing after it and Miguel breathing hard. He gazed around unsure which way they'd come from. Tiny houses with cactus-filled yards lining the block all looked the same. It was early, the sun just up with no one on the sidewalks. A plumber's van passed by and Miguel followed in its wake with Jackson at his side until they reached a commercial strip. The two lucky numbers on the convenience store, same as in Mexico, Miguel entered and found what he was looking for, a box of strawberry frosted, paid, and left.

On the sidewalk he looked left and right with no idea which way to go.

Miguel thought of staring into the mirror at the restaurant and asking his mother if he should return to Nogales or continue to Chicago. He had some money in his pocket and Jackson as a companion, and he closed his eyes and spoke in his mind to her again, saying, *Show me what to do and where to go, because I don't know, mamá, please.* When he opened his eyes she was just down the sidewalk. Dark hair pulled back, jeans and light T-shirt and short black boots and leather bag slung over her shoulder, the woman walking with an intensity that matched his mother's. Miguel knew it wasn't her, it was someone who only looked like her, but it was enough. He followed the woman, sure an answer would be waiting at the end. Down a side street, she moved quickly, it felt like chasing the rabbit, Miguel worried he might lose her but careful not to follow too closely. She turned again and again, on her phone, glancing up at storefronts as if searching for an address. The area seemed familiar to Miguel. He paused in front of the restaurant where he and Jim had dinner and then looked up the block at the car repair place, Otto's Autos. Which meant Jim was parked nearby. When Miguel gazed around for the woman, she'd disappeared.

The answer she'd led him to was Chicago, it had to be, because there he was.

Starting for the truck, Jackson in a happy gallop, Miguel running, and then slowing, then stopping in the street and staring at an empty spot. Where the truck had been parked, it was gone, Jim was gone, he'd driven off and left Miguel behind. The loss of his mother pulsing through him and now deserted. Farther down the block sat a ramp for the expressway. Maybe that was the answer the woman led him to, a way back to Mexico. Miguel started toward it calling for Jackson. The dog stood still, looking in the other direction with her ears up. Miguel called her again but then Jackson let out a single, sharp bark, a greeting as Jim's truck rounded the corner. The look of relief on the man's face as he slowed to a stop and climbed out matched what Miguel felt, neither of them putting words to it. Jim only palmed Jackson's head and held her eyes, saying quietly to Miguel, "You can't do that. Walk away like that, it's too dangerous."

"I'm sorry."

"Just don't do it again."

"I won't," Miguel said, holding up a bag. "I got breakfast." He reached inside for a box, tore it open, and removed a pair of foil-wrapped Pop-Tarts. "Better toasted but still good cold."

"That's what you went looking for?"

Miguel nodded, offering him one.

Jim sighed, took it. "I'll handle breakfast from now on," he said, watching Miguel take a bite, then he did too, and they leaned against the truck with the morning sun warm on their faces.

12

Hernando understood from experience that when Mauricio reached over and turned off the radio, snuffing the music, he was preparing himself for what came next.

He'd done so the previous evening after three hours on the road, quieting the SUV.

Nearing their destination, a filling station in New Mexico. Down the exit ramp with a large sign right there, Red Rock Gas Mart. Hernando had pulled in, parked to the side, Mauricio in the passenger seat, Isidro and Jorge in back. Mauricio stared at the station with the knuckle of a thumb beneath his lip as if meditating in the silent vehicle. A minute passed until he'd wrapped his hands around the back of his head, stretched, and said, "Let's go."

"All of us or just me?" Hernando had asked.

"Just you. Give me one. You too."

Hernando had looked at Isidro who'd reached into the rear of the SUV and turned back with a pair of Glock nines. Mauricio and Hernando had crossed the parking lot then, jangling through the station door. The place lit by fluorescent lights, empty just before eight p.m., the only person there a clerk behind a counter on a cell phone saying in one sentence, "No mom, my shift ends in half an hour, Terry and I are maybe going to the casino, I don't know, I have customers," and hung up. A long braid of dark hair, she'd looked up and said, "Help you?"

Mauricio tapped at his leg signaling Hernando to remain at the door and then stood in front of the counter. "I'm looking for a man here earlier today. Driving a pickup truck."

"That's about ninety percent of my customers." The clerk smiled.

Stepping forward, Mauricio had handed her a photo of Marine Corps and the fair-haired woman he'd taken from the house. "That's him. Look familiar?"

The clerk squinted at the picture. "The atlas."

"The what?"

"The guy bought the atlas. A book full of maps, for a road trip he was taking," she said. "Actually he didn't buy it. I gave it to him—"

"So you did see him."

"Yeah, I just told you—"

"And talked to him. Did he mention where he was going?"

The clerk handed back the photo, stared at Mauricio. "Who did you say you were?"

Seconds of silence thick with Mauricio's impatience, Hernando glanced out at the parking lot and back. "Boss—"

Mauricio ignored him, said to the clerk, "The man has a boy with him who is not his son, you understand? It's important that we find him. Did you see which way he went?"

"We get so many people in and out of here all day long."

"I didn't ask about people in and out. I asked about this man."

The clerk put on another smile, confused. "No, I didn't notice. What direction he went."

"Why do you make that face? Like I'm stupid," Mauricio had said. "Or maybe you're hiding something. Are you hiding something?"

Smile gone, the clerk said, "What do you want?"

Quick as air Mauricio put the Glock in the clerk's face, her expression blanking at the sight of it. "I want those. Nando," Mauricio said, nodding Hernando toward the CCTV screens behind the counter, cameras recording outside, the pumps, and inside the store. Moving then, alarmed, none of it should've been happening in that glassy building where anyone could pull up and look inside, Hernando hurried behind the counter. He went to the monitors asking the clerk how to rewind and she stuttered it out. After a few minutes of watching images of fueling vehicles and shopping customers, Mauricio said, "Hold it."

On a static-filled screen, the truck, the boy behind the passenger window, the old man at the pump. He entered the station, looked at a rack, and made a purchase. Exited, paused. Used a pay phone and then back into the truck and drove off. Hernando had said, "He went east."

"East." Mauricio repeated it staring at the clerk, his eyes empty inside a mask. Over his shoulder to Hernando he said, "Take the tapes."

Hernando glanced at the clerk who seemed cast in plaster. He pulled down the camera aimed at the counter, the one recording Mauricio, then gathered up all the tapes and went to the SUV, climbing behind the wheel. The scene unfolded through the filling station windows with no time to say a word to Isidro or Jorge who watched Mauricio shoot the clerk in the head, a cottony *pop-pop* as the girl deflated like a spent balloon. Jorge remained silent, his baby face empty. But Isidro with his one eye who knew how the cartel worked, he leaned toward Hernando and said, "What the fuck?"

The actual question, a public execution, how was it good for business?

What was Hernando supposed to say?

That the gringo killed Rigo and escaped with the money and boy, and since the clerk couldn't right those wrongs she was useless to the cartel and had to die? Saying so would've explained why Ángel called Mauricio his most relentless lieutenant, and also why the *capo* asked to be kept informed of Mauricio's decisions and movements inside the U.S. Tempted, Hernando glanced down at his phone and then up at Mauricio hurrying for the vehicle. Isidro's question hung in the air and Hernando had said, "Because he's the boss."

Inside the SUV Mauricio put a piece of gum in his mouth and said, "Go."

"Where?" Hernando had asked.

"East. We'll close the gap. The old man can't drive forever."

Hernando returned to the highway then. It was hours until Mauricio had pointed to a ramp, to a highway motel where they could get a few hours of sleep before continuing on. Cutting the engine, stepping from the SUV, Hernando had gazed up at the white stars feeling as if he'd been driving forever, that it was he who'd embarked on a quest that would never end.

* * *

Last thing Mauricio had done before closing his eyes at dawn was to text Emilio again and warn the fat motherfucker he'd better have information by ten a.m. at the latest.

He was on the sidewalk now outside the motel, more of a suburb than a town. Several wide boulevards just off the highway where the shops and restaurants, even a car wash, had the same clean brick-and-stone construction, same pink bougainvillea and neat stone-and-cactus strips of landscaping. Like the safe house neighborhood, one of those perfect TV shows, Mauricio thought, smoking and pacing, waiting for Emilio's call. Across the street Hernando and the other two ate at a pancake house, Mauricio saw them at a booth in the window. Hernando on his phone, nodding.

Mauricio wondered who he was talking to, the girl probably, Juana.

The one with the ripe body who'd acted shy, eyes wide months ago when he sent Hernando to oversee a shipment of pallets while Mauricio had knocked on her apartment door. She'd answered with that innocent face, as if she didn't know why he was there. Juana didn't refuse him, terrified of what would happen to her, to Hernando, if she did. Instead she lay there moaning and begging for more the whole time, bullshitting Mauricio, wanting it to be over.

He didn't care. She wasn't his type anyway.

Circling down the sidewalk he eyed a sports car at the curb, a Mercedes convertible with a woman in the passenger seat. Slim and creamy, honey blond, smiling into her phone. Dressed like she was going to play tennis or something. Mauricio thinking how easy it would be to slide behind the wheel and take her away, the Glock at his back like a golden key, and he heard a voice say, "Hey. You mind?" Mauricio glanced at a guy standing at the front of the car. Tan, tall, long shorts and a pricey T-shirt, body hammered into place at a gym. Two paper cups of coffee, the woman staring at Mauricio now too, the guy said, "Something you want?"

Yeah, to pull the Glock, see the guy's eyes dance on his forehead.

Shoot him once in the mouth and watch him choke on the bullet.

Mauricio picturing it, feeling it, when his phone vibrated. He gave the guy a grin. *Pendejo* unaware of how close he was to death, if Mauricio were in a different mood, if business weren't calling, and he turned away and answered, listening to Emilio explain that Marine Corps used the credit card yesterday at a restaurant in a town called San Pablo. Mauricio remembered passing a sign for it the previous evening, at least a hundred miles back. Emilio saying the card was used again a half hour ago at a gas station in the next county over, a straight shot down Highway 40. Mauricio took the medal from his pocket and ran a thumb over the star's raised surface. "*¿A quién pagamos allí? ¿A quién pertenecemos?*" he asked Emilio quietly. "Who do we pay there? Who do we own?"

13

They made a deal, navigation for gummy bears, so Jim wouldn't accidentally kill them both.

Highway 40, four lanes of vehicles speeding in opposite directions when they passed beneath a sign that said OKLAHOMA CITY—120 MILES, and Jim squinted at the atlas trying to check the route, swerving into another lane to an angry blast of horns, Jackson barking back, and he dropped the atlas and yanked the truck into place. Miguel holding tight to the door, Jim glanced at him and said, "Can you read that thing?"

Miguel picked up the atlas. "What do I have to do?"

"Tell me where we're going." Jim pulled a pen from the truck visor, handed it to Miguel, and pointed at the map. "We're here, this stretch of Texas. The lines with numbers on them are highways. Put an X there, where we are now."

"Okay," Miguel said, marking the atlas.

"See Chicago up there?"

Tracing a finger, Miguel said, "Yes."

"We need to travel from Highway 40, which we're on now, to 54, to 290. Get me?"

"Yes."

"Circle Chicago as our end point," Jim said. "Then trace that line all the way there. It's up to you to follow it and make sure we're going the right way."

Miguel circled Chicago, traced the line, and then looked up at Jim. "What do I get?"

"What do you mean, get?"

"I mean I'm the one doing the hard job. If I stop paying attention we could get lost," Miguel said.

Jim considered it, said, "What do you want?"

Miguel smiled a little. *"Panditas."*

"What are *panditas?"*

Miguel explained and Jim said okay, next time they stopped. Miguel held up the atlas and said we wouldn't even need this thing if you had a phone and asked Jim if the reason he didn't have one was because he was old, some old people were scared of phones, and Jim said he wasn't that old and no, he wasn't scared of phones, he just didn't want one. Miguel said, "Why not? Don't you want to talk to your friends?"

Christine. There at the front of Jim's mind. His wife, his best friend, if only there were a phone that could connect them, he shook his head. "There's nobody to call. Nobody to call me back, neither. Not really."

"Nobody?"

"Well. I know a guy in Detroit. Harold, but . . ." Jim shrugged.

Miguel stared out the window, Jackson

nuzzled against him, and he looked back at Jim. "We follow this line, these highways all the way to Chicago, you think I'll like it there?"

Inside the boy's question Jim heard fear, the large, strange city his destination. "Tell you what. I was a kid not much older than you, I went there with my dad," Jim said. "Summertime, it seemed the whole place was green and blue, the parks, the lake as big as the sea. And the hot dogs, no kidding, they put everything on them, I mean the kitchen sink—"

Bwip-bwip.

Jim's eyes went to the rearview mirror, a Texas state trooper car behind him. He glanced at the speedometer, twenty-some miles over the speed limit, and muttered, "Shit," slowing and signaling into the right lane.

"What's the matter?" Miguel turned, looked back at the car.

"Going too fast is all. Relax and keep quiet, okay?" Jim signaled again, exiting down a ramp to a rural road. At the bottom he cut the engine, the cruiser rolling to a stop on his bumper. A trooper in his Stetson and aviator shades taking his time talking on a cellphone, making Jim wait. Thinking of Sarah, the border patrol surely having issued a bulletin for Jim's plates by now, the truck, a man by his description traveling with a boy. He cursed himself for not watching his speed, and now the trooper was out of the car, middle-aged and stone-faced. He paused at the back of the truck, looked into the bed, moved to the passenger side. Spent a few moments inspecting the bullet holes and shredded side mirror. Around to the front and Jim rolled down the window as the trooper stood there not saying anything. "Something I can do for you?" Jim asked.

"License and registration," the trooper said. Jim gave it to him, the trooper staring at both. "James Hanson. I see Arizona includes the veteran designation. What branch?"

"Marine Corps," Jim said.

"Well. Thank you for your service," the trooper said, and Jim nodded, and the trooper looked past Jim to Miguel. "How you doing, son?"

A hand on Jackson's neck, Miguel looked from Jim to the trooper. "Okay."

To Jim, the trooper said, "Side of your truck, you had some sort of incident?"

"More like an accident. Gun went off while I was cleaning it."

"Carrying any weapons now?"

A pause, Jim said, "I have a .45 in my belt here. Rifle behind the seat in a duffel, got permits for both."

A slow nod and the trooper said, "Step out of the vehicle, sir."

"For speeding? What's the problem?"

The trooper inspected Jim, done with formalities. "That boy isn't your son."

Jim knew then, Sarah had been right. Taking Miguel from the border patrol station without the law looking for them, coming after them, seemed suddenly ridiculous. They'd gone as far as they could go, and Jim sighed saying, "No, he is not."

Stepping back, the trooper told Jim again to exit the truck. Jim climbed out and the trooper said, "Place your hands on the hood and do not move." Jim did as he was told. The trooper took the .45 from Jim's belt, popped the clip, and went to the truck cab. He reached inside, grabbed the duffel holding the M21, two boxes of bullets, Jim hearing Jackson growl from her belly at the man as he took the keys from the ignition. "What you're going to do now is sit in the vehicle with your hands visible on the wheel, understand me?" the trooper said.

"Yeah," Jim said, sliding back into the truck.

The trooper moved off, and Miguel whispered, "Are we under arrest?"

"Seems I am." Staring into the side mirror, Jim watched the trooper place his guns on the front seat of the cruiser and then turn, lifting his cell phone and looking at the screen. The cruiser was parked so close to the truck that Jim heard him answer it.

"They'll send me back?" Miguel asked.

Jim looked at the boy, wanted to say something, it felt like an apology, but could only muster, "I don't know." Miguel leaned into Jackson and Jim glanced at the trooper again in the side mirror, hearing the man utter a couple of words into the phone.

"Marine Corps."

Sounding familiar, spoken that way. Almost like a name, it reminded Jim of the shootout at the border wall. The one in charge calling out to Jim through the steel fence, and now he wondered. Why he and Miguel were sitting in the truck instead of locked in the back of the cruiser. Why the trooper used a cell phone instead of his radio, and Jim bent an ear and listened harder, hearing the man say, "Exit 72, hurry." Jim let go of the steering wheel then knowing he had nothing to lose, and left the truck. The trooper looked around as Jim approached. Quick and nervous, the man drew his sidearm and aimed it at Jim's chest, saying, "Move, you're dead."

"We're dead anyway, aren't we?" Jim said with a slow halt. "How much did the cartel pay you to betray that badge?"

"You don't know shit about it." The trooper backed up Jim with the gun until they were at the truck's open door. "Once they got you, you can't say no, you have to—"

The noise and motion were ghostlike, a blurred rush of gray, hissing jaws. Seeing a gun aimed at Jim, Jackson charged from the truck, teeth sinking into the trooper's forearm, grinding at bone. The trooper screamed and twisted, trying to get a bead on the animal, firing a wavy shot that pinged off the cruiser. Jackson scattered and the trooper took aim again as

Jim hit him hard alongside the head, a loud, bony crack of knuckles on skull. Like an ice skater losing balance, ankles folded, the man went sideways, down and out. Jim looked from him to the exit ramp. Feeling it, almost here, they were coming for Miguel and him. Mind spinning, he went through the trooper's empty pockets and said, "Where the hell are the truck keys?!"

"Here!" Miguel a few feet away, hand in the air, he'd found them on the pavement.

Jim went to the cruiser and grabbed the .45, the duffel holding the M21, and hustled Miguel and Jackson back to the truck. He cranked the engine and rejected the highway, needing to get the hell away without being seen on that open stretch of concrete. Fishtailing over the rural road, scanning for a hiding place, Jim sped along a dusty rise to a construction site, deserted piles of steel railing, idle cranes. He parked the truck out of sight with old instincts nicking at him, do some recon, get an idea what he was up against. An order to Miguel and Jackson, stay put, and he left the truck and climbed the hill. On his belly then, Jim peered down at the exit ramp. Seconds later Miguel sidled up next to him, Jim saying, "I told you to wait in the truck."

The boy's eyes narrowed at the exit, voice low. "I need to see them. Those men."

Jim said nothing and looked back at the road. It didn't take long. A few minutes until the black SUV descended the ramp, eased onto the rural road and stopped next to the cruiser. The trooper pulled himself to his feet, a hand pressed to his head. Four men left the SUV. Jim recognized two of them. The tall one from the driver's seat stood behind the one in charge. His shaved head in pale contrast to black jeans and shirt and boots, the one in charge planted himself in front of the trooper, inked forearms crossed over his chest. When the trooper began shaking his head no, no, no, it seemed to Jim like a physical incantation, that if he kept it up long enough the men would get back into the SUV and drive away. The one in charge, his stance, the way his head cocked to the side as if he were lost in thought, present and elsewhere at once; it flipped a switch in Jim's mind, an old memory from the war of what he was witnessing.

The prelude to an execution.

He could stop it. Save the trooper and take out the one in charge, and Jim scrambled for the truck. It took him less than a minute to return with the M21, snap out the tripod and sight the pale shaved head. Miguel next to him, understanding, whispering, "Do it. Do it," with flat urgency, as Jim's finger grazed the trigger. He took a breath and held it, and paused. Something wasn't right. Slowly withdrew his eye from the scope with the awful sense of having failed the moment, his mission, remembering then that the M21 wasn't loaded.

He'd taken his guns from the cruiser but forgot the ammunition.

Hernando heard the truth in between the cop's excuses, that Marine Corps had figured him out and overpowered him and escaped again, and Mauricio interrupted the cop and said, "You're lucky to be alive."

The guy with his bleeding ear, his shaking hands, he said, "He didn't seem like a killer."

Mauricio nodded. "You're right about that."

Jorge approached Hernando saying, "I found this."

A book open to a page, Hernando inspected it, showed it to Mauricio. "Remember what the girl told us, the clerk, an atlas? See the line here to here?" Hernando pointed at a chain of highways ending at Chicago.

Mauricio looked from the page to the cop. "Is that where they're going? Chicago?"

The cop shook his head. "I don't know."

"You didn't ask?"

Still shaking his head, the cop said, "I didn't know I was supposed to. I mean. I didn't think they'd be going anywhere after here."

"They wouldn't have if you'd done your job."

"I told you. That fucking dog. I tried to kill it."

"You failed. Let me show you how it's done. Last lesson you'll ever learn," Mauricio said, pulling the Glock from the back of his belt and shooting the cop like the clerk, two bullets in the head flinging him against the cruiser like tornado debris, decades of life gone in seconds.

Hernando, unmoving, felt the presence of multiple lanes of highway traffic roaring past up the exit ramp. How many witnesses could there have been, how many cell phone cameras pointed at the scene, and they just stood here now listening to the cruiser's radio saying the dead cop's name, ordering him to check in, where was he?

As Isidro had asked, Hernando now asked himself, *What kind of business is this?*

He answered himself, *Bad business,* and said, "Boss. We have to go. Right now."

Mauricio looked from the head-blown trooper to Hernando with a smirk. "Can you believe it? A fucking dog."

Miguel didn't recoil, staring down the hill as the men got into the SUV and left the trooper's body where it fell. "They want to do that to me," he said quietly. "Kill me like that."

"I won't let them," Jim said.

Miguel glanced at the unloaded weapon in Jim's hands and then at Jim, something more powerful than fear in his eyes, more disturbing.

Doubt.

Jim saw it there like looking in a mirror.

Seeing himself as too old for a fight like this, too out of practice, just thinking of the one in charge sparking another, sharper feeling. Pinpricks of it attacking him all over, making him wince until, as he'd taught himself long ago, he inhaled the feeling. Filled his brain with it as he had when ordered to hide in unseen places and guard his platoon from harm. Knowing there was no greater incentive to keep everyone alive than the awful fear of letting even one of them die.

14

The big box store surrounded on four sides by nothing dominated the Texas landscape with its bland enormity. Jim saw the structure minutes before nearing it. He took his time exiting the highway, crossing the store's vast lot before finding a place to park. Miguel was asleep in his ball cap against the passenger door, a hand on Jackson with the dog's snoring head in his lap.

Jim cut the engine, alert but in no hurry. He sipped whiskey and waited.

Getting behind the enemy without its knowledge was one of a soldier's oldest tactics. Giving it lead-time, letting it travel away from you thinking it was in hot pursuit. After the SUV had sped back onto the highway, Jim turned the truck down the rural road and passed through sorghum and cotton fields following a route that wound back to the highway. Afterward he'd driven the speed limit, letting the day fade, and then sat in the parking lot. Watching people emerge from the store pushing shopping carts, carrying bags, all those purchases, the slow realization and shame at his stupidity warming his face. His credit card, swiped or scanned, how the cartel had been able to track his movements, and he asked himself, why? Had he been so goddamn dense as to use the card when he was traveling with a backpack filled with cash?

Those words again, blood money.

A quiet part of his mind finding its voice then, saying it aloud: how spending the money felt like taking more from Miguel, more of what his mother had already sacrificed for him. Loss and despair were soaked into that cash.

Jim shook the empty pint bottle. He rubbed his face, leaned his head back, and asked his wife what to do, what to do, letting sleep carry him to her.

Christine said, *It's okay, the money, if it helps the boy.*

Jim said, Thank you my darling, my heart, I need you to tell me so.

Although.

Jim asked, Although what?

You know.

I don't, tell me, Jim said.

Just that, what's good for the boy may not be good for you.

And Miguel said, "Jim. Jim, hey."

One eye open, he looked over at Miguel and Jackson who looked back at him. The boy in need of a wash and change of clothes, the dog with that open mouth look of hunger. "Okay, girl," Jim said, meeting her eyes, holding her muzzle. He stepped from the truck and unlocked the equipment box. The red backpack, he unzipped it, removed a sheaf of bills, locked up the box. With a knuckle on the window he told Miguel, "Let's go. We need some things," and led him from the truck and across the parking lot. The boy staring up at the massive store like it had landed from outer space. Through the whooshing doors, the place as cavernous as an airplane hangar, they passed a pyramid of laundry detergent, a display of golf carts and lawn mowers and gas grills, Jim pausing to get his bearings, reading the overhanging signs and turning toward the clothing section. There he flipped through plain T-shirts holding them up to Miguel for size, setting them aside, hearing the boy make a noise, almost happy. Showing a Cubs T-shirt, bright blue with a big red C, Jim said, "You want that one?"

"It's going to be my new team." Miguel smiled.

Jim nodded and they moved on to socks, underwear, toothbrushes, a razor. Then dog food

and then another aisle where Jim found whiskey and water and jerky. Navigating toward
checkout, he glanced at a far wall, a sign there
reading FIREARMS. His thoughts never away
from the four men searching for the boy and
him. Ammo for the M21 and .45, he walked
toward the sign thinking of the one in charge,
how easily he'd killed that trooper with the
other three holding pistols of their own, and
who the hell knew what else they were pack-
ing? He scanned the display of rifles. Paused
at a semi-automatic M4, a solid, medium-sized
machine gun.

"Help you?"

Jim turned to a bearded salesman in plaid
giving him a ruddy smile. "Just looking at the
semi-auto," Jim said.

"Good eye. That there's a certified replica
of the model issued to U.S. special ops forces.
Comes with a thirty-round magazine."

"Lot of bullets."

"Lot of bad SOBs out there." The beard winked.

Jim nodded, moving pieces around his mind, knowing a background check would be like using a credit card, his information sent into the ether. Beyond the Arizona border patrol and state police, the FBI likely on to him by now. The beard gave off a vibe of maybe ignoring regulations in favor of rough justice, maybe a couple hundred-dollar bills would help the man along, and Jim heard his wife's voice then. Asking what he was thinking, using that money for bribery, and how would a machine gun help the boy anyway? If it came down to it, it would be about who was operating a weapon and how versus more bullets. Jim unsure if it was Christine telling him that or if he was reminding himself. Told the beard he needed ammo for a .45, an M21, paid for it and lifted the bag and looked down at Miguel, who was gone.

With dread in his gut he turned to an ocean of people, the ball cap gone.

Feeling a fool, he'd brought Miguel into this wide-open space where the men could be any-where, and Jim forgot caution, going up and down the aisles calling out the boy's name with faces and more faces staring as he went. His carelessness at losing Miguel sparking another woman's voice in his head, not his wife's but the boy's mother, Rosa with agony-eyes beg-ging him to save her boy, he was nearly run-ning when he heard, "Jim?" There at a row of shelves filled with candy. Miguel held greens, blues, and reds wrapped in plastic. "*Panditas*," he said. "You owe me." Jim did not know what he was doing, he went to Miguel and grasped him by his shoulders and pulled him close, a feeling of trying to anchor him to the Earth. Just as quickly let him go. Whatever had been in the embrace started Miguel nodding, a com-prehension there, and Jim said, "C'mon."

By the time they were in the truck he'd decided to get as far from people as possible.

One side road to another, he cut far from the highway until they were crossing flat backcountry. Weathered fence posts standing like sentries, mainly dairy farms back there. A couple hours on they bumped over railroad tracks to a gas station on the other side, a feed store, a liquor store, further down a squat building with MOTEL in neon on its roof. Jim parked at an angle where he could see the truck and pushed into the cigarette-smelling lobby, an older woman in an orange Texas U ball cap behind the counter watching something loud on a screen. She looked up at Jim like she was surprised to see him there and said, "Help you?"

"A room, for me and my boy. Dogs okay?"

"I like them better than people. That's forty-three plus tax. How long you staying?"

"Just the night." Jim laid a hundred-dollar

bill on the counter, looked out at the street and back to the woman. "Where am I exactly?"

"Honey, you got no idea how many times I've asked myself that question." She slid Jim a room key, his change. "Welcome to Midora, home of just about nothing."

"Anywhere to get food close by, a diner maybe?"

"Thirty or so minutes in each direction. I got frozen pizzas and burritos for sale, you can nuke 'em in your room."

"Give me a couple of those pizzas." Jim paid the woman and bid her goodnight. He parked the truck at the back of the motel where it wouldn't be seen and led Miguel and Jackson to the room, turning the key, flipping on the light to twin beds, an old TV, giant microwave and tiny fridge, side table with a rotary phone. "Well. It ain't the Ritz but it'll do."

"What's the Ritz?" Miguel asked, throwing his backpack on a bed.

"Not this." Items from the big box store, red backpack full of money and his duffel bag holding the .45, Jim dropped the gear and opened a bottle of whiskey. He pointed at Miguel. "Take some of that new stuff, the clothes, clean yourself up and change. Bathroom's there."

"Then pizza?"

"Yep," Jim said, pouring a glass. Miguel gathered his things and closed the bathroom door. Jim sipped whiskey. When he heard the shower he went to the phone. It was after five p.m. but maybe she was still there, and he made a collect call and waited, preparing himself, thinking how when she was angry she sounded a bit like her mother.

Sarah knew he'd contact her, didn't know when, everyone in the border patrol office was waiting for it, too. Eyes on her all the time, there'd been zero leads on Jim and the boy since they'd disappeared. Dalton gave her sidelong glances as if she had something to do with it, cornering her twice a day and asking what the fuck her daddy had been thinking, Sarah not bothering to say stepdad, just taking it and waiting like everyone else.

At her desk, stirring cold coffee, her phone buzzed twice.

She lifted it and listened to the operator and accepted the charges and didn't let Jim utter a word, Sarah said, "Where are you?"

Jim glanced at the bathroom door, said in a low voice, "Bad situation here. A state trooper shot dead this afternoon."

"What? Jim, you didn't—"

"No, of course not, no. It was the one from the shootout, the one who came under the wall and tried to kill me."

"The trooper—"

"He was dirty. Must've been paid off by the cartel. Son of a bitch pulled me over. Weren't for Jackson I'd be the dead one."

"What about the boy?"

"Shook up a little but okay. Tough kid."

"Jim. You need to listen to me now." Sarah touched her laptop, stared at the screen. "DEA picked up chatter from Mexican Nogales about a cartel soldier killed at the U.S. border and they worked it backward. The one following you is Mauricio Guerrero. A hit man, now a top lieutenant with his own crew, answers to Ángel Vasquez. The guy you shot? It was this Mauricio's brother."

"Christ," Jim whispered.

"Mexican feds have a mole, said the boy's uncle stole money from the cartel. The guy was hung from an overpass like a side of beef. Word is the boy's mom made off with the cash."

A glance at the red backpack, Jim's eyes rested there. "How much?"

"Same number you gave me, about two hundred."

"Cartels make what, billions of dollars a year, the guy's chasing me across the U.S. for a couple hundred grand?"

A pause, sifting his words, Sarah said, "Chasing you? Or the boy?"

"I told you. I promised his mother."

"Take him somewhere, you get paid?"

"That's right."

"Where?"

"It doesn't matter."

"Jim. My mother would want me to persuade you, make you agree to take care of yourself, protect yourself. This isn't our way, okay, you and me? But I need to say it," she sighed. "I don't want to lose you."

"Listen—"

"And what if you lose the boy? The deal you made, what if it's the very thing that gets him killed?" she said. "I mean, were you even aware that Mauricio and his men were following you until what happened with the trooper?"

The truth of it cut Jim, making him feel less than himself. "No. I was not."

"How were they able to follow you?"

"Credit card. But I stopped using it. I think I lost them."

"They're sophisticated enough to track your card, you don't think they have other means, other methods? Jim. The boy has to come back."

Tingling with the dread he'd felt at the big box store, the idea of Miguel murdered and disappeared, Jim said, "Yeah. You're right."

"Where are you?"

"Texas, near the New Mexico border. Town called Midora."

"Midora, Texas," Sarah said, scribbling the name. "Find the sheriff's office. Whatever's the closest agency, take the boy and explain and have them call me right away. We'll get you back here quick as possible."

"No cops," Jim said, shaking his head at the phone. "Can't trust them around here."

Sarah thought a minute, said, "I'll come myself. Where in Midora are you?"

"Only one motel here. Hey, Sarah?"

"What?"

"I'm sorry. For taking him, what it did it you. Putting you in a bind."

"Don't be sorry. Just don't get killed, okay? I'll be there soon for you and the boy." She added a few more words, so did Jim, and she hung up and closed her eyes, leaned her head back.

"By boy I assume you mean the little Mex your daddy took."

Sarah sat up to Dalton in the doorway with that underwear-a-size-too-small look on his face. "That was my stepfather, yeah," she said.

"They're in Midora, Texas?"

"How long have you been standing there?"

"Long enough to hear you violate protocol. Sharing DEA intel. Saying how you're going to cross two states and pick them, bring them back," Dalton said. "Like hell you are."

"Those cartel guys are in the U.S. They murdered a state trooper for God's sake, and they're pursuing my stepdad and the boy." Sarah pushed out of the chair. "Someone has to help them, get the two of them to safety."

"It's not going to be you."

"He's my family."

"I don't give a shit if he's Jesus Christ himself. You're a desk jockey."

Face hot, unable to hold back, Sarah said, "And you're an incompetent dickweed."

Dalton's neck jerked, he said, "If. Now. I'm warning you—"

"You and your punitive bullshit," Sarah said. "If Lee was aware—"

Movement and a presence behind Dalton, the Patrol Agent in Charge shouldering into Sarah's office, Lee Hurst with his buzz cut and creased expression. "Lee was aware of what?"

he asked. Sarah not wanting to repeat what she'd said, Dalton not wanting to hear himself called the name again, both were silent. Lee looked at Sarah, said, "It's about the boy and your stepdad?"

She nodded. "I spoke to him. They're in trouble, sir."

"Let's discuss it," he said, and faced Dalton. "I'll take it from here."

"But, wait," Dalton said, sounding jilted. "As Deputy Agent—"

"I'll keep you in the loop," Lee said slow and firm, conversation over.

Dalton glanced at Sarah, back at Lee, nodded tersely and left the office.

Sarah took Lee through the paces then, what Jim told her along with the DEA information, Jim's credit card, Mauricio's background, his dead brother and the stolen money. She laid it all out, how her mother's death had affected Jim, frozen and bankrupted him, and the monetary deal he'd made with the boy's mother to transport the boy to safety.

"Where?" Lee asked.

"He didn't say. It got lost in the shuffle when I told him about Mauricio."

She explained about the trooper, Lee wincing. He'd contact someone he knew with the Texas State Police and pass along the information, the trooper's killers and his cartel connections, and when Sarah was done Lee sat on the edge of her desk, crossed his arms. "All of that, trying to protect the boy," he said. "What your stepfather's done still lands on kidnapping. Federal crime, it could be bad for him."

"But if he brings the boy back. If I guarantee it, deliver them myself."

"Then what?"

"I don't know, sir. Maybe it'll be less bad for him?"

Lee looked at her and brushed a hand over

his spiky head. "Maybe. If you get them back by this time tomorrow."

"I appreciate it sir, I do. Jim's a good man."

"Good, bad, or otherwise, you have twenty-four hours. And stay in contact regarding your movements. Dalton's correct about protocol," Lee said. "Even if he is a dickweed."

In his office listening to his wife on the phone complaining about how the landscapers hadn't properly edged the pool, and speaking of the pool she'd ordered new terrace furniture, the old stuff was tacky, and then reminded him to be home soon enough to take the girls to their horseback riding lessons, she had a yoga class, the whole time Dalton thinking about how much it all cost, the woman a money-spending machine.

He was too, no reason to lie to himself. Accustomed to nice things, a supplemented life.

Trapped by it.

His wife took a breath and Dalton said, "I have to go," and hung up and went to the door, closed and locked it and moved to the corner of his office nearest the window. Head tilted against the glass, Dalton looked out at lines of vehicles snaking toward the checkpoints on both sides of the border. He shifted his gaze, staring at his own reflection staring back.

Fucking terrace furniture.

Fucking horseback riding lessons.

Fucking yoga classes, Dalton dialed a number and listened to a voice and hesitated before watching his reflection say, "They're still in Texas. Some little town called Midora."

15

Driving through the night, Sarah traversed the black rise and fall of Arizona punctuated by highway lights and the headlights of big rigs and fast-food oases lit up with sharp reds and yellows. New Mexico drew near and then it would be seven hours to the motel in Texas. Sarah hoped to arrive just before dawn, and she wondered again why she was making the trip. Jim had agreed the boy should be returned to safety. Why not have him get into his truck that moment, and head back? Why had it felt necessary to escort him, to promise Lee Hurst she'd do so, involving herself in Jim's bad decision and making herself more a part of it?

Border patrol SUV going so fast it felt un-moving, Sarah pressed her mother for answers.

When she thought of her, no matter how far or near the memory, her mother was always the same age, dressed the same way. Not yet forty with her long hair up and back, a breezy blue summer dress. Sarah thirteen then when her mother was engaged to Jim, and she'd asked her mother straight out, "Do you love him?"

Standing at a bedroom mirror, her mother had looked at Sarah sitting on the bed behind her and said, "Yes I do."

"Like you loved my daddy?"

"It's not the same thing, darling. Your daddy and I loved one another right away because we were desperate."

"I don't understand."

She'd turned and smiled and sat next to Sarah on the bed. "It had to do with being young. The world felt too big then and we felt alone in it. But what happens is people grow older and become less, I suppose scared is the way to say it. The truth is that in certain ways we stopped needing each other as much."

"But Jim. You need him?"

Her mother had looked away, back with a different smile. "When I first met Jim I didn't know him. I mean, not just that we'd never met but that even after a little while he held himself inside. So did I love him right away, or need him, no. No, darling. But when he was able to explain his past, decisions he'd made in his life, well then I began to understand him and it changed my thoughts and made me love him very much. One part, which leaves him an unusual sort of person," she said, and Sarah remembered her mother's expression, affection and worry entwined. "He can't help but do what he believes is the right thing, whatever that may be. It sounds noble except some of those things made him hate himself, others got him hurt."

Hearing it as a girl had nicked Sarah, it remained with her.

Remembering it now as an answer to the question, why fetch Jim?

Maybe his ironclad independence made it impossible to ask for help, or maybe it was as her mother said, that just because the path he'd chosen was righteous didn't make it right. Sarah thought of those things and then set them aside knowing her quest was more elemental: She feared Jim might die and that losing him would be like losing him twice. If she didn't bring him home she was suddenly sure he'd never make it back, and leaned on the gas. Speeding on in a race, which until that moment, she had not known she'd entered.

It was an old one, the western flashing from the television screen. Jim had seen parts of it for years but to Miguel the film was new. Each on their own beds, paper plates of pizza crust on the side table. Jim stretched out with a glass of whiskey at hand, Miguel sitting against the headboard working on the *panditas*. The part of the story where the sheriff, Gary Cooper, explains to his new wife, Grace Kelly, that he has no choice, he's the law, it's his duty to deal with the bad guys. Love and regret radiated from their eyes, alive on the screen, when Miguel said, "I have a girlfriend at home."

"That so? What's her name?" Jim said, sipping.

Holding up a gummy bear, Miguel said, "Lola. She likes these as much as I do." He popped it in his mouth and spoke while chewing. "I'm going to marry her."

"She said yes?"

"I haven't asked her yet."

"You might want to let her in on it."

"Was it nice being married?"

It slowed Jim, and then he brought the glass to his lips, drank it back and nodded. "Those were the happy years of my life. The happiest."

Gunshots cut the air. Miguel sat forward watching the scene, the sheriff confronting a pair of outlaws, gunning them down, beating them both to the draw. A glance at Jim, Miguel asked, "Is it hard to do that? Shoot someone?"

"You mean fast or just doing it?"

"Both I guess," Miguel said.

"The first part, fast, accurate, I could do it since I was a kid, bottles and targets and such. I never did go in for hunting, my thought always, well, now what did that creature do to be shot? Then I was called into the military during wartime. Just done being a boy. The Marines noticed my skill and gave me training and a job where I did, Miguel, yes. I shot people." Jim sat up on the side of the bed, refilled the glass, and looked at the boy. "I was taught to think that the enemy were not human beings. Supposed to make it easier. Two years passed in which my lieutenant was very proud of what he called my confirmed kills."

"How many?" Miguel asked, swallowing the question.

"I'm not sure," Jim lied. "Quite a few."

"You felt bad about it?"

Jim drank the whiskey, head hot, he ought to quit talking. "Not so much bad as sorry. From the first person I shot in the war to the last, and I remember them both. First was as young as me, but not the last one. He was an older man, in the brush firing at my platoon's position. From my perch I could see that he was leading a small group, him and a few others. Had he ceased fire I would've let them pass. But he wouldn't stop and I couldn't allow anyone in my platoon to be hurt or killed. You understand?"

Miguel nodded, squeezing his hands together.

"I waited. Eventually he raised his head and I did what I did, understand?"

"*Si*, yes."

"Afterward I'm watching to see what those others might do, eye to the scope. They passed by quickly, running hard." Jim turned the glass in his hand, stared at it. "And I saw that it was a woman and two kids and they were carrying baskets, and they left the dead man behind."

Miguel could barely hear himself over the TV when he said, "His family?"

"I don't know but I imagined so. Began imagining the families of everyone I'd shot. I wanted to explain to them that I was doing my duty, which I believed in, and was just as sorry for having done it, both." Jim finished the drink, placed the glass upside down on the side table. "I told myself there was a purpose to it. Country and family, safety, home. Thing is, when I came home the people I killed came with me. I guess it's the price I paid, but. It often feels too costly."

Quietly Miguel said, "My mother paid a price. So I could have a safe home."

"That she did."

"I think. I'll try to be happy there, in Chicago, for my mother. What she wanted."

Jim watched resolution tighten Miguel's face, a step away from childhood. Thought of Sarah en route to take the boy into custody. Hit with that old wave, the need to say he was sorry, Jim felt it in his own face and looked away saying, "It's late. Let's get some sleep." He snapped off the light and lay back, aware of Miguel sitting a few seconds longer before stretching out, pulling at a blanket. Jim blinked at the dark ceiling. Feeling those hundred and five ghosts crowding in, staring down at him as was their way, reminding him of his responsibility, and Jim prayed to himself that he was doing the right thing, sending the boy back to Arizona.

***

Nearly dawn when Miguel was awoken by a cold nose.

Jackson nudged at his hand making a low, whining noise. The first orange crease of sunlight beneath the door, Miguel glanced over at Jim asleep with his hat over his face. He sat up then, a hand on Jackson's head and pictured Jim's expression from the previous evening. Like in the restaurant when the man had been upset about something, trying to push it out of his eyes. An urge to thank him then, Miguel felt it in his chest. For taking him to Chicago as his mother had asked, he didn't care if Jim was doing it for money. The man had lost his home and he seemed so tired, and Jackson was whining again. "You have to pee, I know," Miguel whispered, and led the dog outside. Dense acreage of hazel pine and oak trees, overgrown brush, spread out along the side of the motel. Jackson trotted over there, where Jim and Miguel had watched her nose around the previous day, sniffing at critters as Jim had said. Miguel followed behind the dog as she wandered among the trees, and he noticed an SUV parked outside the office. Through the window a woman was shaking her head at someone else he couldn't see.

A shoulder came into view, a black shirt and the back of a shaved head.

The woman in her orange ball cap was smoking, angrily pointing the cigarette at the exit, and Miguel felt the man in black begin to turn in his direction, and he dropped to the ground and crawled behind a stucco corner. Found his breath, then blinked around the edge of the wall.

With an icy brain Miguel thought, *The second time that man has found me at a motel.*

Watched a few seconds more as the man punched the woman, and she twisted, tumbled, and another man stepped forward, a taller one, and then Miguel was running. Back to the room, the act of shoving through the door got Jim to his feet and Miguel said, "They're here." Jim like a human robot asking not a question, making not a sound, grabbing the .45 from the duffel bag, a glance through the blinds and he threw Miguel his backpack and said put on your shoes and hoisted the duffel and red backpack full of money. He said go into the bathroom, and Miguel went there and watched Jim lift the phone and punch numbers and tell someone on the other end that the motel was being robbed, men with guns, it was happening now, send the police, and he dropped the phone and entered the bathroom too. Nearby the double crack of a handgun went through the air. Jim lowered Miguel from the window and told him to run and hide in the woods, he had to get Jackson, and the boy said, "She's out here, outside!"

"Where?"

"By the woods, I took her to pee!"

Jim's head jerked then, he looked over his shoulder to the motel room door. Men outside, silhouettes behind drawn shades pounding at the doorknob, and Jim climbed through the window. Holding Miguel by the back of the shirt he hurried them into the morning darkness of trees and underbrush, disappearing behind a veil of Spanish moss. Jim knew how to flee an enemy, to become so still as to be undetectable. He took a position behind a thick cypress with a hand on Miguel's shoulder and signaled him to be quiet, do not make a sound. Turning an ear deeper into the trees he tried to locate Jackson, a footstep or a breath, instead hearing cautious movement in front of them.

It was on the other side of the leafy curtain twenty feet away.

Jim knew, could've guessed at the sound of that man coming for them.

The woman, the manager with her loud mouth and orange ball cap and burning cigarette telling them to get the hell out of there and leave her guests alone, she'd been a fucking speed bump, they shouldn't have bothered to ask about Marine Corps and the boy, should've gone room to room, and now they were gone.

But not too far gone. The truck sat just there, unmoving.

Mauricio had been first through the door. Seen Marine Corps slide from the bathroom window, watched as he and the boy ran into the woods. He stood at the edge of the tree line now thinking of a military term: deep cover. The danger of it, pursuing Marine Corps into the unknown with no idea of where he was hiding and catching a bullet through the neck for being a fool. He gestured to Hernando. The tall man hurried to his side. Mauricio told him to distribute the assault rifles, one for each man, they'd spread out and fire as many rounds as it took to clear-cut the woods, cut down the old man and boy. Hernando moved toward the SUV signaling to Jorge and Isidro. Pausing to look back at Mauricio as the shriek of sirens rode the wind, speeding toward the motel. A grin pinched at Mauricio, remembering the phone off the hook in the motel room. Shouting into the woods now, "Marine Corps! You can't hide forever!"

"We have to go," Hernando said, the sirens nearer, determined.

Mauricio drew the nine-millimeter from his waist. Focusing his mind on the boy, their connection, he crouched and fired, one shot, three shots, the entire clip, bullets splintering branches with Hernando calling out his name, warning him until it was too late. Like a bear trap had closed on Mauricio's forearm, the gun shaken free as he lost his feet, on his back, the dog snapping at his face now remembering Mauricio's assault on Jim. Mauricio tried to shove the animal away and felt it then, razor teeth piercing his fingers. Screamed and punched at it and the animal rolled off and dug in its back legs ready to pounce and Hernando was there, Mauricio trembling all over. He grabbed Hernando's gun and lifted it and said, "Fucking dog."

A platoon, everyone it, there's not a single member you fail to defend or leave behind. Not because of duty or an oath but because the shared pain and sacrifice forge you into one living object, like iron in a fire; lose a part of it, you lose part of yourself, and that's what Jim did.

Because if he moved, emerged from the trees, he'd expose the boy.

Jim asked himself, Jackson or Miguel, Jackson or Miguel, knowing that trying to save one would get the other killed, and a harder truth: that it was Jackson who'd saved him and the boy. With sirens in the air, two of Mauricio's men were already hurrying to the SUV. Jackson had halted Mauricio's onslaught, she was a breath from dead, and when Mauricio shot and killed her, Jim shuddered at the agony of it, at losing a part of himself he'd never get back.

16

Looking through the windshield at a man hunched over the steering wheel with a boy beside him, Jim did not know where the man had been driving for the past hours or what he was searching for, knew only that he was that man, it was he who had no wife and no home.

No best friend, not anymore.

Jackson's body cocooned in a tarp in the truck bed, she'd loved Jim because of who he'd been, hers, and with his heart digging at his throat he understood that being the recipient of certain types of love made a soul young forever. With her gone, Jim had become older than old. Salted over, all used up. Dragged along this path not for the first time, feeling again the smothering truth of the loss of love, that it was helplessness. The inability to undo what's been done pulling him down, down, down, resigned to it. He closed his eyes and quit breathing and when the boy spoke Jim reluctantly rejoined his body and glanced over at him.

"How?" Miguel repeated himself. "Can you drive like that?"

Jim did not know if he meant closed eyes or eyes clouded by water, he blinked, sped on.

"Where are we going?"

Grayish plains gave way to the rise and fall of tree-dotted hills. They rounded a bend. Across a long field, Jim eyed one hill taller than those around it. "There," he said, passing tumble-down barns, a silo, a few farmhouses, easing to a stop on the edge of the road. Without a word he left the truck, Miguel following. Jim found a shovel in back, handed it to the boy, and then nestled Jackson in his arms. Heart in his throat now, he thought of carrying her this way when she was a pup, when her head smelled of chocolate, of sweet wood campfire, climbing the hill he whispered, "You're the best girl." Near the top, a level area beneath pines, he dug a hole as deep as his knees with Miguel watching silently. Jim laid the dog inside and stared at her body a while. Then he covered it with dirt, patted it down, and stared at it some more.

"I'm sorry," Miguel said.

Jim nodded at the ground.

"She's in heaven now. With my mother," Miguel said, bending down, hands in the grass. He found a pair of thin sticks and carefully laid them on the fresh dirt in the sign of a cross.

First time in hours Jim looked directly at the boy. He hated Miguel for existing. Hated him for being the reason Jackson was dead. Talking about heaven like that milky preacher with sour breath who'd put a hand on Jim's shoulder at Christine's funeral and said he should be relieved and even grateful the person Jim loved most in the world was dead and gone. As if she'd joyfully passed on to a vacation in the clouds after Jim had watched her fight for life with every inch of her being. He looked across the room and saw her there stretched out in a casket, and shrugged off the preacher's hands, told him to save his fairytale shit for the softheaded. Now he spoke to Miguel, needing to hurt him. "There's no such thing as heaven. People told you that were lying, thought you were stupid. That you didn't know any better."

Miguel stared at Jim, eyes wide and hard, mouth set.

"My dog's buried under that dirt. All she is, ever was, is right there."

"You're wrong," Miguel said.

"Only thing I was wrong about is you. You, understand? *Comprende*? It's you those men were after but it was Jackson they got. She's shot dead lying in a hole and that's because of you."

Jim watched the words hit the boy like daggers, wanting to take it back, but he was spent. "I should have left you at the station. Should not have driven you even this far, it was a mistake," he said. "We're going back to Arizona."

"What about Chicago?" Miguel asked quietly.

Jim shook his head, turned away and reached for the shovel.

"What about those men?"

"Well. I guess. I don't know." Jim thought of Sarah urging him to protect himself. Yet there was the pull, that the world was wanting, and he turned back and said, "Miguel," watching the boy recede. Moving quickly, already down the side of the hill. Jim lost sight of him behind a stand of trees, scanning the landscape until he reappeared, headed due east. A glance at the mound of fresh earth and then Jim left it and went to the truck. He could climb inside with the red backpack and return to Arizona alone, tell anyone who cared that the boy had run away, just another illegal off into the wild. Settle his bank debt and buy a few head of cattle and maybe there was enough of the house left to rebuild on, start over, except Christine was gone and Jackson was gone, and Jim started the engine, turned the truck east, and went after the boy.

Normally Sarah arrived at a scene like this one deep in the desert instead of at a cinder block motel, although the mood was the same, a hub of muffled activity dealing with the recently dead.

She'd spotted twirling cop car sirens, the EMS, from half a mile away.

Pulling up to the motel Sarah had been sure Jim was the one this time, recently dead.

Out of the SUV, badge on one hip, pistol on the other, she'd spoken to a deputy at the entrance of the office, explained who she was and why she was there. He led her inside to the sheriff, a county medical examiner, and the body. A woman in her sixties, folded in a corner near the desk as if she'd slid down the wall for a nap, peaceful with a gray contusion on the side of her face and gunshot wound to the chest. Sarah explained herself again to the sheriff, guy with a rough face and mournful eyes, said she was sure her mission to pick up Jim and the boy was related to the murder. The sheriff asked how exactly, and Sarah told him about the cartel connection, Mauricio and his men's armed pursuit of the boy. The sheriff said, "Emergency call came in, robbery in progress, but the cash register hasn't been touched. Makes me think."

"About?" Sarah had said.

"Just over the border in New Mexico. I got a report of armed men at a gas station off the interstate. Killed a clerk but not a dime stolen there, neither."

The route Jim had driven, the same Sarah had

followed overnight; she wondered now where and when she'd passed the station. "Anyone see anything here, another guest maybe?"

"More like a resident, staying week to week for about ten years," the sheriff said. "What we've learned from him squares with what you're telling me about the man and boy and those cartel people." A camera flashed, the medical examiner shooting images of the woman. The sheriff glanced at her. "Poor old Gladys. Caught up in some nasty business."

"The men that killed her, they're brutal," Sarah said.

"He didn't help none did he, the fellow you come for? Led them right here."

The truth, Sarah nodded at it, said, "Is it possible to talk to the guy, the resident?"

"Don't see why not. I'll send the deputy with you," he said, turning his mournful eyes back on the motel clerk. The officer walked Sarah down a corridor past motel rooms to a door at the end, knocking twice. It opened to a star-tled-looking man who could've been forty or eighty, bearded and skeletal inside a pink tank top that read 'Acapulco is for Lovers,' cargo shorts showing bony knees. The mutter of the TV in the room behind him vied with ban-jo music twanging from a laptop. Sarah intro-duced herself and asked if he'd answer a few questions.

"So you're the feds?" he said, giving off the sweet aroma of vodka and weed.

"I work for the federal government but no, not the FBI. Like I said, U.S. Border Patrol."

Confusion made his face smaller, he said his name was Phil and that he didn't get what the border patrol had to do with dead dogs. Sarah paused, asked what he'd meant. Phil said, "Told the sheriff I was here chilling and out of nowhere heard this zip-zip and knew it was a gun, I grew up around guns. If I'd known it was Gladys got shot, damn. Tough as nails that lady but she didn't deserve that shit."

"What about the dog?"

"Right, so. I heard the gun and went to the window. Somewhere down the walk this kid appeared, like a Latino kid maybe, and then this other guy not Latino, white guy, and the two of them hauled ass into the woods." Phil patted himself down, found a butt and lit it. "Almost right away this other guy shows up and now see, he was Latino I think. All in black like a bald Johnny Cash, waving a pistol and yelling at the woods. I opened the window a crack to hear what he was saying but only caught one little bit."

"What was that?" Sarah had asked.

"Something about the Marine Corps and then bang, bang, bang, he shoots into the trees, and that dog come out of there like a fucking rocket. I mean to tell you that thing was a shark, it had that guy by the arm, and the guy was screaming and went down on his ass. Swear to God I thought it was going to bite the guy's face off." Phil inhaled smoke, blew it out. "Got to his feet and the dog backed off growling and shit, and then the sirens started. Loud as hell out here, nothing but fields and clouds and this other guy runs up, tall dude, he had a gun, too. Johnny Cash took it from him and that was it. He shot the dog."

Throat tight, knowing the answer, Sarah said, "Brownish-black. A border collie?"

"Like ones that herd sheep, I seen them on TV." Flicking the butt, Phil squinted. "Animals, man. I feel them, you know? That guy, he didn't just shoot the poor dog. He emptied the clip into it."

Sarah's heart thudded, guessing what Jim felt, knowing what she'd felt for Jackson. "What happened next?" she said.

"Those guys took off. Then the other guy

and the boy came out of the trees. You know that guy?"

"I do."

"Hm. Well. The man's face when he went to the dog and picked it up and looked at it?" Phil ran a hand through his beard, said, "I wouldn't want to be Johnny fucking Cash is all."

Sarah asked a few more questions, Phil saying nope, he didn't see the boy and guy drive off, and she thanked him and left. On the way to the office she passed a room with its door ajar, curious. To the deputy she said, "It's open. Let's take a look."

Almost a kid, the deputy touched at his ear. "Maybe we should ask the sheriff."

Sarah said, "It's okay, just a quick look," and knocked and got no response and pushed inside the shadowy room. Beds unmade, blankets kicked back, a pair of kid's socks on the floor. A bag of gummy bears on a side table, a dead pint of whiskey and glass upside down. Pizza boxes and empty bags from a big box store. Sarah looked inside one bag and then the other and found a receipt. Ran a finger down the items and stopped at six boxes of ammo for a .45, six boxes for an M21. Sarah knew the weapons. Jim had taught her to shoot them when she was a girl. What she thought of each time she put on her service piece, Jim telling her not to be fooled by the power a gun gave her, it would make her regret she'd ever touched one.

Out there somewhere was a man who'd shoot a dog while cops were approaching.

Less about carelessness than the power to kill, and Sarah looked around the room. Into the dark corners that seemed to look back, she said, "Jim. Wherever you are. Please be careful."

An hour of driving slow, the hilly landscape having flattened out again, Jim was sure he'd spot the boy crossing a field or hiking at the side of the road, but nothing. He passed by farms and prefab warehouses, a regional airport, a link of strip malls hawking pedicures and hot wings and hardware and lap dances, and then made a long green light that took him into a town called Hollister, Oklahoma. After an acre of truck dealership and a row of tidy brick houses Jim spotted Miguel at the same moment he saw Jim. A dry, hot day, the boy sat on a bench under a chestnut tree with a soda in hand talking to a youngish man in shorts and a T-shirt and boots and gloves, a lawnmower at his side. Behind them crouched an old clapboard church with a high steeple. As Jim pulled to the curb Miguel rose and crossed the grass and entered the church, and the man rose too, gave Jim a wave. Jim climbed out of the truck and met him on the sidewalk. The man removed a glove and offered a hand. "You must be Jim. I'm Charlie, good to meet you."

Jim shook back, said, "What's going on here with Miguel?"

"I was cutting the grass and he showed up. Asked to use the restroom," Charlie said. "The kid was sweating, I offered him a cold drink and we got to talking."

"You work here?" Jim asked, glancing at the church and back.

"Yep."

"It's okay Miguel went inside? The preacher or minister, they won't mind?"

Charlie shrugged. "I don't mind at all."

It took Jim a few seconds until he said, "You're him?"

"What'd you expect?" Charlie grinned.

"I don't know. A collar or something."

"While I cut the grass?"

"Well. Why are you cutting the grass?" Jim asked.

"The whole congregation pitches in, does what needs to be done," Charlie said. "It's a solid bunch of folks, we look after one another. Like you're looking after Miguel."

A pause, Jim said, "He told you about that."

"Some of it. Enough. It's hot out, you want a beer?"

"Beer with a minister?"

"I wasn't born one." Charlie led Jim back to the bench, a cooler there. He handed Jim a cold can and popped one himself and they sat and Charlie said, "Seems some things went down at the border in Arizona."

"That's an understatement."

"Miguel told me about his mother, what happened to her. To lose someone he loved and needed that much, it's traumatic for a kid."

"Not just for a kid," Jim said, sipping.

"You lost someone recently?"

"My wife. About a year ago."

"Then you know. You have an idea what Miguel is feeling." Charlie drank and held the can on a knee. "His mother asking you to take care of him, get him to Chicago, that was no small request. Not to be all preacher-y but she must've had faith in you."

"Seems so."

"It's a gift to be trusted that way. Performing an act that important for another person."

"Sounds like something my wife would've told me."

"Sounds like she was an intelligent person," Charlie nodded. "Listen. Miguel went into the church—"

"To get away from me."

"To pray for his mom." Charlie finished the beer, stood. "I'm going to take care of the rest of this lawn. Maybe you should talk to him."

Charlie started the machine and pushed it away, and Jim glanced around at the faded whitewash, the bright stained-glass windows of the church. He hadn't been inside one since Christine's funeral, thinking of the prayers and tropes, none of it had touched him. It was months later when he realized he'd at least needed the ritual, the acknowledgment of his wife's transition from being alive to living in some other part of himself, and who the hell was he, anyway? To tell Miguel he was stupid for needing the comfort and relief of his mother being somewhere else, too? Like a fist to the gut he felt what he'd said to the boy, the bitterness of it. He rose and crossed the lawn to Charlie. Got his attention over the buzzing mower and spoke to him for a few minutes. Charlie nodded and Jim went to the church. Cool and empty inside, it smelled of candle wax and wood polish and Jim heard his boots echo down the aisle. In a pew alone, head back, Miguel stared up at the altar. Jim sat in the pew in front of the boy. He looked around at the statues, emaciated Jesus on a cross, and turned to Miguel. "You shouldn't have done that," Jim said. "You promised you wouldn't disappear again."

"What you told me," Miguel said, gaze fixed ahead. "It's my fault Jackson got killed."

"I was wrong about that. Miguel. Look here."

The boy's eyes shifted, resting on Jim's.

"I was wrong to have said it and I'm sorry I did. All that stuff about heaven too, I shouldn't have. If you feel your mother's there then okay, she is," Jim said.

"I know it. She's watching over me like always."

Jim nodded slowly. "I was thinking. Maybe you'd want the preacher to talk a little bit about her. Say some words for her if you want that."

"Like a funeral?"

"Yeah, like a funeral."

"I want it, yes," the boy said, holding the rosary his mother had given him.

He and Jim turned to Charlie then, moving down the aisle, brushing grass from his fore-arms. The man leaned in and asked Miguel a few questions before ascending the altar and reading a passage from the Bible. He began talking then about how Miguel's mother had taught him to be a strong person and that made her a part of him and in that way she was still with him. Charlie said everyone makes mistakes but the point is to turn something unfortunate into something good, and said he believed Miguel's mother had done that by getting Miguel into Jim's hands. Listening now, Jim shifted in the pew, wondering if the boy had told Charlie about the backpack full of stolen cash. In simple terms the preacher saying the money was a catalyst that had brought Jim and Miguel together, it was true, but Jim knew the money was a curse, too. It put the scent of blood on them, there'd have to be a reckoning with it, and Charlie was talking again, his words snagging Jim, making his heart beat harder. How losing someone we loved most was losing how that person made us feel, not only loved but also courageous and smart and honorable, and it was our responsibility not to let her down, to go on being those things even though she was gone.

Moving a hand over his face, Jim felt the years after he'd returned from war.

Barricaded behind work and alcohol until one day Christine sipped her coffee and shook her head and said, *No, wrong, you're not just one man but many men in one.* How they met and the months when he loved her when she did not love him back, what mattered was that her statement fragmented Jim, broke him into pieces and freed him so he could actually talk to her. And she answered him, saying, *See, all those pieces? Those are you, too. You're not just a young man inside an older man who regrets having used a rifle that way. You're also courageous, smart, and honorable, and now come be those things with me,* and he did, and Christine loved him, all of him. So much that she worried over him in a rolling way, like the weather. For her too, for everyone, love came with a fear of loss, and she'd say, *Follow those instincts of yours but please be careful,* and so he apologized to her now. Told her he was sorry for not being more careful but Miguel needed him, and Jim knew Christine would understand, and apologized to her again for whatever else he'd have to do to get the boy to Chicago.

Charlie descended the altar, and Miguel said, "Thank you," in a quiet voice.

"Okay," Charlie smiled, turning to Jim. "What can I do to help?"

Things he wanted to say but Jim stuck to the practical. "Got a phone I could use?"

Inside the idling border patrol SUV parked in a fast-food parking lot, Sarah looked at the screen and sat back and looked through the windshield and said, "Motherfucker."

The call with Jim had lasted less than ten minutes.

Her phone had rung and he'd said her name and Sarah had put it all aside, everything that would come next, and said, "Jackson, Jim. I loved that old girl."

"I know you did," he'd said, sounding like he was at the bottom of a hole.

Both of them quiet a beat until Sarah got to it, asking if he and the boy were okay and saying that she'd been to the motel, Jesus, and where were they now, she'd come for them and drive them to Arizona nonstop.

Jim had interrupted her with, "No, Sarah. The boy's not going back. That's what I called to tell you. I'm doing what his mother asked, taking him to Chicago. I have to."

"No you don't."

"He has family there. It's where he belongs."

"That isn't up to you."

"His mother gave him to me, not the border

patrol. He goes back to Arizona, he'll get de-ported, and Mauricio will kill him in no time. Came this close to getting us at the motel."

"He can apply for asylum," Sarah had said. "His mother's murder, he has a strong case."

"Yeah? You guarantee he'll get it?"

Sarah had squeezed at her phone then, un-able to guarantee anything, aware Jim had made decisions, locked them in. "You under-stand, right? I can only help if you let me."

"You already did," he said.

"I did? How?"

"By coming after me. I know it's not all about your job."

"Jim," Sarah had said, unsure of what she intended to say next.

"It reminded me, something I guess I'd forgotten, that I'm not alone in the world. It showed me how alone this kid is. So I have to," Jim had said. "I have to take him."

"Mauricio and his men are out there. They won't give up, you understand that."

"Yes," Jim had said.

"I wish there was some other way, something I could do."

"Or not do," and Jim had said it wasn't any secret, his ignorance of technology, hell, he still didn't see the need for a cell phone, but that he'd been taught. Years ago as a kid in uniform, the way to cover his ass and stay alive was to concentrate not on what he knew but on what he didn't know. Last time they spoke Sarah had said to him, means and methods, didn't Jim think Mauricio had other ways of tracking him beyond a credit card? The question stuck. Because technology aside, it still didn't explain the motel, "How they knew we were there," Jim said.

Sarah had remained silent, trying to catch up.

"I didn't know where I was going or where we'd come to," Jim had said. "We left a big store with too many people, it scared me, so I drove back roads. Stumbled upon the motel in Midora and paid cash. We weren't followed, I would've noticed, it was as deserted as the moon out there. Plus Mauricio didn't show up until hours later, the next morning."

"What are you saying?"

"How Mauricio found us. Only way I can figure, it was you."

"Me?"

"Not on purpose. You got superiors. You got to report what you learn."

"Oh. Shit," Sarah had said, removing her sunglasses.

"The cartel, Mauricio, they must have a connection inside the patrol. I told you, Midora, Texas, and he showed up there."

"Shit," Sarah said again, putting Lee Hurst on one side of a scale, Dalton on the other. Lee with thirty years of experience and commendations, it would've been near impossible to exist that long without being detected as a cartel mole. Then there was Dalton, with his protocol, his rules, everything by the book to the point of obsession. Or cover, Sarah saw it now. Saw the dickweed and his shiny new Escalade, overheard him talking about his vacations, she'd assumed his wife came from money. All of that plus his habit of protecting agents who didn't question him, undermining those who did, Sarah said, "Jim. I never would've guessed, I didn't know—"

"'Course you didn't."

"Is there any way I can help you?"

"Yeah. Like I said. By not doing something."

"What?"

"Your job, Sarah. Your duty."

They'd spoken a while longer and then said goodbye, and now Sarah sat in the SUV watching cars take turns at the drive-thru, thinking of the no-win position Dalton had put her in and cursed him again, motherfucker too small of a word. She looked at her phone then. The call she'd have to make. Walking back over the last minutes of talking to Jim when he'd said he was transporting the boy to Chicago, to an aunt there, he was telling Sarah in case something happened to him, and asked her to lie to her superiors. Tell them she did not know where Jim was taking the boy. She'd asked him then if he'd ever ignored his duty, even when he'd felt it was wrong, and hearing him pause before saying no. Hearing him say, *I'm asking you to do what I never did, it's your decision, and I'll understand either way.*

Phone in hand, Sarah began to dial.

Thinking of what she had not told Jim.

That it was always in the back of her mind but now at the front that she wore a uniform because of him, wanting to be like him, a person who'd served honorably. So far she'd done that. Her career was uncompromised. She'd never stood for harassment or kissed ass or been dishonest, believing the narrow path was the right one, even if it caused pain along the way.

Listening now to a voice answer on the other end of the phone.

Jim's words coming back to her, saying it was her decision.

Sarah talking to the voice, telling it she'd spoken to her stepfather and knew where he was taking the boy.

Dalton sounded impatient when he asked, "Where?"

A pause and Sarah said, "North Carolina. Raleigh."

17

All over his brain and in his chest as he gazed out the window passing a city called Joplin, the sense of peacefulness surprised Miguel. Steady and secure inside the truck, it was jarring, he'd been sure he'd never experience anything like it again, tinged now with guilt. Feeling this way without his mother present. Remembering what the priest had said, Charlie, that being strong meant she was alive in Miguel, and he wondered and said, "What was your mother like, Jim?"

In profile at the steering wheel, a grin lifted the edge of his mouth. "Mine? Tell the truth she was something of a firecracker."

Miguel shrugged. "I'm not sure what that means."

"It means explosive, but not in a bad way. Had a temper and would get to hollering and such, but somehow she'd end up laughing, we all would, couldn't help it," Jim said. "You want to know about my mother, hardships aside, she loved life."

"She died, yes?"

"A while back. I was older than you. Home from boot camp, you know what that is? Military training, Marine training, she'd been sick a while so it wasn't that big a surprise. Still, never an easy thing." He glanced at Miguel. "One of the last times I saw her, you want to know what she told me?"

"Yes," Miguel said.

"She said, *Don't always be like everybody else.* Meaning I should go my own way when I needed to. Don't be scared to be alone, and she was right."

A nod, Miguel thought of his mother pointing out boys in the neighborhood, young men. Lola's brother Felipe with his thin mustache and pistol, fear behind his eyes. Miguel's mother saying they were going backward, devolving, being taught to act like *animales*. Reminding Miguel she couldn't always be with him. If they tried to put a gun in his hand he'd have to say no and mean it, and he looked out the window again. Wondering, instead of the peaceful feeling emanating from his connection to his mother, if it came from being far away from someone else.

The man from the motel, Jim called him Mauricio.

There'd been countless Mauricios in Nogales.

The ones who owned Felipe, whom his uncle had angered, Miguel aware since he was small that all those cartel men wanted something from him, too; not an object but something inside him that made them seem angry and possessive when they'd spot Miguel on the street.

Joplin was behind him then and his peacefulness went with it.

Because back in Nogales he knew which corners to avoid and streets never to cross, how to spot cartel men before they spotted him, but here he was lost. Not knowing where Mauricio was suddenly felt more dangerous than if he and his men were following right behind them, and Miguel turned and looked through the back window at empty road, Jim saying, "You okay?"

Miguel nodded

Jim said, "Fuel light," and signaled down an exit ramp. At the pump he asked Miguel if he wanted gummy bears. Miguel said okay. Jim said he'd be right back and locked the doors and walked to the station taking cash from his wallet. It was hot in the truck. Miguel rolled down a window, jumpy all over, hearing a voice nearby say, "*Ahi esta!*"

"There he is!"

Sitting forward, Miguel blinked at the side mirror, at the islands of gas pumps. A black SUV parked two cars away with a figure at the wheel. Miguel turned to see a man hurrying back to the vehicle, head and shoulders visible. Bald in a black T-shirt. Miguel sure the man had spotted Jim in the station. Going to get a gun to kill Jim. Miguel opened the glove compartment to the .45, loaded, he'd watched Jim palm a clip into it this morning. A little big but it fit in his hand. He slid from the truck without closing the door and crouched down, moving toward the SUV, heart racing in his ears. He wouldn't say a word to the man, *You murdered my mother, burned my friend's house, killed his dog*, nothing. Just start firing. Shoot the man and when he fell, shoot the one behind the wheel, whoever else appeared, Miguel almost there hearing the voice again. *"En la estación. Estabas por las dulces,"* it said. "In the station. He was by the candy," and Miguel moved behind the man and aimed the .45 and pulled the trigger to nothing. Spinning around, the man's eyes flew from Miguel to the gun. He whispered, *"Madre mia,"* and Miguel saw the little boy, three or four, in the man's arms. The man's roundish face, gray goatee, eyebrows back on his shaved head as a woman at the steering wheel leaned out and saw the .45 and began screaming, and Miguel's arm went into the air.

Jim behind him locking it there, immobilizing Miguel, he said, "Easy now."

The man held the little boy tighter and said, "What the hell? Is this?"

"A mistake," Jim said. Miguel feeling the gun yanked from his hand as he was turned toward the truck, Jim pushing him ahead. Stumbling that way, inside his head Miguel saw the little boy shot dead and began to shake all over. He was in the truck then with Jim driving fast from the gas station, saying, "You have any idea? What could've happened back there, do you?"

"I thought. I thought . . ." Miguel said into his hands.

"Jesus god." Jim reached for the pint of whiskey.

"It was him, I thought. Mauricio. I wanted to protect you." Miguel wiped his face, stared out the window. "The gun didn't fire."

"It's called a safety. Near the trigger, so it won't shoot."

"That man had a little boy. If the gun had gone off—" Miguel spoke quietly to his reflection, shedding tears without crying.

"Until we get to Chicago. If you're going to be around a gun, you should understand it," Jim said. "What to do, yeah, but what not to do is more important."

Miguel turned from the window to Jim, wiped his eyes.

"We'll find someplace up ahead, somewhere safe. I'll teach you," Jim said.

The road nearly empty, GPS set, they were making good time, and Mauricio was trapped.

That place with shadowy edges, more asleep than awake, suffering his father.

After a phone call with Dalton he'd re-routed them to the long, unbroken line of a northbound highway, headed to Raleigh. Days burnt chasing Marine Corps and the boy, and now they were embarking on an even longer journey. Isidro and Jorge flicking glances at Hernando, the three of them talking without uttering a word. Mauricio knew they'd comply. They suspected he would kill them if they didn't, their suspicion as strong a motivation as fact. The four of them blazed ahead now in the SUV, Mauricio allowing a bit of sleep to enter his consciousness, hearing the clink of metal bracelets before he saw them, and tried to run.

Thirteen years old, he'd made the mistake of going home, if it could be called that, home.

Taken by the cartel three years earlier, made a *halcone* first and then a soldier, he'd proven himself as fearless, some said reckless; a wire had been tripped inside Mauricio, weapons put into his hands and he was not a powerless boy anymore, so valuable to his bosses that he was not poor anymore, either. One afternoon he found himself on his old street outside his old apartment building thinking of his mother, unsure if he'd gone there by accident or on purpose. It hadn't been her fault that he and Rigo had been taken away. He'd been told by people in the neighborhood how she tried to get her sons back, made inquiries, pounded on doors, had guns put in her face until she went away, a futile effort from the start. Mauricio also believed the men who'd taken him and

Rigo had been right, that they were better off with the cartel.

Still, he wanted to give his mother money, do something for her.

He wanted to see her face and remember it.

Standing in the street beneath windows covered by plywood, the door spray-painted with a large black X. He understood. It didn't surprise him the building had been condemned, slated for demolition, the place just barely above a slum. Curious, he pushed inside and climbed three floors passing door after door bearing black X's. The hallways were silent. Outside his apartment, he paused before entering, something popping underfoot. He looked down at a crushed glass vial and then up and around, his eyes and nose growing accustomed to the dank light, the airlessness. The kitchen table and chairs were gone, pots and pans and spice rack gone, the walls stripped of pictures, the rosewood crucifix. No trace of his mother. Moving deeper into the apartment, Mauricio glanced at bags of aluminum cans, boxes of scavenged metal, hubcaps, dented pipes, shit worth a few *pesos* at the city dump. Only things he recognized were the ratty old couch and scarred coffee table. Mauricio noticed its overflowing ashtrays, more glass vials, used needles, blackened spoons, a smell he'd come to know working for the cartel, the stink of scorched crack cocaine. A junkie cave, some zombie squatting there, dumpster diving to support his habit. Of all the abandoned apartments in the building he wondered why this one had been chosen, hearing a soft footfall, he spun and squinted at a ghost he knew. Gaunt, with an edge of authority in his burnt voice, Mauricio's father said, "*Hijo.*"

"Papa," Mauricio said quietly. "I thought you were dead."

"I'm working on it," his father said with a faint smile. "Why did you come?"

"Looking for mama."

"Me too. Someone on the street, I asked around. They said she left when you boys left. That she went to Hermosillo, or," his father shrugged. "I don't know. Somewhere. She's gone."

"We didn't leave," Mauricio said.

"What?"

"We didn't leave, Rigo and I. We were taken, after you disappeared."

Standing a little straighter, his father said, "You boys join the cartel, it's my fault?"

Mauricio could only grin at what his father didn't know, that he and Rigo had been adopted by a whole family of fathers, ones who would never desert them. He nodded at the coffee table and said, "Having a party, huh? All by yourself?"

"This is how you and your brother make money. From me, my blood, blood money, it's a sin," his father said, rolling up a shirt-sleeve to a pale forearm slit with needle tracks.

"This addiction, it's the cross I bear. You think I like it?"

"I think you're like every other crackhead. Weak and a liar, lying to yourself more than anyone else."

"Even if I'd been here I couldn't have stopped you from going to them," his father said, blinking slowly. "But I know now. I'll be cursed to hell for doing nothing. God will hate me."

"God?" Mauricio laughed. "The same one you used to mock my mother about, your own wife, calling her a fool for believing, a dumb bitch for saying the rosary?"

His father spread his arms like crucified Jesus. "I'm saved. I found him."

"Where, cooking in a spoon?"

Trudging to a splintered wardrobe his father pulled a drawer, threw aside an old screwdriver, a cracked hand mirror, scavenged junk, saying, "God has a plan for all of us."

"He's forgotten about you. There's nothing

you can—" Mauricio said, shocked at his father's movement, faster than he could've imagined. An elbow wrapped around his neck, his
father pinned Mauricio's arms and removed the
knife Mauricio had hidden at his back, tossed it
aside. Then his father slapped a rusty handcuff
around one of Mauricio's wrists and dragged
him across the room, locking the other cuff to
the radiator. Stunned and lunging, Mauricio
yanked at the bracelet locked to an iron pipe
screaming, "What?! Why?!"

"I can't let God hate me," his father said,
swallowing his breath.

"Open them! Unlock them, you're stoned!
Fucked up!"

"This is my penance. Trust me, *hijo*. Trust
me." His father shoved all the loose drugs and
paraphernalia from the coffee table into a bag
and slung it over a shoulder. "Only in death
will you be free," he said, making the sign of
the cross in the air and withdrawing as if the

shadows had eaten him, the front door clicking into place behind him.

Silence then, cut by the muffled bleat of traffic three stories down.

Hours passed with Mauricio sitting still, eyes pinned to the front door knowing he'd never see his father again. The man so fucked up he might not even remember what he'd done. No one would enter the apartment, the spray-painted X telling the demolition people it was vacant. Mauricio folded onto the floor, back against the pipes, and woke in darkness. Throat dry, wrist swollen, he called out but heard nothing, and noticed a tall figure standing over him. His father, it had to be, Mauricio found the words and said, "Papa. Please. Help me."

"Why should I?" Marine Corps asked with a squint.

"Because. You're a hero."

Marine Corp wagged his head. "You got the wrong man."

"No, it's you. It's you, see?" Mauricio used his free hand to dig into a pocket and came up with the medal, a star cut from silver. "You can save me."

"You think that's what the medal's for? Saving people?"

Yanking at his cuffed wrist, Mauricio said, "Please. Free me."

"You want to be free," Marine Corps said, pity in his face, "—someone's got to love you enough, that's the only way."

"Please, help me," Mauricio said, pulling away from the radiator and sitting up in the SUV. Looking out at the rolling landscape. Wheat fields next to strip malls, he glanced over at Hernando at the wheel, Hernando turning back to the windshield. A dulled sensation like being unplugged, Mauricio touched at his head with Marine Corps still in there. Knowing something then without knowing how, trying to work it out, he found his phone and called Dalton. Three rings until he answered, Mauricio said, "Your information has been reliable so I made a mistake, stopped asking where it came from. Doesn't he have a daughter? I saw a picture in his house."

"Hanson?" Dalton said. "A stepdaughter."

"In the picture, she wore a Border Patrol uniform. Is she there, in your station?"

Quiet a moment, then Dalton said, "Yes."

"This woman has bad feelings toward her stepfather? She hates him?"

"I. No, I don't think so."

"She loves him?"

"Well. I assume she does," Dalton said.

"So she wouldn't want anything to happen to him, see him get hurt," Mauricio said. "She's the one who told you North Carolina?"

Quiet again, a longer pause, and Dalton said yes.

Mauricio hung up without another word, took a breath and let it out. To Hernando, the men in the backseat, he said, "We're going the wrong way."

Jim's question to himself, walking through a field next to an abandoned airstrip, was why deserted structures inspired so much beer drinking. Empties lying in the tall grass like Easter eggs, and Jim heard Miguel behind him call out, "I found another one!"

Jim said, "That'll do!"

They met at the truck. Nearby, on the bones of a small Cessna, Jim set a dozen cans and bottles in a row along its rusted wing. It was noon, the sun high in a cloudless sky. He indicated each component of the .45 to Miguel, what it meant, its function. The basics then, he began with the boy's body position. How he stood, knelt, or lay was critical to the point of aim, which led to trigger control. He showed Miguel how to squeeze rapidly, not pull back at it, not yank it, and explained that steady breathing, even holding his breath for a ten count, was vital to keeping a gun steady. Miguel nodded, eagerness brightening his face, he said, "Am I ready?"

"Not yet. Something you have to know, you ever been in a fight?"

Miguel thought of streets in Nogales where it was inevitable, part of the landscape. "Yes," he said. "So?"

"You ever lose?"

"Sometimes."

"Why?"

Miguel shrugged. "They were bigger. Stronger."

"Maybe, but more likely it was hesitation. You waited before throwing a punch or thought too much. Too late, you got hit," Jim said. "Same with firing a gun. When your body's ready, your aim and trigger and breathing, you have to quit thinking and take the shot, get me?"

"Yes."

Jim loaded the .45, feeling how he loved guns and hated them. They'd been placed into his hands when he was so young the choice hadn't been his, and time had melded them to him, and here he was. "See the targets? You're aiming at the green bottle on the end."

"Okay."

Jim gave the boy the gun. "Get into a crouch."

Miguel didn't move, staring at the weapon, pausing before the unknown of squeezing a trigger. Jim thought of what he'd been told over the years by his father, his COs, his buddy Harold, that in the same way craftsmen wielded their tools and artists their brushes, a machine with a scope and trigger had been Jim's equivalent.

He'd known better.

That killing was the pure opposite of creating a thing.

But the truth had come to him early, that it

was a world where sides were drawn, sides had to be chosen and often defended. The other truth, undeniable to Jim, was that firing a gun was never arbitrary. There were such things as just and unjust, or at least levels of each. When he'd defended the just side, he loved guns, and when he'd found himself defending the unjust, he hated them, and himself. He'd learned to live with it, had known what box to put it in, seal it up, or it would've ended him, and now he said, "The crouch. Like I showed you."

"This way?"

"Knees a little more, bend them. Good."

"Aim?" Miguel said.

"Yep, then fire—"

The .45 popped once, throwing Miguel's arms back, surprise on his face at the power in his hands. The green bottle was intact. He glanced at Jim saying, "I didn't come close."

"Try again. Like I told you, find your breath. Hold it steady, shoulders loose."

Another crouch, Miguel inhaled and then squeezed off two shots, turning the bottle into green fragments. "I did it! You see that, I did it!" he said with a hop up and down.

"Not bad," Jim said, feeling a bump of pride for the boy. They fired at the remaining targets, and then Jim instructed him on the M21. When Miguel shot it the violence expressed by the rifle was different than the .45, a quiet slice through the air that jarred him more than physically. This time it was confidence on the boy's face realizing what he and it could do together, Jim saw it there and said, "It was made to kill people. No other reason. Good people or bad, it can't tell the difference. Using a gun is a choice, you understand?"

Miguel nodded, handed over the M21 without asking to fire it again.

"I guess we're done for today," Jim said, moving toward the truck.

"Jim."

He turned to the boy in the field who stood with his arms at his sides.

"Mauricio murdered my mother," Miguel said. "Someday I'm going to kill him."

Quiet then, looking away and back, Jim said, "Nothing feels good about killing a man. Not one damn thing."

"I don't care."

"You'd better." Jim went to him, took him by the shoulders. "You'd better be ready to kill a person, take his life away. Because for a long time afterward, maybe forever, you're going to feel like the one who's dead."

Miguel held Jim's gaze, said, "If I had the chance I'd kill him right now."

Jim looked over the boy's head at nothing, knowing the truth when he heard it.

18

Hernando descended through the young trees reaching from branch to branch so he wouldn't lose his feet and tumble down the muddy incline. A cement footbridge just below spanned a wide, brown river, far enough away from the rest stop where the SUV was parked, a spot where he wouldn't be seen or overheard. Thinking of Juana as he stepped onto the bridge. Her hair, the silk of her thighs, the puppy he'd bought for her, gray and curly white, they called it Diego after her favorite movie star. Hernando loved Juana, loved that little dog, he pulled out a blunt and a lighter and his phone from a pocket while hating Mauricio and feeling guilty at the same time.

A glance down at the flowing water, he flicked the lighter, inhaled the smoky sweetness. The phone buzzed twice in his ear before Ángel said, "*Diga.*"

"*Es Hernando.*"

"So I hear. Tell me you have my money, that the woman and boy are dead."

"The woman, yes," Hernando said, listening to silence, forced to say it. "The boy escaped again, with the money. The gringo has him."

Ángel said, "Where are you?"

Hernando explained then, the atlas pointing them to Chicago and the dead state trooper, the gas station clerk and motel manager, Ángel interrupting to ask, "All of that death, that risk, for what, two hundred thousand dollars?"

"That's why I called."

"When it was a short time and quick, into Arizona, back, okay. But this, bad information, North Carolina, Chicago?" Ángel made a noise, said, "What the fuck is wrong with Mauricio?"

Hernando hit the blunt, said, "I don't know, but in his sleep? He was begging for help."

That late time of day when the sun lingered on one side of the sky while the moon hung translucent on the other, Jim told Miguel they'd have to find a motel soon, get some sleep and then drive back out to the highway first thing in the morning, and Miguel said he was hungry. Starving. Jim decided he was, too.

He looked out at the orange fields of Missouri, wondering if he'd been careful enough.

Jumping on and off the highway after Oklahoma, alternating with rural roads, never traveling in a direct line. Not sure what Sarah had said to her bosses, if Mauricio was on his trail. He'd told Sarah he was determined to get the boy to Chicago, but it didn't mean he wasn't scared. Not sure of what, something cool and empty at the back of his heart. An abyss he was inside of and traveling toward, both at once, and Miguel said, "How long will it take?"

"To get food?"

"Until we're in Chicago."

"Another day of driving, maybe a little more."

"Then how long do you think? Until it feels like home?"

That was it, the boy capturing the abyss in one word: home. After he delivered Miguel to his aunt, it hit Jim that he himself would not have one to go back to. A burnt-out old house, a ranch owned by the bank, that red backpack full of money, pieces of a life that didn't feel like his anymore, and in a quiet voice he said, "I'm not exactly sure. Everyone's different. I guess you'll know it when you know it."

"Maybe you could stay in Chicago for a while," Miguel said.

"See a ballgame," Jim said. "Have a hot dog or two."

"Ride the train," Miguel said.

"Sounds good. It's just that I'm not much of a city person. More of a wide-open spaces type, I suppose."

"Hey." Miguel sat forward. "Look."

"What's that?"

"Up there, see? It's like yours," the boy said, pointing through the windshield.

Jim followed his gaze over the horizon to what looked like a thin tree with a single leaf moving in the wind, taking on its true form as they drew closer. A flagpole with stars and stripes riding air currents, the sun nearly gone behind it, and a pang of hope touched Jim's chest. Far beyond the age now when he sought out signs and ascribed meanings yet it felt personal to come upon it, beckoning him to the little grocery store beneath it. The threat of Mauricio didn't fade then but changed, like the many losses Jim had experienced, he understood this journey and his life afterward was out of his hands. The only way beyond the abyss went through Chicago.

The men's room, Jesus, the odor like something had been butchered in there, Mauricio approached the SUV waving his wet hands in the air, ready to get on the road, unhappy at what he didn't see. Isidro leaning on the hood smoking a cigarette, Mauricio said, "Where's Nando?"

Isidro's sunglasses reflected twilight looking left and right. "He was just here."

"He said he'd be right back," Jorge said from the front seat.

Mauricio looked around at the sparsely populated parking lot, the humming highway, nothing else but trees and reddish hills. "Back from where?"

"I don't know." Jorge shrugged.

Mauricio tilted his head thinking, a slip of

breeze passing by with a familiar scent. Like fresh hay, that Cali perfume, his crew's weed of choice. He followed it toward the restrooms, then behind the building to the slope of a hill. Peering below the trees, Mauricio saw moving water, a river, and waited for the wind and then trailed it downhill. Twenty feet away, through the brush, he spotted Hernando standing on a bridge. Phone pressed to an ear, he was smoking and listening with an intense expression on his face, emotion there. Hernando was probably talking to Juana, saying how he loved and missed her. The tall man took a final hit, flicked the butt, and spoke into the phone. Moving closer, Mauricio heard him say, "*No lo sé, pero. El estaba pidiendo ayuda.*" Wondering whom he meant, who'd been begging for help, and Mauricio remembered waking from his dream, Hernando at the wheel looking quickly away. Hernando nodded at his phone, said something else, and hung up. Mauricio started toward the bridge, almost there when his phone vibrated. He looked at the display, Ángel's flashing name.

One call ended, another demanding to start, Mauricio's gut said, *Don't answer.*

He walked on quickly. On the soles of his feet onto the bridge, moving soundlessly, he stood next to Hernando and said, "What does he want from me?"

Hernando jumped a little, tried to hide his surprise as he turned to Mauricio, that flat mask with its concealed eyes. Knowing not to lie, he said, "It wasn't my idea."

"Tell me."

"He wondered about you."

"In what way?"

Turning so they faced one another, Hernando stood as tall as he could. "After what happened at the border wall. Rigo, you know, and then the gringo taking the boy away. Ángel told me I had to. He called and told me, said I should watch you."

"Watch me? Why?" Mauricio smiled with his mouth, nothing else.

"In case. You went too far, I guess."

"What does that mean, too far?"

Hernando shook his head then, gesturing to the river, the trees, the never-ending United States, he said, "This isn't our world. This is the middle of nowhere."

"We always get what's ours."

Still shaking his head, Hernando said, "Ángel said he doesn't care about the money anymore. He cares about the bodies we left behind. A trail, if it leads to us it leads to him."

"No one can get to him over there," Mauricio said. "Hidden away in his villa."

"But they can get us. We killed a police, you think these people will let it go, just forget about it?" Hernando felt the color rise in his neck. "You know better. You taught me, murders are bad for business. You said kill only when necessary, to make a point, to scare the shit out of an enemy, a rival, so what the fuck did killing that girl at the gas station do for us? That lady at the fucking motel, there was no reason, except," he said, and stopped, sealed his lips.

"Except what?" Mauricio asked slowly.

"Nothing," Hernando muttered, heading for the path up the hill.

Mauricio turned and blocked him. "Say it."

The conversation with Ángel, what the capo had promised Hernando, he was wary but emboldened as he pointed at Mauricio's face. "That, whatever's behind there. Whoever you are. That's why those people are dead. That's why we're here, and no matter what you say, none of it has shit to do with business."

"You might be right," Mauricio shrugged. "You want to know? Who I am?"

Wind through the treetops, the rush of water below them, Hernando stared.

"The boy. I'm him, he's me." Mauricio tapped his cheek, the raw bullet slit there from the gringo's rifle. "Behind flesh and bone, we're made the same way."

A light touch at the pistol concealed behind his shirt, Hernando said, "Is that so?"

Mauricio nodded. "When I was his age, life did things to me like it's doing to him.

"He'll grow up the same way, become like me. I can feel it in him, so he has to die, so I can live. It's his fate, what the universe wants for him."

"You know what the universe wants," Hernando said, not a question. "Okay. Let's get on the road, head back."

A different type of smile, Mauricio said, "You're suggesting? Or telling me?"

"Ángel wants us to return to Nogales. He'll tell you himself, call him."

"What's he's giving you? Make you a *teniente*, my crew is yours now maybe?" Mauricio said. "Enough money you can get a nice apartment for you and your girl, huh?"

"Can't we? Just turn around and go home?" Hernando said, tired of all this.

Shaking his head, moving in a tight circle, Mauricio said, "Fuck Ángel and fuck you, the boy will die. If we go anywhere it's Chicago."

"Mauricio—"

"Listen to me, you—" Mauricio said, turning quickly, his words smothered by a mouthful of blood as Hernando swung the butt of the pistol against his face. Mauricio staggering, clutching at air, and Hernando hit him again, a crack of iron against skull, he went backward, tangled on the bridge railing, blinking through pain.

Hernando pointed the gun and said, "Enough of you."

Mauricio gasped, knees bowing.

And Hernando wondered why it had taken him so long to see that Mauricio was like everyone else, a human body that could be stopped, and he pushed the gun into his belt and made a fist with his big right hand and connected it to Mauricio's jaw while his left hand had already been thrown. Raining down punches, he was bigger and heavier, Mauricio shrinking before his eyes, Christ, did he think Hernando didn't know what he'd done to Juana? Did he really believe Hernando would follow him across the country on a murder spree waiting to be shot down, and now he controlled the universe, too? Mauricio trying to crawl away, Hernando kicked him in the stomach, the kidneys, given carte blanche by Ángel to bring him back to Nogales or not, it was up to Hernando, and he'd tried, hadn't he? To be loyal, to get him to abandon this fucking goose chase, trying was the right thing to do after everything Mauricio had taught him, even in a situation like this. When someone has a gun but you don't, what you do is absorb the pain and wait for your chance, Hernando remembering the lesson too late as Mauricio slipped a knife from his boot and buried it in Hernando's calf. The chunky sound of cut meat, pain like fire in Hernando's brain as Mauricio yanked the blade downward, sliced through tendon and bone, removed the knife, rolled to Hernando's other leg and did the same to his other calf, the tall man collapsing to his knees unable to scream. Mauricio on his feet then, he grabbed Hernando by the hair and held him that way so he wouldn't topple over, nothing to say, he made a fist around the knife handle and drove it into Hernando's chest like an uppercut. Pulled it out and showed it to him, cherry syrup on steel, all Hernando could say was, "I can't, die. I have a dog," before Mauricio slit his throat.

Released the body then, Mauricio wiped the knife on his jeans as Hernando folded.

Finding his breath, Mauricio went to the railing, leaned over, and made himself throw up the blood from the beating, expelled it. Two broken ribs, he felt them on his lungs because he was alive. Because he'd said it to Hernando, he said it to himself inside his head every waking minute between every breath, that from the day he'd been taken by the cartel he'd been in survival mode, and would always have to save himself, every time. He'd save himself from the boy and thought of it looking into the brown river, watching it flow west toward the Gulf of Mexico. A glance at Hernando, he went to the corpse. Dragged it to the edge of the bridge and kicked at it until it splashed into the water. Like Hernando was swimming on his back, face and feet visible as the river carried him away. Mauricio turned and left the bridge, chest burning and face aflame. He climbed the hill to the restroom and used cold water from the sink and stared at his reflection, erasing the pain from it. Mask in place. He walked to the parking lot smoking a cigarette, Isidro and Jorge standing at the SUV, they couldn't have missed the swelling on his face, the blooming bruises, but said nothing. Instead Isidro asked where Hernando was.

"He went home," Mauricio said, staring at Isidro with his single eye behind sunglasses, and turned to Jorge. "You're driving."

The young man nodded, and they climbed into the SUV and headed off without a word.

Inside the moving vehicle Mauricio felt the lost hours between him and the boy. Marine Corps probably close enough now to Chicago that there was no way they'd catch them, at least not on their own. He dialed the safe house in Arizona. Buzzing in his ear until that fat fuck Emilio answered. Mauricio explained the situation, gave him Marine Corps's vehicle information, and then said, "Also? Get me the Cousins."

Jim had an idea of them by the life in their voices, the quick consonants traded across the aisles of the small, well-organized grocery store. An older woman close to his age working the cash register, a middle-aged man and woman stocking shelves, helping customers, and a girl maybe fifteen behind the counter next to the older woman, clearly her grandmother, an identical smile. The sound of Vietnamese a surprise to Jim out here in somewhere Missouri but only a small one, the country a patchwork, how it was meant to be. He approached the register with Miguel at his side, placed some items on the counter and said, "*Xin chao*," sounding like *zeen chow*, a little stiff tinged with his Arizonian drawl.

The girl and woman exchanged a look, with the woman's smile brightening as she said, "*Xin chao.* How are you today?"

"Good," Miguel said with a smile of his own.

"Fine, thanks," Jim said, laying out cash.

"You speak Vietnamese?" the girl said, ringing him up.

"A little," Jim said.

"Cool. Need anything else?"

Jim glanced past her at liquor bottles lining a shelf, finding his whiskey there, he said, "Nope. I guess we're all set." A nod and goodbye, and he and Miguel exited the store, pausing to look out at the vista turning dark purple. "Not a cloud. It'll be full of stars soon."

"I'd like to see it. Fall asleep under it," Miguel said, gazing skyward.

"Pretty nice feeling."

"I've never done that," Miguel said.

"You've never camped?"

Miguel shook his head.

"If things were different," Jim said quietly, watching the middle-aged man leave the store in his starched apron. He walked to the pole and lowered the flag, began to unhook it from the rope. Jim had an urge then, almost like a memory of himself, and said to Miguel, "Come with me. I need to do something."

At their approach the man, turned, said "Something I can do for you?"

"Well. This might sound a little odd." Jim pushed his hat back. "Would you mind if I folded up that flag the military way? Get it ready for tomorrow morning?"

The man's gaze lingered on Jim's face. "You serve?"

A nod, looking across a windswept field and back. Like talking to himself, Jim said, "Marines. Viet Nam, three tours. Long time ago."

"Well, then. Wouldn't mind at all," the man said.

"Good of you, thanks. Help me here Miguel, we'll do it together." Jim finished unhooking the flag, made sure it didn't touch the ground. He reached one end to Miguel and lifted the other himself. "Hold it as flat as you can. Now flip it over," Jim said, folding it in half, then in thirds, and then in triangles, the boy following his lead.

"Like this?" Miguel said.

"Perfect. Just right."

"You've done this before," the man said.

"Couple of times." Jim took the flag from Miguel, tightened the edges, and handed it to the man. Dusk was in the air. After the experience with Mauricio and his men, the cinder block motel with its narrow bathroom window as an escape, the idea of staying another night in such a place seemed foolish. Jim turned to the man, said, "Listen, your store there, how're you fixed for sleeping bags? Blankets and such?"

"I think we can get you set up."

"Someplace nearby, safe, where we can camp the night?"

The man led Jim back to the store, telling him about forestland west of the River Road, offering directions. Half an hour later Jim and Miguel left behind the last of the sunlight, shadows drawing them toward a stretch of low green hills. They found the place the man had told them about, a glen surrounded by pine trees not far from the road, and parked the truck right there. Jim opened a sleeping bag in the back of the truck for Miguel, told him in a couple hours the midnight sky would be his own personal nightlight, and then showed him how to build a campfire. Thinking of Sarah when she was a girl. He and Christine taking her into the cold desert for a sleepover, Sarah a natural staking a tent, sparking a flame on peppery mesquite, naming constellations. Now Miguel gathered armloads of twigs and leaves for kindling while Jim searched out thick, moist branches that would burn like charcoal. Soon enough they had a snapping fire encircled by rocks. Jim sat on one side and Miguel on the other. Listening to the wind move the trees, Jim called attention to the call of birds or huff of little animals. They roasted hot dogs on sharpened sticks and ate oranges and shared a bag of sugar cookies, and Miguel sat back, quiet a while before saying, "I wonder what she'd think now."

Jim knew who he meant, how it was to have someone on his mind. "As brave as you've been, doing what she hoped you'd do. She'd be proud of you, that's my guess."

"It's hard when," Miguel said, inhaling tears. "I just, remember she's gone."

"Like a bad surprise all over again. You forget for a while somehow."

"You still get sad when you think of your wife?"

Jim nodded, turned to the boy. "Thought she and I would be together until we got old, or older at least. After she died I just couldn't understand how I'd been so wrong. Now though, what I mostly feel is gratitude. Thankful we had each other as long as we did." Jim moved his gaze to the fire. "Life doesn't always work out how you want it to. Still, you're lucky if there were more good times than not. If you can remember, no matter how you feel, things get better."

"For everyone?" Miguel asked.

"I like to believe so."

Miguel faced him across the burning sticks, light in his eyes. "Then that means you, too. Things will get better for you."

"Well," Jim shrugged. "I guess that's possible."

"I know what she'd think, my mother. That she was right about you." Miguel sat forward, hugged his knees. "Thank you for taking me to Chicago. For taking care of me."

"You don't have to thank me. I needed to do it," Jim said quietly, feeling his wife nearby. He thought into his words then, finding a hard truth, that what he'd needed was to leave the ranch behind; that he hadn't been working himself to death as much as he'd wanted to die there without Christine. Get buried on the hill next to her so they could be together again, except she wasn't there, she was here with him, and he reached for the backpack. Pushing it toward Miguel he said, "This money. It belongs to you."

Miguel shook his head.

"Your mother meant for it to take care of you."

Still shaking his head, Miguel said, "It wasn't my uncle's or mother's. It's cartel money, and it got them killed."

"Well then. What do you want to do with it?"

Blinking into the embers, Miguel shrugged.

A pause and Jim said, "Fire's getting low. I'd better get some kindling." He unzipped the backpack and took out a banded brick of hundred-dollar bills, glancing from it to Miguel, his eyes telling the boy what he intended to do. Miguel saw it there, smiled and nodded and Jim threw the money onto the fire. It sat for a few seconds until it began to crisp, a dark line eating at the edges, and then hissed and popped into greenish-yellow flames. Jim handed Miguel a brick and he did the same, the two of them watching that one burn too, the destruction of paper, cotton, and ink that had caused such pain. Staring into the fire, Jim felt a sense of being cut loose from the desert land he'd tied himself to, that place of grief and mourning, aloneness and blind toil; even more strongly, he felt Christine's approval. Miguel peeled open a brick. He fanned out the currency and released it from his grip. All those sly gazes from Ben Franklin scattered over the flames like falling leaves, the moment shifting from somber to thrilling as they crushed and tossed money into the fire, shredded it into bits that became orange confetti, Miguel's smile glowing when he said, "You know the best part?"

"What?"

"The men who killed my uncle and mother for this money will never get any of it."

Jim nodded with a flat thought of how right

the boy was; that if they'd had a bargaining chip it had just been turned to ash. Deciding then it didn't matter, the determined way in which Mauricio had pursued them, they'd never had a bargaining chip at all.

19

Subtracting a short roadside nap Sarah had been driving for fourteen hours. Round trip to the motel in Texas and back, she glanced down at the speedometer seeing it was many miles per hour over the limit. Bristling, breathing hard. Adrenaline and caffeine and rage, but it was the memory of impending death that caused her to speed. How she'd felt during the months that led to the end of her mother's life, nothing she could do to stop it. Always grinding with a need to blame someone or something besides the cancer itself, illogical, she'd known that, but grinding nonetheless. The circumstances were vastly different now, yet Sarah felt the same sense of inevitability that Jim would soon die. Her step-father existed in the dangerous unknown with no way for Sarah to help him, but with another difference.

This time there was someone to blame.

She was aware of passing the exit that led to her home, accelerating around an oil tanker, dusting into the border patrol station parking lot right before the afternoon shift ended. Sarah parked near a white Escalade waxed as shiny as a pearl, watching officers come and go. She pushed her hair behind her ears. Checked that her pockets were buttoned, gun was on her hip, waiting, and then she slipped from the SUV and moved toward the Escalade saying, "Dalton."

He turned, pushed sunglasses up on his head inspecting her dishevelment from hours on the road. "Jesus, your uniform looks like shit. I ought to write you up."

Sarah stepped forward, said, "My question,

which will come first, bitch or cunt? Guy like you, my money's on bitch."

Dalton stared for a beat and then put on a grin. "Whatever this is, I'm too busy for it. I suggest you go home and get some rest."

"Aren't you even going to ask? About my stepdad and the boy?" she said. "Or do you already know what happened to them?"

Moving off, he stopped and turned again, the grin gone.

"I know things, too," Sarah said. "About you and your cartel buddies, your arrangement. You guys are tight, huh?"

"You're not making any sense," Dalton said. "I have no idea what you're talking about."

"No? Well. It was either you or Lee Hurst. But Lee's been around too long, done too much. Man's tough but fair, versus you," Sarah said. "Forget balls or a backbone. I just wonder if there's even a little bit of honor left inside you."

"Watch yourself," Dalton said, eyes pinched.

"Or what? You'll have Mauricio take me out?"

"Fuck you, bitch—"

"There it is."

"—you don't understand a goddamn thing about it," Dalton hissed. "There's no choice left, not anymore. I have to tell them what they want to know. I have to protect my family."

"And get paid for doing it," she said. "Nothing's for free, right?"

"Ah. Okay," he said, lowering his voice, moving toward her. "Forget all this. Forget what you know, I'll make it worth your while."

"Yeah? How much?"

"Ten. Fifteen thousand, cash."

"Fifteen thousand dollars to abandon my stepfather and an innocent boy and betray my oath? Wow. It's not Escalade money but I could almost buy a used car."

Dalton shrugged. "Okay. So fuck your stepdad. Fuck my oath, Lee Hurst, the entire patrol." His own smile now, etched there, he said,

"Because see, one thing I made sure of, there's zero proof. How I communicate with the cartel, how it pays me. Not a shred, not a trace. My word against yours. You reassigned once before for whatever it was, refusing to let someone get in your pants? Go ahead and do what you need to do and we'll see how it works out."

Sarah nodded and unbuttoned her shirt pocket and removed her phone. Looked at it and held it up to Dalton. "Got it. Every word."

His expression, it was his whole world there gone pale. "Give it to me."

"Your lawyer will get a copy. At the moment I need to talk to Lee," Sarah said, ready, a hand at her hip.

"I said give it to me," Dalton repeated, his voice hot now as he went for his holster, his pistol, eyes widening at Sarah already holding her gun on him.

"Put your hands behind your head and walk toward the station," she said.

"Fuck that, you cu—" was all he could say before Sarah pivoted and threw a fist from her shoulder that shut Dalton's mouth, sat him down hard on the concrete. Sarah understanding the term then, stepfather, the steps Jim taught her as a kid, how to protect herself, leading up to now.

20

Brothers born three minutes apart, the only thing identical about them were their eyes like green marbles, and as they grew, a familiarity with violence, which came in handy in the drug trade.

The Tejada brothers, Nestor soft and pudgy and all business, a quiet, brainy shark, Osvaldo fueled by steroids, looking like he was chopped from granite. Both so fully inked with gang symbols that long-sleeved shirts buttoned to the neck were necessary in the civilian world. Growing up they'd watched their father beat their mother with a drunken ferocity that burnt their brains, and their mother swing bottles and lamps at their father aiming for a death blow, and then each parent took turns working out their mutual hatred on the twins. For Nestor at least, it wasn't monsters he feared, freaks in hockey masks wielding chainsaws; real fear was what might happen if his father was hung over or his mother was in a mood. As boys he and Osvaldo beat the shit out of each other until Nestor told his brother to do the math, versus one another they were less than themselves but together they were strong enough to survive, and from then on they functioned as a single operating unit. Their parents owned Tejada Produce, a tiny storefront vegetable market in the Austin neighborhood, the farthest west corner of Chicago, boxed in by railroad lines and expressways. The streets and sidewalks of Austin had been a gang battleground for decades. Nestor was nine, maybe ten, when he decoded the constant warfare, concluding that there were two types of gang violence. The first revenge-based, an exorcising of demons that ended badly for all involved, like at home. But the second was a business practice. Everything from ass-kicking to murder committed in the name of profit, which made perfect sense; shedding blood was the way of the world in Austin so why not get paid for doing it?

By the time Los Primos came for Nestor and Osvaldo, they were ready.

Born of Incan mythology, built on modern bureaucracy, Los Primos was interchangeable with its English name, the Cousins. It was the largest street gang and preeminent drug trafficker in the world, headquartered in Chicago, and Nestor and Osvaldo had been sixteen when they were recruited like osmosis. Drawn in by older members who plied them with weed and the intimacy of doing small crimes, then larger ones, sharing the spoils with old folks and single moms and kids in the neighborhood until the sense of being part of something expansive and mythic dwarfed their own beat-down lives.

Inking a blood oath on their skin and soul felt like admission to an alternate universe where they were protected from the outside world.

In Chicago alone, fifty thousand Cousins had their backs.

The *corona* of Los Primos, the king, Raymond G, preached fealty and discipline to his tribe, a strict hierarchy and even stricter rules assuring that Los Primos remained orderly and pure. Cousins who violated those commandments were fined until they got into line. If that failed they were beaten on sight, then murdered, the cancer removed, purity restored. Nestor interpreted that gospel for Osvaldo, explaining how it existed in the service of making money. That the constant influx of dollars was lifeblood to Los Primos, without it their universe would crumble, that getting product onto the street without internal strife or interference from other gangs or the law was more than a vocation, it was their purpose. Los Primos reaped huge profits from the sale of weed, coke, crack, and heroin supplied by the Vasquez cartel, trucked over the border and distributed outward from Chicago. Nestor's grasp of the importance of the supply chain caught Raymond G's attention early on, as did Tejada Produce, the tiny storefront.

A legitimate American business was a valuable asset to Los Primos.

The vegetable market offered a multitude of uses, the most immediate as a distribution center, the most important its tax ID number, a business in good standing with the IRS; with so many transactions made in cash the place was prime for laundering drug money. When the twins turned eighteen, Nestor explained to his parents that ownership of the market would be transferred to him and Osvaldo, no questions, no arguments. The parents laughed first and then protested. Then they threatened the twins, who now towered above them. Their sons' allegiance to a new family was rock solid. Nestor listened to his parents shout about the law, calling the police, and then he glanced at Osvaldo, who punched their father twice, dropping him, and slapped their mother until she was on her knees. Through bloody teeth their father said that he'd never give up his market to thugs, going silent at the .44 Magnum Nestor put in his face, Nestor saying, "Think of it as early retirement." The market was signed over to the twins soon after. Several years passed while the parents grew smaller and slower, staring at their sons in disbelief; they died within months of each other, one of a heart attack, the other eaten by cancer, escaping into death. Afterward Nestor hung their portraits on the wall of the glass office in the market, not as a memorial but a reminder that exorcising demons had no place in business.

Where he sat now, behind the desk, staring out at *abuelas* squeezing avocados.

Across from him, Osvaldo leaned forward and said, "So? Then what?"

Nestor looked at his brother, a Mexican-American Hulk on the edge of his seat. Anxious to hear about the rest of Nestor's talk with Raymond G, not every day the *corona* called about something other than sales numbers, the volume of weed moved, crack versus coke. Today it had been about their supplier, the Vasquez cartel. Nestor explaining how one of its intermediaries had contacted Raymond with a request for Los Primos to help locate a gringo driving into Chicago with some kid from Nogales. Impossible to refuse the favor, it might fuck up the supply chain, and Nestor paused, held Osvaldo's gaze. "You remember Mauricio?"

Osvaldo said, "With the knife."

"He's on his way here."

"He's in the States?"

A slow nod, Nestor said, "Mauricio wants

that kid. Raymond don't know why, don't care. Told us to find the gringo. He'll issue the order, we'll have as many Cousins as we need."

"When's he arrive, the gringo?"

"Any day now."

"Got a vehicle ID?"

"Yeah." Nestor slid a sheet of paper across the desk.

Staring at the information, Osvaldo said, "Where's he driving from?"

"West."

"So, I-90 and 290, stake out the side roads, ramps, and overpasses. Tunnels and tolls, get some cars on the road, drive those expressways. We'll need a lot of eyes."

"Like Raymond said, as many Cousins as we need."

"Better we find the gringo as far outside the city as possible."

"Then we hold him and the kid for Mauricio, take them to the warehouse," Nestor said, referring to another asset. The large, bland structure the twins had purchased for Los Primos using cash laundered through the market. Located west of the city in the middle of rural nowhere; jump on the expressway and forty minutes later take exit 38 to a back road, the corrugated metal warehouse a perfect storage location for drugs and weapons coming from across the country. The brothers stared at each other for a few seconds sharing a thought, which Nestor spoke aloud. "Raymond says do something, we do it. Not up to us, we don't question, but. We both know, don't we? There's a problem here."

Osvaldo said, "Mauricio."

Both of them thinking a few years back when Raymond sent them to Mexico to oversee a shipment. Ten tons of coke packed into lettuce crates, Nogales to the Tejadas' warehouse outside Chicago via big rig. Raymond had grown increasingly unhappy about a couple hundred pounds of product that went missing on the Mexican side during recent shipments. Mauricio had picked up Nestor and Osvaldo at the Nogales airport telling them to relax, every grain of coke would be accounted for this time. Smiling through a mask as they entered a low concrete structure on the edge of the desert, Mauricio saying he practiced quality control. Men lined up at tables bagging cocaine, other men slow-walking among them with AR-15s, cameras tracking everyone's movements. Mauricio's presence stilling the room, he said loudly that these two men represented the cartel's largest customer and that someone here had stolen from them. No way of knowing who the thief was so from now on if product went missing he'd blame everyone on the line. A scuffle, a yelp and a plea as Mauricio's guys, one tall, the other thick, dragged a man to the front of the room. The man folding in on himself saying, "No, no," with hardly any voice left as the tall one handed Mauricio a billy club, short and blunt.

In two minutes the young man was dead but not from that length of hardwood.

Mauricio battered the man around the head, torso, and knees in order to terrify the other men in the room, purposeful, yes, but it wasn't enough. Behind that mask, his eyes danced as he threw away the club and drew a knife from a sheath at his waist. The young man bled from his mouth and ears, he stood quaking while Mauricio circled him saying things under his breath, and then began methodically slashing with the blade. A suspension of sanity. Nestor had seen it in his parents. In Cousins and cops who may or may not have enjoyed hurting people, killing people, but needed to, like sleeping and breathing. Like they were killing a specific person over and over again, whoever that person was, they couldn't kill him enough. Nearly dead on his feet, the man offered no defense as

Mauricio paused face-to-face and then quietly stuck the knife into the man's stomach and pulled it upward like zipping a jacket. A collective intake of breath, the man's last and the men's in the room, as the body crumpled. The tall one handed a cloth to Mauricio. He cleaned the knife while announcing that next time it would be two men, then four, then eight, so they'd better keep close watch on one another. Afterward he'd taken Nestor and Osvaldo to dinner. Steak and seafood, chatting at them as breezily as if they'd just attended a sales conference. In the SUV back to the airport, pulling onto the tarmac, Mauricio assured the twins that the problem would not repeat itself. They had his word, an oath so solemn there'd be no reason for them to return, they should stay in Chicago where they belonged, Nestor understanding then, the knife display had been as much for the men in the warehouse as for Osvaldo and him, a performance and a threat.

Basically telling Los Primos to fuck off, mind its own business, and now they were expected to help this Mauricio, this professional psycho?

Nestor weighing it now, he said, "The gringo, who is he, who's the kid?"

"You told me, Raymond G don't care," Osvaldo said.

Folding his hands, Nestor kneaded his knuckles. "What I'm saying is, where's the money in it? The profit? Because if we're doing it for any other reason, it doesn't make sense. It could be bad for everyone involved," he said. "That means us."

Her husband finally told her with a patient smile to stop with the pastries, that the house was beginning to look likc a *panaderia,* cakes stacked on top of cakes. She didn't even like baking much, wasn't great at it, but. Needed to do something to occupy her mind. She was an accountant's assistant, in sync with numbers just like her brother. Normally she got pleasantly lost in columns and computations but since receiving the postcard from her nephew she'd been suffering mental helium, always drifting back to the same thought. Wanting a distraction but unable to handle anything more complicated than flour, egg, sugar, milk, heat, and at least baking felt like preparation. Like taking steps to welcome Miguel into their home, which was what Anna couldn't stop concentrating on, the boy alone, why her nephew had not mentioned Rosa in his postcard. Not even the plural 'we.' *I am safe, I am on my way, I will arrive in Chicago soon.* Anna had stared at the precise handwriting thinking of what an adept student Miguel was of both classroom and street, knowing how close he and his mother were, and saw what was not on the postcard versus what was written there.

She slathered frosting on a lopsided cake, thinking.

The last time she'd spoken to Rosa, her older sister calling from a motel in Aqua Prieta, saying they were with a group of people who'd be driven into the desert the next morning. From there they'd be led on foot into Arizona. Afterward, another van, another coyote would take them to a safe house for a few days. And then they'd begin the long trip to Chicago, Rosa saying it quickly, her usual intensity heightened. Anna had the same feeling now with the postcard as she'd had then, information was being withheld, and she'd said into the phone, "What else?"

A pause, long seconds until Rosa spoke. "*Carlos esta muerto.*"

Whenever Anna thought of her brother, his job and the people who paid him, it was accompanied by a tight line of dread, of what

could happen to him. Quietly, she'd heard herself ask, "How?"

"I don't know."

"When, Rosa?"

"Sometime today. This morning."

"But. You're sure?"

"Anna. It's us. Carlos and me and you, it's
always been just us three," Rosa had said. "You
think I can't feel it, that he's dead? Now that
you know, tell me you can't feel it too."

Finding her breath, Anna had said, "You.
And Miguel, there's no reason. Promise me
there's not."

"Reason for what?"

"You know what. They wouldn't kill Carlos
just to kill him. He did something, or took
something," Anna had said. "Is that it? How
you were able to pay the coyotes, to get away?"

"Stop. Enough—"

"The ones who killed Carlos, is there a reason they'd come for you and Miguel, too?"

Rosa had made a sound, some part sigh and groan. "No. There's no reason."

Anna had listened to the lie woven into Rosa's words, her tone. It had been that way since they were children. When their father left for a mining job in Yucatan and never came back, and their mother was snuffed by grief, the hopeful untruths Rosa and Carlos and Anna had told one another to survive. Little to eat, nowhere to live, but they said it would be okay. Said it over and over, moving through those dark years guided by incandescent lies until they became real. Rosa found factory work and was married, and life did get better, and Carlos earned an accounting degree, and it was better still, and then Anna turned seventeen and it all came crashing down.

A cartel man fat with rank spotted her and decided to own her.

Anna was full and bright and he wanted her outside of his family, *un pedazo de caramelo.*

She refused to be a piece of candy. In return the man vowed to cut off her nose and ears, throw acid in her face, he screamed it from the street below their tiny apartment, so Carlos gave himself up. The cartel had tried to force itself on him when he was a boy, more strongly since it became known that he was good with numbers. He found his way to Ángel Vasquez. Made the deal, Anna would be left alone while Carlos went to work at the big drug depot in the desert where the trucks came and went. Not trusting the cartel, they'd have been fools to do so, Rosa and Carlos scratched money together to send Anna to the U.S. That had been ten years ago with Carlos working his way up until he was put in charge of the counting room, always looking for an opportunity. Revenge for his sister, for taking away his life, Anna was sure then that he'd stolen money, and had said to Rosa, "How much?"

Rosa breathed into the phone. "Not so much."

"Enough to kill our brother. Why would they treat you any differently?"

"It doesn't matter. They don't know where we are. Tomorrow we'll be in Arizona and then there's no chance anyone can get us," Rosa had said. She'd promised to contact Anna as soon as she and Miguel were at the safe house, and then nothing. A week passed in alarming silence. Finally the postcard arrived from Missouri, a bluebird on one side and Miguel's evasions on the other, and Anna knew.

Ever since opening the mailbox, she'd known. As she'd sensed with Carlos, she could feel Rosa was dead too, both gone, and Anna moved the frosting-covered spatula in a slow circle before stabbing the cake with it. Hacking at the motherfuckers who'd murdered her brother and sister, arm going like a piston until only a crushed smear remained, pinkish streaks up her arm and over the countertop. Remembering what it felt like as a girl, that Rosa and Carlos would not let the world harm her. And then she sighed and cleaned the kitchen. Drifted into the front room to do what she'd done each day since receiving Miguel's postcard. Anna stood at the picture window and looked up and down the street that lay in the heart of Pilsen. Her neighborhood, hers and her husband's and daughter's, a small, functional paradise carrying echoes of life in Mexico; it was Latin America and the United States of America and Chicago all at once, and she wanted it for Miguel. Except that today, this minute, the blood connection flowing between her and her nephew felt broken. That he'd never make it to Pilsen and so she closed her eyes, considered asking the Virgin for help but was as good at praying as she was at baking. Instead she visualized Miguel. Trying to bend the universe to her will so that when she opened her eyes he would be walking up the street toward the house, having found his way there, alone in a strange country.

It forced her eyes open, the question there all along.

There was no way Miguel could cross the country alone, so who was he with?

Traffic on Roosevelt Road crept or flowed but never stopped, an artery crossing Chicago westward from the lake where it passed the glassy, boxy FBI field office.

Helen Wu stood at a window looking out at the line of vehicles thinking of Lee Hurst.

They'd met a few years back at a federal law enforcement convention, the two of them part of a panel on the interdependency of U.S. street gangs and Mexican cartels, drug commerce the lifeblood of both groups. She'd liked Lee right away. Twenty years her senior, a deep intelligence behind the blunt talk and buzz cut. Interested in how Helen had graduated top of her class from University of Chicago law and declined big job offers in favor of the FBI, returning to Chicago to work on the gang task force. She'd explained how as a girl her family's restaurant in Chinatown was caught between warring factions, Chi-Town Rangers versus Los Primos, drive-bys in the street while kids hopscotched on the sidewalk. All of that bad enough but it was her brother Henry who sealed her decision to become a Fed. In and out of rehab since he was sixteen, sweet and smart and funny, and then a year into junior college he bought a bag of crack cocaine mixed with something that killed him. Not a pleasant death, messy, Henry found by their mother, and Helen wanted to kill someone in return.

After the panel, agents and cops drinking at the bar, Lee had said, "The dealer?"

Helen had sipped her bourbon and shrugged. "I wasn't sure who to blame. In the end I settled on the gangs."

"The distributors. The ones who put it on the street," Lee said.

"In Chicago that's mainly Los Primos. Henry died when I was fifteen and I had this fantasy of getting a machine gun and just mowing down a bunch of those fuckers. Except I hated guns then as much as I do now."

"You don't carry on duty?"

"Not often. In my time with the task force, it's rarely come to guns. Los Primos is a family structure, the idea that they become cousins through a blood vow. The rules and codes of honor, the hierarchy, it's all based on Mexican mythology. Like any other cult the bosses use that stuff to manipulate the ones at the bottom, put the true believers to work. Fifty, sixty thousand in Chicago alone toiling in the family business."

"Selling drugs supplied by the cartel," Lee said.

Helen had nodded. "That's why in the end, what progress we make, whatever we call a win, is transactional. The Cousins spill too much blood, or import too much product at once? Basically become too present in the lives of tax-paying citizens? Before reaching for guns and warrants we go to the bosses. If they know what's good for them, and they always do, they take a loss and give us what we want, and we allow them to stay in business."

"Even if it violates a rule or code or something?"

"In Los Primos one rule trumps the rest," she'd said, finishing her drink. "Go out and make money, and when you're finished doing that, make more money."

Looking at Roosevelt Road now, Helen recalled the certainty she'd felt saying it to Lee.

The intervening years had only confirmed how profit-driven the gang was.

Lee's phone call today surprised Helen, they hadn't spoken in some time, Lee getting right to the point. After an hour they said their goodbyes, and Helen had gone to her office window to parse what she'd been told. A shootout at the Arizona border between a U.S. citizen on one side and three Vasquez cartel men on the other, one a lieutenant, Helen's ears perking up since Vasquez was the supplier for Los Primos. The cartel men were pursuing a woman and her young son as the pair illegally crossed into Arizona. By circumstance they came upon the citizen, James Hanson, a Marine veteran. The shootout occurred when Hanson refused to hand over the woman and boy to the cartel men, shooting and killing one of them through the border fence, the dead man the brother of the lieutenant, Mauricio Guerrero. Mauricio, Lee had said, we'll come back to him, and went on to explain how the woman later died from gunshot wounds. Her son was taken into custody by Lee's agents and held at the patrol station to be processed and sent back. And that's when Hanson showed up and took the boy.

Helen had said, "What do you mean, took him?"

Lee sighed, said, "Security lapse. The man entered the station and walked the boy out of the holding area and drove away with him."

"For what reason?"

"Guess."

"Well. I'd say money, but who had it, and why?"

"Vasquez money, stolen by the woman's brother so she and her son could make it into the states," Lee had said. "Dying out there in the desert, she told Hanson the cash was his if he got the boy safely to Chicago. To an aunt there."

"How do you know all this, Lee?"

"Hanson's stepdaughter is one of my agents. She'd been in contact with him as he drove the boy cross-country. As Mauricio and his men have pursued them."

"Wait," Helen had said. "The lieutenant is in the U.S.?"

"Chasing two hundred grand, more or less."

"That's it?" Helen had asked, incredulous. "He pursued the woman to the border, planned to grab the money, probably kill her, that's cartel behavior. But entering the U.S. for such a small amount? It's too much exposure. I can't see him getting the okay from his capo. Two hundred K is a drop in the bucket to the Vasquez people."

"My agent wondered if it was revenge, Mauricio hunting down the man who killed his brother. But Hanson told her different," Lee had said. "That Mauricio wants to kill the boy."

"How old is he again?"

"Eleven."

"Okay, well, if he was there to be killed, either at the border with his mother or if he was back in Mexico, like I said, cartel behavior.

But crossing an entire foreign country to do it doesn't make sense," Helen had said.

"Right. And there's this." Lee had read excerpts to Helen then from the DEA file on Mauricio and told her about the dead state trooper, the dead gas station attendant and motel clerk.

"Jesus," Helen had said quietly. "All that for one kid?"

"Look, I called you because Mauricio trying to find Hanson and the boy in a city that size, he'll need help. Who better to contact than one of the cartel's best customers?"

"Makes sense. Los Primos has an army at its disposal."

"Hanson and the boy have to be close to Chicago by now," Lee had said. "You can probably guess my agent is worried about her stepdad."

"She should be."

"It's a long shot, Helen. The longest of long shots, but with your gang contacts, is there anything you can do?"

"Honestly? It's between no and absolutely not," she'd said, both of them aware she was being optimistic. She'd taken down information from Lee about Jim Hanson and then stared at the mostly empty sheet of paper. Promised Lee she'd call with any developments, hung up, and gone to the window. Nothing out there but cars and trucks, and she sighed knowing that was all she had, data on Hanson's vehicle. A late model pickup with Arizona license plates, Helen called Chicago PD and spoke to a commander she often worked with. A conversation they'd had about carjacking, she remembered the commander mentioning license plate reader—equipped squad vehicles, two hundred LPRs rolling on city streets. Add a plate number to the database and the onboard computer would ping if it scanned a match, the commander taking Jim's information, saying he'd send out an alert to non-equipped squaddies too, eyes on the lookout for an old truck with AZ plates. Helen thanked him, said she owed him one. A final glance at Roosevelt Road, mostly empty, a lull before rush hour, she knew she'd done all she could. No transaction to be made, she had nothing to offer Los Primos. It came down to the gang helping a lieutenant in the Vasquez cartel, their supplier, versus the lives of two innocent people.

Helen shut the window blinds, hating the truth, that the boy and Hanson had no chance.

21

The sensation, foreign in a desert existence, returned to Jim as he and Miguel entered the slipstream of traffic flowing toward a metropolis. Like magnets pulled by the steel skyline that would soon ascend on the horizon. The vehicles around, ahead, and behind them were all headed to Chicago, each for different reasons and every one for the same reason, because it was there.

Jim touched at his breast pocket, reassuring himself.

The piece of paper inside with Miguel's mother's handwriting on it, her blood, Jim had memorized the address. The aunt's name was Anna, Miguel had explained, his mother and uncle's younger sister. She'd become a U.S. citizen a decade earlier, married to a man who worked for the transit authority. He operated a train, something like that, and they had a three-year-old daughter, Miguel's cousin. Yes, the aunt knew that Miguel and his mother and uncle were going to try and make it to Chicago. It was Jim's idea then, guessing she'd be worried, to send her a postcard. He'd had Miguel select one from a rack at the little grocery store in Missouri, it showed the state bird, a bluebird, and he'd dictated to the boy who wrote it out in Spanish. That Miguel was on his way to Chicago and was safe and would be there soon, nothing more. Nothing about his uncle or mother, or about Jim, all of that needed to be explained in person. The man at the grocery store had mailed it for them and sold Jim a map of Chicago, the kind that folded. Jim assumed the aunt had received the postcard by now and would be expecting her nephew. He'd found her street on the map and memorized that too, the names and directions of other streets that led to the address in a neighborhood called Pilsen. Glued to the window, Miguel pointed at a highway sign. "How long now?" he said, excitement in his voice.

Jim glanced out as the sign sped past. "About an hour and a half. Not even that long."

"I think I'm ready. Ready to be there."

"That's good."

"The only thing," Miguel said, looking at Jim. "What about you and me?"

"What do you mean?"

"Will we see each other again? After?"

"I drop you off with your aunt?"

Miguel nodded.

"Well now. I'm not sure," Jim said. "But just because we don't see each other, it doesn't mean we're not friends."

"I know. But it would be better if we did. It's easier that way."

"I guess that's true."

"Like that friend of yours you told me about. What's his name?"

Jim paused, remembering what they'd discussed. "Harold Richman."

"Don't you wish you could see him?" Miguel asked. "Just to know what he's doing?"

It made Jim think. Harold married his high school sweetheart after being discharged and had a kid right away, a daughter, then divorced later on, Jim knew that much. Harold had taught school in Detroit for decades, likely retired by now but Jim wasn't sure. Miguel was right. He'd like to know some things and was about to say so when a rocket shot past, a neon-green Porsche, low to the ground, leaving the old pickup in its wake. Jim moving in the middle of three lanes of eastbound traffic, and then here came another car just as fast, and another, one of those impromptu races with drivers catching speed fever from each other. A truck came up so quickly it looked like inches in the rearview mirror, Jim glancing at the driver on his phone chattering like crazy. Moments later the truck sped past, the name of a plumber displayed on its side panel, with a beater Honda on its bumper like a pilot fish. Jim looked at the Honda's driver as he passed by. Pale and solemn, dusting of goatee, the guy looked back blankly and then roared after the truck, Jim watching him go, hearing Harold's voice. The tone, the gravel at the back of Jim's mind, a thing Harold said when the two of them were scouting a position. A place high and hidden where Jim set up his rifle and began eyeing the scope, Harold at his back prepared to feed him ammo and a fresh weapon, he'd say to Jim, *Some are born and some are made. Sure as hell man, you were born.* Jim asked what he meant the first few times then quit asking because he knew, his affinity for a rifle, any kind of gun really, although it occurred to him Harold meant more than that. A thing inside Jim that first whiskey and then Christine had kept at bay, he didn't like thinking of it but knew it was there.

Flaring now in all this traffic, maybe because they were close to Chicago.

Call it bad or good, all Jim knew was the thing inside himself had kept him alive in the jungle and saved Harold's life; after the war it ranged around his gut and brain searching for an exit, some way out, the routine of exhausting work a necessity. Now the thing was squatting behind his eyes while he drove. Examining the blank gaze of the guy in the beater Honda as traffic slowed and separated into lines at a toll plaza. Jim eased to a booth, dropped a handful of quarters into a basket, and drove on. Miguel said, "Any more tolls before Chicago?"

Jim shook his head. "Nothing can stop us now."

22

In the rear of the market, the refrigerated backroom, Nestor supervised a delivery of tomatoes and onions, Chihuahua cheese and cooking oil, making sure his guys stacked it all in front of the crates of bundled weed and plastic-wrapped vials of heroin, ticking off items on a clipboard, when Osvaldo filled the doorway. Nestor told the guys to take a break and close the door behind them, he and his brother watching their cold breath rise. "We got a hit," Osvaldo said.

"Where?"

"Outside Rockford."

"When?"

"Five minutes ago," Osvaldo said.

"So. The gringo's getting close to the warehouse. I got to call Raymond. Shit."

"What?"

"It's Saturday," Nestor said, thumbing his phone. "Ballet."

Mauricio could see it in the glance Isidro exchanged with Jorge. Their confusion at why after such a grueling drive across the States, a hell-bent quest to reach Chicago, they'd stopped to get the SUV washed. It was one of those places where a driver walked slowly down a glass-enclosed hallway watching his car on the other side of the windows ride a conveyor belt through soapy water and twirling brushes and flashing lights. Mauricio said to wait outside, that he wanted to be alone in the hallway. Isidro nodded behind sunglasses and led Jorge into the cool evening, handing him a cigarette. Mauricio turned his attention to the conveyor belt, gazing at the spray of bubbles and foam, refusing to arrive in a vehicle caked with road dirt and insects. Not wanting the old man he would soon kill to think badly of him, that Mauricio was sloppy and undisciplined. Unprepared.

A notion he'd had for miles, the closer they got to Chicago.

How in another life he could've been Marine Corps.

Mauricio lifted the Silver Star and gazed at its five points, flashes from the carwash coloring the medal bluish-orange. If his birth had been different, where and to whom, he might've grown up to earn the sort of honor as Marine Corps. Human lives erased by the old man during wartime in order to receive that medal; those men had been soldiers too, doing their duty on an opposing side. Just as Mauricio was doing for the cartel, which was an army like any other. He'd said it to Marine Corps at the border, that they were both soldiers, telling him they were alike. Meaning that fateful thing inside Mauricio, the ability to decide who lived and who died, it existed just as strongly within Marine Corps.

Staring into the glass wall, water beads melted Mauricio's reflection.

His eyes narrowed, remembering Marine Corps's response.

The old man had shaken his head with an unmoving gaze and said, No, they were nothing alike, Mauricio laughing to himself now, saying to Marine Corps in his mind, *Oh yeah, is that right, what's the difference between you and me?* Surprised at how fast the answer came back to him, Mauricio spun, unsure if someone had actually said it or if he'd conjured it up.

In the hallway alone, Marine Corps's voice in his ear, *The difference is, I don't kill kids.*

Mauricio stared at his reflection, said, "I shot his mother. He'll want revenge."

Wrong, that's not why you want to kill him. Not because of what he might do. It's because he has someone waiting for him—

"No," Mauricio shook his head.

—his aunt, who won't let anyone steal him away. Like you and your brother were stolen.

"Fuck you, *no*," Mauricio said loud enough to make other people in the glass hallway glance in his direction. He stared them away and then looked at the Silver Star in his hand. A piece of metal, that's all it was. He shoved it in a pocket, picturing it now, two bullets through the boy's heart and one in the head. Marine Corps on his knees by the boy's motionless body, a barrel pressed to the old man's temple as he echoed Mauricio's own nightmare, *Please, please, set me free*, his fear making Mauricio tingle as a siren blared. Warning car wash employees that the conveyor was pulling through another vehicle, the SUV outside being toweled off. It was time to get back on the road, Mauricio headed for the exit when his phone vibrated. He answered to music plinking in the background. Raymond G said his name, speaking low, the *Corona* of Los Primos nearly whispering. Saying the gringo's truck had been spotted and was being followed, nearing a secure place where Mauricio could take care of the gringo and the boy. Mauricio asked what secure place? Raymond saying the Tejada brothers had arranged it. The smart one and the steroid one, Mauricio remembered the twins, he asked where, and Raymond told him, nearby, you're closer than the gringo. Explaining that Cousins in cars would wait for Mauricio at a rendezvous point, exit 38, and that he could take over from there.

Mauricio said, "The Tejadas set it up. I want the big one to be part of it."

"Osvaldo. Okay. Then what?"

"What do you mean?" Mauricio said.

"The gringo, he's American. We disappear

a U.S. citizen, we got to be ready if someone comes looking for him. Family, friends, they alert the police, what's Ángel's plan?"

"Don't worry about Ángel," Mauricio said slowly, an icy threat between each word that silenced Raymond. A few more details and Mauricio hung up. He went to the SUV, Isidro in the backseat and Jorge behind the wheel. Heading off toward the rendezvous, Mauricio closed his eyes, folded his hands over his stomach, picturing it again. Watching Marine Corps ask for mercy. Mauricio nodding, benevolent, removing a knife from a sheath at his waist and telling the old man that begging for his life is no way for a soldier to die.

All the tiny ballerinas onstage in pink taffeta doing their thing to a plinking piano, a dozen five-year-olds and not a single one moving to the same tune, cutest thing he'd ever seen.

Saturday morning watching his daughter, the ringer on Raymond G's phone turned off but still vibrating loud enough for his wife to lift a shush-finger with its bejeweled nail, giving him a death glare.

All of his officers knew not to call him during Saturday ballet unless.

Raymond had left his seat then, excusing himself past the other parents and up the aisle into the theater lobby where he found a corner, answered the phone. Nestor Tejada apologizing but saying they'd located the gringo outside Rockford, he'd be near the warehouse soon. Raymond listened to everything and then called Mauricio and gave it all to him, whatever this shit was with the gringo and boy. Los Primos had done its part. Asking nothing in return for having mobilized a squad of Cousins to find the truck from Arizona like a needle in a haystack, wanting only the basic assurance of a plan from the cartel if something went wrong, and what did the *corona* get? Staring at his phone after Mauricio hung up, repeating the man's words in his head, *Don't worry about Ángel.*

Fuck that. Raymond did worry. It was his job to worry about Ángel.

The Vasquez cartel was the main supplier of Los Primos, any supply chain issues would weaken the Cousins, rupture the organization, and Raymond flipped a mental coin knowing what he had to do before it landed. Hitting a speed dial number, two beeps and then a voice asked him to identify himself. Raymond did. A few seconds until Ángel Vasquez came on the line with a murmured greeting. Treading lightly so as not to make the *capo* feel he'd lost control of his own *teniente*, Raymond carefully asked Ángel if he'd spoken to Mauricio recently.

An intake of air, angry or impatient, maybe something else, Ángel said, "Have you?"

Shit.

Occurring to Raymond then that Ángel

knew exactly where Mauricio was and what he was doing. Asking Raymond's own question back at him because he knew the answer, testing Raymond's truthfulness, and Raymond hesitated. Just the facts then, tell it as if Ángel already knew everything, and see where it went, and Raymond said he'd spoken to Mauricio twice. First about a gringo bringing a boy to Chicago, Mauricio asking Raymond to muster his forces, have Los Primos help locate them. The second call minutes ago. Raymond letting Mauricio know the boy and gringo had been found. Mauricio and his men were en route to apprehend the pair, take them to a location arranged by Los Primos to dispose of them there.

Ángel grunted softly. "Mauricio's men. Which men, did he say who's with him?"

"No."

"You don't remember him mentioning a Hernando?"

"He didn't say any names. Just men," Raymond said.

"How many?"

"I don't know."

"Because this Hernando, I spoke to him a few days ago, he said they were headed to Chicago after the boy and the gringo," Ángel said. "And Chicago means you, that Mauricio would reach out to you for help."

"He did, yes, as I said."

"And since then I've not heard from Hernando."

"Ah."

"But you've spoken to Mauricio?"

"Yes. As I told you," Raymond said.

"Why?" Ángel asked. "Has he contacted you, but not me?"

Raymond hearing the vague accusation, Ángel wondering if he was withholding information, maybe doing some side deal with Mauricio. Flipping it back with all due respect,

Raymond said, "You're the only one who can answer that, capo. No one knows your men as you do. Fact is, I know Mauricio only by reputation. A real killer."

"When it's good for business."

Seeing his chance, taking it, Raymond said, "And how is this good business for any of us? Your men entering the States illegally, crossing the country with guns to kill a boy? Coming to my city, asking me to do something that could fuck up my business for years?"

"What thing?"

"You know. Disappearing a U.S. citizen," Raymond said. "It goes wrong, I'm the one on this side of the border. It's Los Primos who suffers."

Another grunt from Ángel and he was silent.

"What did the boy do?" Raymond asked. "For Mauricio to chase him so far?"

"His family stole from me. Mother and uncle, they're dead. The boy has the money."

"How much?"

"A little over two hundred thousand American."

Raymond silent now, he wouldn't say a word. Because if he did, the only appropriate reply to Ángel would be what the fuck, you wipe your ass with more than that each time you take a shit. Instead he said, "Your man doesn't seem to care if he draws attention."

"He already killed three people on his way there. One a police," Ángel said.

"Mm." Raymond boiling inside now, the blood Mauricio was trailing to Los Primos.

"You read history?"

"Not much," Raymond said.

"Long ago a flea bit a rat, infected it with the plague. That rat bit the people, and the people breathed and bled on one another, and empires fell. I've had Mauricio since he was a boy," Ángel sighed. "He's become the flea."

Raymond waited, silent.

"This place you arranged. Will any of your men be there?" Ángel asked.

"One. A good one."

"So. Mauricio shows up with his men, and your man joins them to help kill the gringo and the boy. When it's done your man opens fire. Mauricio first. Don't underestimate him. Don't think he'll go down easily. Listen to me Raymond, it must be an automatic rifle, a full clip," Ángel said. "And then your man, he takes out Mauricio's men afterward."

"Now I have more bodies to get rid of," Raymond said

"For a discount on your next shipments," Ángel said. "It's all about business, yes?"

He hung up, placed the phone screen-side down on the desk and was staring at it when Osvaldo entered the office. Nestor looked up from the phone to his brother and said, "Raymond says we have to kill him, Mauricio. By we he means you."

Osvaldo nodded slowly. "What's the play?"

"A deal with Ángel Vasquez. Mauricio dead, thirty percent off the next three shipments."

"What about Mauricio's guys?"

"Them too, dead."

A ripple through his triceps as Osvaldo squeezed an imaginary trigger. "The AK-203. I only ever used it out in the boonies to cut down trees."

Nestor said, "How Raymond wants this to go is, you meet with Mauricio and his guys at the exit. They'll stop the gringo and boy there. You take everyone to the warehouse. Stand back while Mauricio kills them, and then no small talk. Blow his fucking head off. Slice him up, Raymond made me promise you would."

"Like, what? Mauricio's some walking dead?"

"Just do it. His guys after, right away."

"That's a lot of blood."

"Like I said. Thirty percent off the next three shipments."

Osvaldo shrugged his big shoulders into a black satin jacket, *Tejada Produce* stitched in red letters. "Van or truck?"

"Take the van." Nestor sat forward holding his twin's gaze. "Remember, stand back and let it happen. Then wipe him out, *hermano*. No fucking around."

"I'm not worried," Osvaldo said, going for the door.

"No, be worried. Be scared too," Nestor said. "You know, it's the best way to stay alive."

23

The day had turned bright blue, sunlight so sharp it was like a laser beam through the truck's visor. Jim squinted into the windshield as they sped beneath an overpass holding a large sign that indicated forty-seven miles to Chicago. Miguel said it out loud, voice vibrating, and Jim nodded along, although it wasn't the sign he'd been staring at.

Standing on the overpass, he could've sworn someone was looking down with binoculars.

Emerging on the other side, Jim hoped he'd imagined it and glanced into the rearview mirror and did not see a man back there.

He saw three of them.

No law, he told himself, there was no law

against people standing on overpasses, and continued on with his heart ticking against his chest like a timer, get Miguel to his aunt before the buzzer went off, as the road ahead revealed itself to be a small miracle. How it happens sometimes like driving into another dimension, all lanes in both directions suddenly empty. That vast, flat, concrete-covered Midwestern plain held not a single vehicle, and Jim leaned on the gas feeling free. Miguel reclined and popped a *pandita* into his mouth, looking straight ahead. Then sat forward abruptly saying, "Should they? Be there, doing that?" Jim fought the sunlight, catching a flash of neon green. The Porsche from miles back making a U-turn from the right side berm, the beater Honda doing the same from the left, the pair of them blocking the highway as Jim cranked the wheel and roared down an off-ramp, seeing its sign at the last second, EXIT 38. Shaking all over, Miguel asked, "Where are we going?"

"Back roads. Got to lose those guys," Jim said, death-gripping the wheel.

Miguel turned and looked through the rear window. "No one there. Just dust."

He was right, the pavement giving way to gravel as the truck kicked up a whirlwind. Eyes flicking to the road, the rearview mirror, back to the road lined by shoulder-high corn and nothing else, Jim heard Miguel make a noise. A gasp, the boy's gaze glued to his own window. Jim looked past him at the rapidly approaching intersection where a pair of headlights glowed off to the right behind a stand of trees, seeing what Miguel saw: not a phantom or a demon because those things weren't real but this was, the black SUV opening up in a furious dash to block their path. Jim realizing then that no matter how far he drove Mauricio would be there, only one thing to do now, and he said, "Hold on tight."

"Is it him?" the boy asked, gripping the edge of the seat.

Jim answered by accelerating, pushing the pickup to its limit. The SUV came within twenty feet of the intersection, then ten, a collision course with Miguel bracing himself as Jim tapped the brakes seconds before impact, Mauricio and his men sailing past. Jim hit the gas then but too soon, the pickup's front bumper snagging the SUV's back end as the world went into a mad spin, the SUV flung one way and the pickup crashing through a fence, juddering to a halt in a cornfield. From chaos to silence in a moment, Jim swiveled his head on his neck, and Miguel groaned a little. Jim turned, peering through stalks at the SUV across the road balanced at the edge of a culvert. Time to go, right now, he turned the key. The truck rattled to life. Jim dropped it into gear and began cutting down corn, aiming for the road, hoping to God almighty it led somewhere safe.

***

Osvaldo sat shaken in the back seat, gripping the AK-203, the SUV set at an odd angle. Half an hour earlier he'd arrived at the exit, left the van in the underbrush, keys in the ignition for a quick getaway, and hurried to where Mauricio and his men waited. Mauricio looking at the 203 and saying, *This fucking guy, he's hunting elephants,* even though he and his men had 15s, not exactly popguns. Osvaldo telling Mauricio the warehouse was a couple miles ahead, the best way to stop the gringo's truck would be at the intersection, they'd gain cover from the trees there. That's what they'd done, piled into the SUV, parked and waited, he and Mauricio in the back seat, a baby-faced guy at the wheel, an older guy in sunglasses riding shotgun. The pickup truck appeared soon after, herded down the road by Cousins on the highway, Mauricio instructing baby-face to wait, wait—now, go fast! They'd flown from the trees with Osvaldo watching the old truck accelerate like a race to cross the intersection, neither vehicle slowing down, Mauricio telling baby-face to crush the motherfucker. Osvaldo thinking Jesus Christ, they might all die, closing his eyes and hearing the whoosh of the SUV as it passed by the truck's hood with just inches to spare, and then it was a merry-go-round at hyperspeed. Spun out at the edge of the road, bumping to a stop, teetering in the breeze. Looking around at the guys in front barely moving, Mauricio palming his eyes, it occurred to Osvaldo to kill them all right now. This Mauricio, what Nestor would call a liability, get it done with, Osvaldo's hands tight on the 203 when Mauricio said, "Where are they?"

The one with sunglasses pointed through the windshield. "There."

Osvaldo looked at shards, cornstalks, cutting across a field like a giant termite at work.

Mauricio screaming, "Go! Get them, go!" as the SUV roared and found the road, Osvaldo sinking back then, cursing himself for hesitating.

Jim knew. Hearing the SUV plow into the cornfield behind them, feeling the old pickup strain beneath him, he and Miguel wouldn't get much farther. He pulled at the steering wheel and burst through the edge of the field onto the dirt road, punched at the gas. The truck rallied, climbing a short hill, pushing them a quarter mile ahead as Jim scouted for cover among the endless rows of stalks. The windshield suddenly obscured by steam, pouring from beneath the hood with the acrid smell of scorched iron, the patched radiator blown. Jim accelerated once more, the truck shuddering as he yanked the wheel to a sideways stop across the road. A glance down the hill, he saw the SUV still navigating the cornfield. Jim reached behind the seat for the pistol, shoved it in his waist, and grabbed the M21. "Get out."

Miguel frozen in his seat, he said, "We should keep going. He'll kill us."

To the boy, to himself, Jim said, "Not if I kill him first."

Their eyes joined until Miguel slid from his side, and Jim from his. Jim set the boy against the rear tire, had him curl hard against it, then chambered a round into the M21 and stretched the rifle across the hood. Blinking through the scope, aiming at the top of the hill, he began to count and breathe until numbers and the rise and fall of his chest were joined. When the SUV appeared he locked it in his sights and would not let it go.

Seven, eight, nine—the vehicle came quickly, Jim squinted, steel grazing his finger.

"Ten," he whispered, pulling the trigger to a single crack that cut the air, split glass in the near distance. An abbreviated moment and then the SUV skidded like it had hit black ice, unable to find its footing, a rubbery stutter before it flipped twice and landed with a shattering crunch.

Jim's eye on the scope: leaking undercarriage and spinning tires but no other movement.

He waited, counting and breathing.

They'd sped up the rise, and there it was at the top of the hill as if it had been abandoned, Marine Corps's truck set sideways, Mauricio wondering about it for less time than it took to catch the flash of gunmetal and yell, "Get down!" A shriek of glass then, a *vip* of air carrying the bullet that pierced Jorge's face, his body slumping over the steering wheel of the SUV that was traveling eighty miles per hour. No chance to do anything as the heavy vehicle succumbed to G-force, to physics, and began to roll and do battle with the rock-hard earth below until coming to rest on its side. Jorge's body folded against the driver's side window, one eye open and the other a black-flecked hole where the bullet entered his skull and snuffed his brain. Isidro made noises deep in his throat. The Tejada muscle-head, Osvaldo, saying *Madre de dios, madre de dios*, while Mauricio wiped at blood. Flowing from old wounds re-opened, new ones from glass biting into his shoulder, his shirt soaked purple. On his back, he kicked at the window until it was empty. Told Isidro and Osvaldo to grab their weapons and follow him, ease out and get down. In a crouch, he directed them to opposite sides of the beached SUV while remaining in the middle and giving the order, shoot on three, fingers up, and they stood and fired. Battering the pickup truck like a tin can, exploding windows and deflating tires. Mauricio raised a hand. Silence, the clink of falling debris, and then the sharp, solitary snap of a bullet ripping through Isidro's shirtsleeve, making him yelp. Infuriating Mauricio, Marine Corps with his fucking rifle, he'd had enough. "I tell you, walk and fire and don't stop, pop a clip and keep on. *Órale cabrones! A chingarse a ése hijo de puta, ahora!*" he said. "Kill this motherfucker, now!"

On the move then, shredding the truck with bullets, hunting down the man and boy.

When he was a child in the desert a rare spring storm might hit the tin roof of Jim's family home with a barrage of hailstones, the ceaseless violence of it like the men's gunfire. No way he could take on three of them from a distance that was growing shorter by the round. He was out of moves and tried to shield Miguel, whatever good that might do, smelling gasoline. Seeing a rivulet flow from the truck like its last bit of lifeblood. It snaked toward a chunk of burning debris, a fuse, and he yanked Miguel's hand and said, "Run! Right now, run!"

Not a dozen steps away when the pop and flash of fire slowed the men's onslaught.

Seconds now, Jim sprinting and dragging Miguel, and then the truck exploded, buckling into a furnace of thick black smoke. The cover Jim needed, he pulled Miguel from the road and into a field dotted with round bales of hay. Weaving from one to another like running slalom, there'd be targets on their backs when the smoke shifted, when Mauricio realized they'd made a run for it. Feeling the ground beneath his feet descend, Jim spied a barn at the bottom of the hill. That old familiar noise then, a hot hiss like the wind traveling backward, he shoved Miguel behind a bale and dove next to him as a spray of bullets sliced the hay above their heads. A choice, fire back or keep running. Jim shifted and looked at the barn maybe fifty yards away, heavy timber walls versus hunks of rolled grass. "Listen now. On your belly and follow me. Lift your head they'll shoot it off." Miguel nodded furiously and Jim said, "When I say go, you stand and run like hell. Don't stop until you're inside that barn." Miguel nodded again and Jim began to crawl with the boy behind him. Over the slope of the hill, inching lower, sure the men were combing the field behind them, closer now, closer, Jim said, "Go!" and they were off.

Both dead, Jim was sure of it until he kicked open the door and they slid inside the barn.

Quiet sunlight fell in dust-filled columns. A rusting tractor, a pile of busted seed bags, nothing else, the place cool and mostly empty. Jim looked at a landing above them. He hurried Miguel up a flight of stairs and situated him in a tight corner, protected on both sides. "Stay put, keep quiet," Jim said. "Something happens to me, you get out of here. As far away as you can."

"Okay."

Nodding at a ladder bolted to the wall, Jim said, "I'll be up there."

"Okay," Miguel said, his voice shallow.

Jim slung the rifle, scaled the ladder to crossbeams leading to three small windows, and took a position at the one in the center. He lifted it, nosed open its shutters with the barrel of the rifle. An eye to the scope, he scanned the landscape below looking for a certain type of movement, like he used to tell Harold, no-muss-no-fuss, when the enemy was unaware of being watched from a vantage point. If he were lucky, Mauricio and his men were still searching the field and hadn't yet figured out that he and Miguel had reached the barn.

Jim thumbed sweat from his forehead feeling the furthest thing from lucky.

* * *

Fuck this shit, Osvaldo's sole thought as he crept through the field searching for the gringo and boy, pausing before aiming the AK-203 around the corners of hay bales expecting a rifle in his belly each time. They were spread out, Mauricio in the center of the field, the one in sunglasses on the other side, Osvaldo bringing up the rear.

Barely an hour out here, he'd almost been killed two, three fucking times.

That terrifying game of chicken with the pickup truck, the SUV flipping after baby-face took one through the eye. Christ, that sharpshooter shit, the gringo almost clipping sunglasses from what, a hundred fucking yards?

Channeling his brother, Nestor told Osvaldo to cut his losses and get out of there now.

Back far enough, he could turn and run for the van before the other two men knew he was gone, except. Raymond G had been clear. Ángel Vasquez wanted Mauricio dead to the tune of thirty percent off the next three shipments of product. If the gringo and the boy survived, well, that wasn't any of the Cousins' business, was it? Osvaldo was there to kill Mauricio, rip the crazy fucker to pieces, and he quickened his pace, breaking into a trot. Almost in range, nearing an old barn, take out Mauricio first and then sunglasses, Osvaldo crossed between hay bales lifting the AK-203 and stumbled, losing his breath. Couldn't catch it like he was choking and paused to cough into his hand looking at blood there, looking from his fingers to the sticky hole in his chest as a second bullet passed through his heart and he went down thinking of Nestor, the last thing he felt, wanting to apologize to his twin for leaving him alone.

＊＊＊

Two shots like firecrackers and Mauricio took cover and turned to Osvaldo on his back, his chest a jumping red geyser. Peering around at the barn, a window near the roofline where Mauricio spotted a ghost trying not to be seen. Across the field Isidro crouched behind a hay bale. With a low whistle Mauricio drew his attention and signaled: Marine Corp at the window, *I'll shoot first, then you.* Isidro looked at the barn and nodded back, rifle ready. Deep breath, Mauricio stood, fired a full clip and crouched. Isidro followed, the frame and shutters, the square area surrounding the window pounded to bits like eaten by a wood chipper, and then Mauricio again, the pulsing AK cold in his hands as he waited for the ghost to fall to Earth.

* * *

Those bright scarlet letters on a black satin jacket may as well have been a bull's-eye. The big man carried a cannon, moving like he was in a hurry and also trying to be secretive, both. Squinting into the scope, Jim keenly aware he was about to announce his presence in the barn, he pulled the trigger once, twice, remaining at the window only long enough to watch the body drop before dropping to the ground himself. First one hail of gunfire chewed holes in the timber, then another, and another, then a pause. Jim crawled from the bombardment to the far window in the corner, above the ladder. Leaned over it and spoke to Miguel in a low voice, "Come up here."

The boy's face a mask of alarm at the assault, eyes wide, he hesitated.

"Miguel. I need your help," Jim said, extending a hand. Moving then, Miguel nodded, climbed the ladder, Jim pulling him up and setting him against the wall. Took the .45 from his belt saying quickly, "We need a diversion. I'm going to find a position on the ground. Soon as I leave, you count to thirty then reach out that window, fire two shots, and get down. Right away, cover your head, get me?"

Miguel said, "Count to thirty. Two shots. Then down."

"Show me, is the clip in right?" Jim said.

Miguel popped it out and clicked it back into place.

"The safety, so you can shoot," Jim said.

The boy thumbed it back.

"Good. Start now. One, two—" Jim said, going to the ladder, listening to Miguel whispering behind him. On the landing and then down the stairs, he hurried across the barn counting along in his head, reaching the door and easing it open a crack. A tumbledown shed just there, Jim spied a figure through the slats creeping along the opposite side, he lifted the rifle thinking, Twenty-seven, twenty-eight, twenty-nine—

From above, the .45 pierced the silence twice.

The figure emerged from behind the shed with an AK aimed up at the window, sunglasses throwing off a dull glint as Jim fired. Blowing out the man's shoulder, the automatic weapon flung from his grip, he turned too stunned to move and Jim shot him twice, throat and chest, and swiveled back behind the door. Still counting but a different number: three down.

One left.

Mauricio was still out there.

A slow creak sounded and Jim spun and peered into the afternoon shadows filling the barn. A footstep or the wind or a door pushed open, impossible to tell but he couldn't wait for it. Going cautiously toward the noise with the M21 aimed from his shoulder, listening into the darkness, and then a splintering from above followed by a smear of noises, a wooden crash mixed with Miguel's screams. Flooded with panic, Jim called the boy's name and began to move and heard the *snik* of a clip being readied. Hit the deck as a storm of gunfire perforated the wall above him, sunlight spilling through dozens of bullet holes, hands clasped over his head until it ended and the metallic clatter of something heavy fell to the floor.

On his elbows, Jim pulled himself around the corner, seeing a spent AK-15 lying there.

Somewhere nearby Miguel began to scream again.

24

Count to thirty, point the .45 from the window and fire twice, what Jim told him to do, at twenty-one, twenty-two, twenty-three, Miguel slowly raised his head and peeked outside.

Seeing Mauricio down there gesturing to another guy in sunglasses.

Twenty-four, twenty-five, twenty-six, Mauricio edging around the side of the barn while sunglasses crept behind a shed, Miguel wanted to call out to Jim, warn him, except that wasn't the plan, twenty-seven, twenty-eight, twenty-nine, and he reached the pistol from the window and pulled the trigger, louder than he thought, and got as close as possible to the floor.

Sure of another assault but quiet, then Jim's rifle, *crack-crack-crack,* and quiet again.

Miguel rose carefully. Blinked out at Sunglasses lying on his side with ankles crossed as though he were napping in the grass. Seeing Mauricio pressed against the barn waiting, and then slipping in through a side door. Miguel went on his hands and knees along a crossbeam, peering down at the ground floor. Watching Mauricio cross the floor below. The pistol in Miguel's trembling grip, just a few feet more and the man would be an easy target, he lifted an arm to aim the .45 as the crossbeam complained, then splintered, then the world disappeared beneath him. With a scream of shock he tumbled through the air, landing in the pile of seed bags, flipping over and desperately digging through the heavy material as Mauricio said, "*Buscando esto?*" with a boot pressed on the .45. "Looking for this?"

Miguel gazed up at him slowly, the man soaked in blood, holding a rifle.

Jim called out then, close and searching, "Miguel?!"

Mauricio turned and shoved a clip into the rifle in one motion, Miguel could only watch helplessly as he emptied it in the direction of Jim's voice, the gun like a jackhammer through thin slats until it clicked empty. No movement on the other side of the wall but Miguel could feel it, Jim was there, still alive. Mauricio must've felt it too, tossing aside the rifle and lifting the .45, yanking Miguel to his feet. An iron arm wrapped at his neck, Miguel resisting, screaming as he was dragged deeper into the barn, telling Mauricio he'd never get away with it, he'd never kill Jim, and Mauricio said, "Maybe you're right. Maybe I'm not the one who will kill him after all."

***

Movement across the floor, muffled voices, and Jim got to his feet and said, "Come on out and let's finish this!"

No reply, the silence waiting for him, it drew him forward.

Around a corner, Jim stepped into the center of the barn where sunlight fell in a cone over Miguel, Mauricio directly behind him. Mauricio pressed Jim's own .45 to Miguel's temple with one hand, his other tightly clutching the boy's throat. "Put the gun down," Mauricio said evenly.

The terror in Miguel's expression made Jim take a quick step.

A crunch of skin and windpipe, Miguel choking as Mauricio tightened his hold on the boy's neck, lifted him by it, and Jim froze. "Drop it," Mauricio said.

No options, Jim lay the rifle on the floor

without shifting his gaze from Mauricio. "Let him go."

Relaxing his grip as Miguel gasped for air, Mauricio smiled a little. "Let him go? No, no, he'll make an excellent soldier. This boy will learn from the best, I'll train him myself." Mauricio shifted his gun hand, his arm snaking back around Miguel's neck; with a free hand he went into a pocket and came up with the Silver Star. "He'll become a real soldier. Medals, trinkets, they won't mean shit to him. Doing his duty to the cartel will be its own reward," he said, throwing the star at Jim's feet.

A fast-spreading nausea, Jim recognized it as dread, he said, "He'll never kill for you."

Mauricio shrugged. "I was like him once. We all learn what we have to do to survive. You and I both know that's true."

"He's not like you. Or me," Jim said.

"Not yet."

"We made our choices," Jim said. "Let the boy make his own."

"I never had a choice." Mauricio stretched his arms around Miguel. Grasping the boy's hands in his own, forcing the .45 into Miguel's grip. The boy trying to fight, but Mauricio was too strong as he circled his fingers tightly around Miguel's hands, the pistol, pulling back the hammer, chambering a bullet and aiming the weapon at Jim.

"Jim," Miguel whispered, a plea.

Nothing to say now, Mauricio wrapping his finger around Miguel's on the trigger, Jim found Miguel's eyes, shifted his gaze to the .45 and back again, reassuring the boy. Telling Miguel with a look that he had confidence in him.

Fighting the pressure of Mauricio's hands against his, Miguel was suddenly back in that deserted airfield where Jim set cans and bottles along the wing of an old airplane before explaining the components of the .45: the hammer and safety and sight and grip, how ammunition was loaded into the magazine, a clip lined with brass bullets, and how to remove it.

Miguel watched Jim's eyes flick to the gun's grip and then back to Miguel.

A button there, the magazine release, Miguel pressed it feeling the clip fall from the gun.

As Mauricio forced him to pull the trigger, Miguel remembering another lesson too late, how a gun with a bullet already in the chamber can fire, and he jerked the .45 as hard as he could but it didn't matter, the gun discharged, and he shot Jim.

Either age or shock but he spun too damn late, too slow, and it hit him below the ribs, the bullet took a sharp, deep bite and kept going, Jim grunting, feeling the blood flow, turned and saw Miguel rip himself free from Mauricio and slip into the shadows.

Saw Mauricio looking down at the .45's clip and bending for it.

The M21 was just there but Jim went for Mauricio instead, sending a boot hard into his stomach, both the .45 and the clip launched from the man's grip. Mauricio finding himself, vaulting up with a swinging kick against the side of Jim's head. Stunned, bouncing off a pillar and seeing Mauricio advance, Jim leapt. Hit Mauricio like a linebacker, drove him against a wall hammering fists into the man's gut, once, twice, then cracking him across the jaw. Mauricio huffed and stepped into the momentum and swung back with rapid punches to Jim's bullet wound, bloody knuckles digging hard as pain sucked the air from Jim's lungs, and then the knife. Mauricio's forearm pressed against Jim's neck, the steel blade advancing in his other hand as Jim seized his wrist. Weak all over like he'd been unplugged, the knife on a steady path to his heart, hooking Jim's shirt, biting into the flesh underneath and then piercing it nearly to bone.

The explosion above their heads covered them in dust and splinters.

Jim gasped for breath, seeing Miguel there, pointing the .45.

Mauricio turned to the boy, a split second when Jim drove a knee into his stomach doubling him over. Used his knee again against Mauricio's nose just short of jamming bone into brain, and snatched away the knife. Mauricio buckled then, leaning against the wall. Everyone stood quiet and unmoving, Mauricio leaking blood, blinking at Miguel. "So. Show me," he said. "What kind of soldier you are. Show me."

"Miguel," Jim said urgently.

The boy's gaze stuck on Mauricio. Examining him, Miguel said nothing while his hands didn't waver and gun didn't move.

"*Que de tu madre*? What about your mother?" Mauricio said. "Avenge her."

"Miguel, wait—"

"Avenge her! Kill me!" Mauricio screamed. "She's dead and gone, so do it!"

Taking aim, Miguel stared down the sight as Jim stood rigid. Knowing the boy's expression, he'd seen it before. On the faces of men he'd served with long ago, trying to see beyond the moment, what they'd become after they pulled a trigger, but different now. Rage and agony and vengeance, all of it for his mother, all of it passing over Miguel's face like shade from fast-moving clouds, he adjusted his stance, bent his knees, and took a breath.

"You're nothing! Unwanted!" Mauricio said. "Do it! It's your fate!"

The boy's eyes changing then, they showed a darker light as if seeing what pulsed behind Mauricio's words, Jim somehow at his side. Saying quietly, "Give me the gun."

Miguel stared up at him. Without relief but with a choice made, he extended the .45.

Jim took the gun, the weight of it lifted from the boy's hand along with the weight Miguel wouldn't have to carry. Touching his shoulder, Jim said, "Go outside now." A look between them, Miguel stepped from the barn, walked away from it. Jim watched him go and then turned back to Mauricio. On his knees raging at Jim, he made bitter oaths and promises, pausing to fight for a breath and to spit blood.

Jim raised the gun.

Locking eyes with Jim then, voice low, Mauricio spoke of what was inside him, had always been there, and how it was his decision whether he lived or died, not Miguel's or Jim's or his father's or the cartel's, and about the universe, his place in it. Some of what he said was in English and some in Spanish. Jim couldn't translate all of it but understood it all.

Soon Mauricio became quiet.

Jim waited. He made sure the man was done talking. Then he pulled the trigger.

25

In his concerned way her husband told her that her behavior was becoming obsessive.

Not the baking, Anna had given that up. She didn't care if she ever saw another cupcake or *concha* again as long as she lived. No, what her husband meant was how she waited for Miguel to appear, standing in the picture window at precisely the same times every day. Not that she thought he was right, that she was obsessive, she just didn't want to explain herself. Growing more certain each day that something terrible had happened to her nephew, Anna feared that revealing her method might disrupt its power to draw Miguel to her, to bring him home from wherever he was. It was no different than seeking a miracle by lighting a daily candle to Our Lady of Guadalupe, or manifesting one's heart's desire through meditation.

In Anna's case it involved counting cars and trucks and vans.

Three times a day, morning, noon, and dusk she stood in her home's picture window waiting for six vehicles to pass by, one for each letter in Miguel's name, an arbitrary decision that felt fateful. Willing one to stop in front of the house, not a hero or guardian angel, just a normal person who'd help a boy, who'd bring her nephew home. Sometimes it took only minutes for six vehicles to appear, sometimes much longer, and often they didn't slow down. Anna was convinced that Miguel would appear if she were there in the window waiting, and panicked if she wasn't at her post each day at the appointed hour.

Where she stood now as number four rumbled past, a rusty Cadillac.

Early evening, the sky peach-colored, she felt Rosa next to her, counting along with her, Anna saying aloud to her older sister, "I don't know what else to do."

I understand.

Number five approached, a Volvo packed with kids, it turned at the end of the block and disappeared. Anna said, "All I want is for him to be safe. To take care of him."

Mi hermana, I know. I know.

Anna turned to number six, a car with a siren-like glow inching up the street as if searching for an address. She sighed then, that's what it was doing, searching. A restaurant delivery cone glowed on top of the car looking for an address; it picked up speed and traveled past, gone. All six vehicles come and gone and no Miguel, and Anna said, "I'm sorry, Rosa."

Silence, her sister gone, too.

Turning from the window, unsure if she wanted to weep or scream in frustration, interrupted by the squeal of brakes. Anna pivoted, peered out at a van at the curb lettered with *Tejada Produce*. The driver's door opened and a man emerged. Older, tall, and rangy with gray hair, face tilted at the house with a weary gaze. His head turned at the sound of the passenger door closing, a figure moved around the van, and Anna's hand went to her mouth.

Not the little boy she remembered but still such a child.

Miguel saw her in the window, his face brightening as he lifted a hand. Anna waved back, frozen, hardly believing her eyes as they headed up the walk, the man moving slowly. Grimacing, he stumbled and went down on a knee and couldn't seem to catch his breath.

A stain of brown and red coating his midsection, Anna saw it and knew it was blood.

She was out the front door then, hurrying down the porch steps to help the man who'd brought her nephew home.

26

The glass office felt like a transparent prison cell. Looking out at the old ladies and other shoppers tapping melons and sniffing tomatoes, Nestor tempted to take the .44 Magnum from the desk drawer and kick open the office door and blow away every fucking one of them, the entire market, every row of green apples and pile of jicama and pyramid of bananas, expend his sorrow and rage through the rending of flesh and fruit, but. Silly from a business standpoint, and besides, it wouldn't be enough.

Nothing would bring back his twin.

Without Osvaldo he was trapped in this life alone.

Which was an endless slog of investments and profits and debt, which meant he was owed for his brother. For killing Osvaldo, that debt was owed to them both. Nestor sat pushing chess pieces around his mind, brought back to the moment by someone approaching the office who wasn't a customer, who'd never normally be at the market when it was open, and he sat up straight, too late to rise from his chair for the *corona*.

Raymond G, bone-thin beneath an oversized hoodie and jeans, hair slicked back.

He entered the office with a gaze like two black coins, said, "She here?"

Nestor held back from asking Raymond what he was doing at the market, unannounced visits were never good, but calmed himself, took a moment and said, "She who?"

A beat, those coins fixed in Raymond's head. "I was summoned."

Unsure what he meant, Nestor glanced at

the office door. A petite woman there, staring with cool eyes, and then a smile and she entered without knocking. "Raymond," she said by way of a greeting.

"What's it about?" he said, dropping into a chair.

She sharpened her smile. "No introduction?"

Raymond spoke then as if he were talking to himself. "Helen Wu. Agent Wu from the FBI, who we deal with."

"Condolences for your brother. Osvaldo, right?" she said to Nestor. "Bad way to go."

"There's a good way?" Nestor said.

"Versus gunned down in the middle of nowhere, dead in a hayfield? I can think of a few," she said. "Bloodbath like that, nasty, the farmer who found the bodies soiled himself before calling the cops, who called the Bureau. It was three Vasquez cartel figures, one of them well-known, a lieutenant. Mauricio something or other. You two are familiar with him, right?"

Raymond inspected his Timberlands while Nestor sat motionless, both silent.

"And there was Osvaldo. Just pitching in? Helping Mauricio kill a boy and an old man?"

More silence as Raymond and Nestor exchanged a blink.

"Yeah, I know about that," Helen said. "Just like I know you guys do nothing for free. So whatever poor, dead Osvaldo was up to, it had a price tag on it. Sit there like mummies, tell me nothing, fine, I'll tell you. The balance between my organization and yours, how and why we allow you to exist, is delicate. You don't want it to tip, bring the full weight of the federal government down on your ass? Take my advice. Get out of the business of murdering children."

"We don't do that," Raymond muttered.

"So Osvaldo was out there what, enjoying nature?" Helen said.

"Where's his body?" Nestor asked.

446

"On the slab with the other three."

"Three," Raymond said, not a question but surprise in it.

"That's right," Helen said. "Two bodies missing. The man and the boy."

"They're alive?" Raymond said.

"Seems that way."

"The old man," Nestor said. "He killed everyone?"

Helen shrugged slowly. "All I know is from today on, their fate is none of your concern. That's why I'm here," she said, eyes narrowing. "I find out anything has happened to them, to the boy especially. I'll make it my business to fuck with yours."

"Threaten Los Primos," Raymond said, tilting his head. "You must really care about some *viejo* piece of shit, some kid."

"Yeah, well. It's my job," Helen said.

"I mean. It's not like we'd hunt them

down. There's no profit in it," Raymond said. "Right, Nestor?"

Nodding along, Nestor agreed with his *corona*. Said, "Right," since it wasn't profit he wanted, no, but an outstanding debt he needed to settle.

Knowing now who owed him.

An old man with a rifle, somewhere out there alive in the world.

27

A few days into it Jim thought, I'm an interloper, I don't belong here, it's time to go.

After surgery, orders to rest and heal, Miguel's aunt and uncle insisted Jim stay with them and recuperate. The brick house was warm and bright, and they treated him like he was someone special, which made him uncomfortable. His ribs too, they ached, but Jim ignored it, watching Miguel learn to know his toddler cousin, the little girl holding onto his finger while they walked, looking up at the boy like she was seeing a miracle. It was natural, how Miguel spoke to his aunt, and she caressed his hair, how she and her husband listened intently while Miguel recounted their journey across the country. Jim nodding, adding a detail here and there, catching Anna staring at him with tears in her eyes, he guessed it was gratitude and had to look away. When he called Sarah to tell her he was okay she cried a little behind her words, trying to hold it back. Somehow it was easier for Jim to take. She wanted to come bring him home, but Jim said no, he could make it back on his own. Sarah insisted then, either he got a phone or she'd be on the next flight out. Jim gave in. Miguel's uncle took care of it, got Jim hooked up, showed him how to use it, and he was able to admit that he liked having it, a phone made good sense.

Another day passed, morning broke with Jim still halfway inside a dream.

Semi-asleep, his ribs taut and hot, Jim was in the barn with the gun pressed to Mauricio's head a second before pulling the trigger, then the boom and the blood, silence, and the man slumped on his side. Then Mauricio raised his dead eyes to Jim and spoke, he said, You did what you had to do, I'm gone. Now it's your turn Marine Corps, what are you waiting for?

A start, snapped awake, Jim's fingertips touched wet bandaging across his torso.

He'd been a young man absorbed by a jungle, an old man joined to the desert, Jim knew his body's signs and signals and warnings. Knew what was approaching, what belonged only to him and his wife, and what he would never allow Miguel to witness. All of the years, all of the miles; he was long past tired. As if he could close his eyes and sleep hard for as long as it took, but not here, not in this house full of life, he rose and changed the bandage. Ignored the fever around his ribcage and smiled accepting a cup of coffee. It was a cool, green morning. He asked Miguel to come outside with him.

Sitting side by side on the porch he said, "Well, amigo. I have to go."

Miguel's face folded and he wrapped his arms around Jim's neck and wept into it. Jim held onto the boy, he hadn't felt that way since right before Christine died, that impending loss. But different, he thumbed his eyes and smiled at Miguel and said, "We'll see each other again, I promise. Just, you have to get on with it now. It's time."

A nod, Miguel said, "I'll be here when you need me. We're friends."

No other words could've meant as much to Jim, still feeling them hours later standing on the curb outside the Greyhound Station on Canal Street, Chicago flowing around him. Anna had asked him, Why a bus, that long, slow trip, why not an airplane, be back in Arizona in four hours? Jim had replied that a long, slow trip appealed to him, watching Miguel's final wave through the car's back window. When the boy was out of sight, Jim turned with effort and entered the station. Gazed at the departures board, listening to Christine's whisper. Reminding Jim she'd be with him wherever he went, he just had to choose, and he exhaled. Pain from the wound and with gratitude, he approached the window, considered the destinations before purchasing a ticket, and then boarded a bus. He went to the back row, empty. Settled into a seat, tilted his forehead against the cool windowpane listening to the bus hiss and growl, it made Jim smile that he was unable to remember.

Where he was going, he suddenly could not recall.

Knowing only that it felt like the beginning of his trip with Miguel. That there was a purpose to it only he could accomplish, and that someone waited for him at the end of the line.

Jim closed his eyes and rested then, because it was enough.

The End

If you like *The Marksman*, you might like . . .

Con Crazy by Addison J. Chapple,
Danny Kravitz, and Eliza Marsh
Inspired by the hilarious true story. When a
brilliant but bankrupt con man chooses an
aging, eccentric French aristocratic family as
his next mark, he gets a whole lot more than
he bargained for.

Faster by Alex Schuler
The birth of self-driving cars through the eyes
of a brilliant but self-destructive machine-
builder and the computer programmer who
helped revolutionize the technology . . . while
breaking his heart.

Death Valley by Eden Francis Compton
In a dark and seedy part of Las Vegas that few
know about, two brothers with a violent past,
battle over a woman they love and the money
she wins at a casino.

Stay up to date
Follow Robin on Amazon & Goodreads

https://www.amazon.com/author/robingmercier